CALL TO A KILLER

Several drinks later he was still thinking. The Sambuca was not making him sleepy.

Maybe it was because he had killed two men.

He took off his horn-rimmed glasses, laid them on the table, and rubbed his eyes. He could not be arrested. His mother would never understand. It would be the end of his job. His career as an author would end before it really began.

The telephone rang. He looked at his watch as he reached for the telephone.

"Hello."

"Mr. Biddle. This is Detective C. R. Payne with the Atlanta Police Department. Homicide."

Colin froze. My God. How could they know so soon?

"Mr. Biddle, I'm calling regarding a double homicide that occurred several hours ago."

Colin swallowed and waited a moment.

"I'm sorry to call you so late. But I know from the older officers you like for us to call you when there's a big story."

Colin slowly let out a long, quiet sigh and closed his eyes in relief.

"That's quite all right," Colin said. "Tell me about the homicides. . . ."

Robert Coram

ATLANTA HEAT

A SIGNET BOOK

SIGNET
Published by the Penguin Group
Penguin Putnam Inc., 375 Hudson Street,
New York, New York 10014, U.S.A.
Penguin Books Ltd, 27 Wrights Lane,
London W8 5TZ, England
Penguin Books Australia Ltd, Ringwood,
Victoria, Australia
Penguin Books Canada Ltd, 10 Alcorn Avenue,
Toronto, Ontario, Canada M4V 3B2
Penguin Books (N.Z.) Ltd, 182–190 Wairau Road,
Auckland 10, New Zealand

Penguin Books Ltd, Registered Offices:
Harmondsworth, Middlesex, England

First published by Signet, an imprint of Dutton Signet,
a member of Penguin Putnam Inc.

First Printing, November, 1997
10 9 8 7 6 5 4 3 2 1

REGISTERED TRADEMARK—MARCA REGISTRADA

Printed in the United States of America

PUBLISHER'S NOTE
This is a work of fiction. Names, characters, places, and incidents either are
the product of the author's imagination or are used fictitiously, and any resem-
blance to actual persons, living or dead, events, or locales is entirely
coincidental.

This book is for Myrlene Tye, a teacher

ACKNOWLEDGMENTS

First, to the Division of Forensic Sciences at the Georgia Bureau of Investigation, where Kelly Fite, chief firearms examiner, is the best ballistics man in the country. He and his two able assistants, Bernie Davy and John Collins, loaded a Walther TPH with Stinger ammo and spent a half day demonstrating the ballistics. Larry Peterson explained fibers and linen.

At the Atlanta Police Department, Major Mickey Lloyd paved the way. Carl Lee Price and Kenny Raines, homicide detectives and friends, were unstinting with their time, advice, and counsel. Investigator Dale Kelley in Sex Crimes explained the gathering of DNA evidence.

At Manuel's, that most enduring of Atlanta pubs, Susan Strack, Danny Jones, and Pat Glass were escorts on a memorable visit to the Clermont Lounge, that strange and wonderful place where one can earn a Ph.D. in life science.

Don Farmer and Don Johnson, both of WSB-TV, explained certain technical aspects of television.

Chris McLoughlin, shooter extraordinaire,

knows all there is to know about guns in general and the Walther TPH in particular.

Finally, a special thanks to Ned and Karen McCarthy, forever friends, who let me work in their Key West house.

Man's great guilt does not lie in the sins that he commits, for temptation is great and his strength limited.

Man's great guilt lies in the fact that he can turn away from evil at any moment, and yet he does not.

—MARTIN BUBER

1

Colin Biddle was angry because the waiter had dropped four coffee beans instead of three in his last Sambuca.

This was Colin's big night. His first book had been published and tonight there had been a party for him at Nathalie DuPree's home in Ansley Park. People who made their living as writers were there, the heavy breathers of Atlanta's literary community, and they were there to pay homage to Colin and to celebrate the publishing of *Street Smarts*.

He shot his cuffs. In the light from the instrument panel he admired his new gold cuff links. He turned down the air conditioner, leaned back, and glanced at his wife. "Aside from that rather stupid waiter, how do you think it went?"

"Keep your eyes on the road."

"My eyes are on the road."

She shrugged. "Nathalie's food was wonderful."

"She's written about fifteen cookbooks. Plus how many cooking shows on TV? It was supposed to be good. I meant—"

"You meant do Atlanta writers think you are a real writer instead of just a little old police reporter?"

"I'm not just a little old police reporter."

She snorted.

Colin covered the police beat. He could have covered politics or education or the environment or anything else he wanted. But he chose the cop shop. So maybe the cop shop is not exactly at the top of the journalistic food chain. But because of the rapes and robberies and homicides that occur with numbing regularity in Atlanta, his byline was on the front page of *The Atlanta Constitution* three or four days every week; far more often than were the bylines of reporters on the prestige beats. Even so, those novelists there tonight knew, as did he, that journalism is not really writing. They knew, as did he, that journalism is little more than typing notices on an ever-revolving bulletin board. It is a business—not a profession, not even a craft—but a business that attracts the insecure; those who find esteem in a byline, those who find gratification in having politicians call them by name, those who never understand that their popularity comes from what they do rather than who they are. And all their breast beating about being protectors of the public weal, all their secret self-images of being knights errant on white horses will not change a jot or tittle. They are psychological puppies, trembling and yapping in the midnight hours as they wonder what comes after journalism.

Colin clicked his tongue. "You must have had a bit more to drink than I did."

"Those people were generous. They treated you as a full-fledged dues-paying member of the exalted brotherhood." In her lap, she curled her forefingers and used the fingernails of each to push at the cuticles of her thumbs.

He nodded.

"Not like some literary outrider," she finished.

"Thanks," he muttered.

"Well, I did think your suit looked smashing." She looked out the window. "Just smashing."

He looked down at the sleeves of the new blue pinstripe. It had been made in London. Savile Row. Henry Poole.

"It should. It cost—"

"Sixteen hundred dollars. I know." She shook her head. "You perspired. Your collar was wet."

"There was no air-conditioning on the deck, my dear. And in case you haven't noticed, the temperature outside is almost eighty degrees. I was slapping mosquitoes all night." He paused. "God, there are a lot of mosquitoes in this town during the summer."

She looked out the window. "You perspired because you kept your coat on."

He did not respond.

"You were afraid they might notice that little gun you wear on your belt. You think you are the only person in Atlanta who carries a gun? You think all those writers are liberals? Most of them are in their forties or fifties. Liberalism is an affliction of the young. It's like smoking dope or marching and protesting. Those people there tonight probably are more conservative than you. I wouldn't be surprised if most of them were carrying guns. This *is* Atlanta."

She looked out the window and slowly shook her head. "You don't see many old liberals. They are very sad people."

She turned and looked at him. "You are a writer. You have all these special insights that we mortals lack. Don't you know that?"

Colin stopped for the red light where Piedmont and Cheshire Bridge Road forked. "Writers don't carry guns."

"Does that mean you aren't a writer?"

He turned right onto Cheshire Bridge. "We've had this conversation before."

"I know. Your job takes you into rough places. Sure. Like the bars in north Atlanta? That's why the people at the paper call you the King of Buckhead."

"I go into the projects. The police know I'm armed. I'm what they call a stand-up guy. I'm an unofficial backup."

"Unofficial? Right." She laughed. "And I have a Ph.D. in theoretical physics."

She leaned forward, turned on the radio, and punched buttons rapidly until she heard rock music. She twisted the volume button.

"Is that *really* necessary?"

"Yes." She turned and smiled. "Yes. Yes."

"I need this tonight."

"Don't get pretentious, my dear. It was just a paperback crime novel. I mean, we aren't talking *Gone With the Wind* here."

"*That's* your idea of good writing?"

"Think yours will sell one-tenth as many? A *hundredth* as many?"

"It *could* be a best-seller."

"Monkeys *could* fly out of your ass."

"Don't be crude." He pressed harder on the accelerator. The big Mercedes gathered speed.

She smiled. "I noticed how you weaseled when they asked you about the press run. And when they talked about their advances you stood there and nodded sagely, smiling as if yours was too big to talk about."

"It's my first book."

"Eight-thousand-dollar advance. Maybe, *maybe,* a hundred thousand press run. Paperback. Now *there's* a book that will change the course of western civilization."

"If it catches on they will print more." His voice had risen. He was on the edge of losing control. He caught himself.

"If you build it they will come," she intoned. "*If* frogs had wings they wouldn't bump their asses."

"Brilliant logic. Unassailable."

"Those people *knew*. This is their business."

"They had to start somewhere."

"Under the basement?"

He sped up again. His face was tight.

"Well, you got a *sweet* review."

His mouth twitched. The *Constitution* did not usually review first books by local writers. That is, not unless they were published by Longstreet Press, a local publishing house owned by the newspaper. And the book editor was a fey creature who breathed such rarefied literary air that he would never deign to mention a paperback novel, especially a paperback crime novel.

But because Colin's mother owned a hefty block of stock in the newspaper, his paperback crime novel was being reviewed in the Sunday paper. He had seen the review when the mid-runs came up Thursday. Very clever it was. "Promising" is how his book was described. "Seamy" was another word used. Damned with faint praise. In a few hours when Atlantans were having their Sunday breakfasts they would read the review and chuckle.

She turned to look at him. He was an extraordinarily handsome man, tall with hair so blond it was almost white. He would be thirty-nine in November but looked ten years younger. His horn-rimmed glasses were dark against his fair skin and gracile features.

But how could a man who had inherited so much money be so insecure? Those successful writers there tonight had something he was missing. She sensed it in talking with them. Each of them had a fire in the belly. She sensed that they wrote because they had to; because they could do nothing else.

They would write whether they sold their books or not. They were passionate about the act of writing, not about the acclaim of being a writer.

Colin? Colin was passionate about nothing. For a split second she wondered if his lack of passion and his insecurity came *because* of the money he inherited.

She quickly dismissed the thought.

"You think your cop buddies won't give you a speeding ticket?"

He looked at the dials but did not answer.

She smiled triumphantly. "Are we about to go into another of our childish rages?"

"Your car needs petrol."

She looked at her watch. "It's after one o'clock. I'm tired."

She was a feminine version of her husband, tall, slender, and very blond. If he was the whitest white boy in Atlanta, as his friends at the newspaper often said, then she was the whitest white girl. And though she did not want to think about it, her insecurities were as great as his. In public she was cool and aloof and reserved and intimidating; the prototypical ice maiden. But her eyes gave her away. Her eyes and her fingers. Those brilliant green eyes, if one looked deeply enough into them, revealed roiling turmoil, a fur-ball of emotional spiders fighting to be released. And the fingers of both hands constantly picked at her cuticles. At any given time, two or three fingertips were wrapped in Band-Aids to protect raw and bloody cuticles. And even then, even if one hand was gesturing or being used in some quotidian task, the forefinger of the other hand would ritualistically push at the cuticle of the thumb and then march relentlessly across the tips of the other fingers.

Theirs was a marriage made at a Halloween carnival.

"Your car needs petrol," he repeated.

She sighed. Colin was an ardent anglophile who often used British colloquialisms. Usually she ignored them. But petrol? Who the hell in Atlanta called gas petrol?

"Don't stop around here."

He pressed hard on the brakes and swung into a small gas station.

She looked out the window, then swung around in amazement. "This is where . . ."

He drove under the overhang, moved forward, and braked to a stop at the last pump.

"Yes. A man was killed here a few months ago; a customer who stopped for gas. I wrote a story about it. Front page. I remember it because it was my twentieth front-page byline that month."

She looked out the window at the oil-splotched concrete. "I don't believe this."

"The things we must endure in our passage through this vale of tears." He stepped out and slammed the door. She locked it.

Colin was about to pick up the hose when he noticed the scratch that ran across the trunk of the Mercedes. Someone had keyed the car while he was at the party. He ran his finger along the deep gash. The brownish-red primer coat underneath was visible.

"Oh, no," he sighed.

He walked forward and tapped on the passenger side window. The radio was too loud and his wife did not hear him. He tapped again. Louder.

She looked over her shoulder with startled eyes. Then, relieved, she put her hand to her throat and pressed the switch that rolled the window down a few inches.

"Someone keyed the car." He was almost shouting to overcome the radio.

"They must have read your book." The window whirred up.

He turned and walked back to the gas pump, picked up the hose and turned around to press the access cover over the gas tank. It was locked. When his wife locked the doors, she also locked the gas tank. He tapped on the fender with his hand but the radio was blaring and she did not hear him. He tapped again. She did not hear.

He tried to walk forward a few steps with the hose but it was too short. He backed up, reinserted the hose into the pump, then walked forward and slammed his hand against the window. His wife jumped. She glared at him, then lowered the window a few inches.

"Would you please unlock the gas tank?"

The window whirred up.

He turned, pushed the nozzle into the tank, and

pulled on the grip that released gas. Nothing. He pushed the nozzle farther and again pulled on the grip. Nothing.

He sighed and turned around to read the instructions on the pump. Again he placed the nozzle inside the tank, this time not as deep, and pulled the lever. The gas burbled through the hose with an explosive *whoosh* created a backsplash that covered his hand and arm and drenched the sleeve of his suit.

He groaned in anger and frustration.

He pressed the nozzle a bit deeper and with his left hand reached into his rear pocket for a handkerchief. He patted his hand and arm, sopping up gasoline. He looked at the pump and stopped when the indicator showed $5.00. Tomorrow she could fill up somewhere else. She was right. He should not have stopped here. He hated it when she was right.

Holding his arm up high and waving the handkerchief to dry it, he walked briskly across the brightly lit concrete. He reeked of gasoline.

Inside, no one was at the cash register.

The store seemed exceptionally bright. The fluorescent lights imparted a burning white cast to everything in the store. He narrowed his eyes to protect against the blinding glare.

He looked around. A radio on the counter was on the same station his wife had tuned in and it was even louder.

"Hello," he said.

No response.

"Hello," he shouted.

After a pause he heard a distant voice. "Just a minute."

His lips tightened into a thin line when the rear door opened and a young man looked at him impatiently, then walked toward the cash register. The man was thin and very neat. There was something vaguely familiar about him.

"You don't keep someone out front?"

The young man pushed his glasses higher on his nose and flicked his wrist in dismissal. "I was busy, busy, busy. What is it?"

Colin stared in amazement. What the hell did the guy think he was there to do, inquire about the Concorde's flight schedule?

"I would like to pay for my gas."

"Well, fine." The attendant held out his hand.

Colin looked up as another young man, this one black, emerged from the rear room, propped the door open, and sauntered forth. "You didn't wait for me," he said plaintively.

"Oh, don't be that way," said the first young man. He paused, smiled at his friend, and ignored Colin. "Are we through back there?"

The black man smiled. "We're through replacing the videotape." His smile widened. "But we're not through."

Both men giggled. They stood behind the counter, so close they were touching. One turned the radio louder. Colin flinched. He hated loud radios. He slapped at a mosquito that had bitten him on the neck. He missed. The mosquito landed on the wall near the front of the store. Colin took two steps and smashed the mosquito. He wiped his hand on his handkerchief.

"Oooooohh," said the attendant. "Now you've made a mess on my new wall."

Colin stared. "Would you please take my money?" He had to shout to be heard. He slapped a twenty-dollar bill on the counter.

The attendant pushed his glasses up and stared at the bill. "Have anything smaller?"

"No."

The two young men stared at him. "You shouldn't take out your hostilities on other people," the first one said.

Colin's anger ratcheted upward. This kind of platitudinous nonsense from a gay gas station attendant?

"And repair your pump." Colin held up his arm. "Look at this. Gas all over me."

The first attendant wrinkled his face. Then his eyebrows arched. "No one else has had any trouble. Do you know how to use the pump?"

He looked at his friend. Both squeezed their lips and tried not to laugh.

Colin looked from one to the other. Then he spoke very slowly. "I know how to use the pump. Any idiot can operate a gas pump. But yours is broken and it sprayed gas all over my suit. This is the first time I've worn this suit. I'm sending you the cleaning bill."

"You just make sure your return address is on it. Because we will send it right back."

The second attendant moved closer to his friend. He nodded. "We don't pay laundry bills for people who've been drinking and can't figure out how to use the pump."

He touched his friend's shoulder.

The first attendant nodded. "Yes, you can just take your old laundry bill and . . ."

Colin slapped his coat aside and wrapped his fingers around the little Walther TPH holstered at his waist. "Stop the simpering and give me my change."

He pulled his hand away from his pistol and swung at another mosquito. The mosquito landed on the remote cash register display that was at Colin's eye level. He slapped again, missed, and connected with the display. It snapped and fell into a forty-five-degree droop.

The two young men stopped giggling and jumped back, arms clasped in front of their bodies. Their eyes were wide. "Now you're in trouble, mister," the first one said. "You've broken the cash register."

He stepped forward and punched the keys on the cash register. The twenty-dollar bill went inside and the drawer was shut.

"My change." Colin held out his hand.

The attendant pushed his glasses up again and

glared at Colin. "You broke the cash register. I'm keeping your money to pay for it. You better leave now or I'll call the police."

Colin's voice rose. "Give me my change."

The attendant picked up the telephone. "I'm calling nine one one to you, mister."

"Give me my goddamn money."

Colin realized he was losing control. He never used profanity.

"Operator, this is the Quicky Gas Station on Cheshire Bridge just south of Happy Herman's. Can you send someone over? I have this"—he looked over his shoulder—"this abusive man here. He's talking ugly and I want him arrested." The man paused. "Less than five minutes? Okay." He hung up.

Colin saw that during the conversation the attendant had held down the button on the telephone. The little faggot was trying to run a con on him.

Colin jerked his gun from the holster, leaned across the counter, and brought the butt down hard on the attendant's fingers. He felt the bones snap.

The attendant screamed.

The second man jumped back. "That was totally uncalled for, mister. Just totally. You are going to jail. Definitely."

Colin fired twice. The first bullet shattered the lens over the attendant's right eye and careened around inside his skull. The second bullet was close behind. The man collapsed as if he were boneless. As Colin swung the pistol, the second man put his hands over his eyes, said, "Nooooo," and froze. Colin pulled the trigger. The weapon malfunctioned. Moving quickly and with no hesitation, Colin thumbed the magazine release, let it drop several inches, racked the slide back and ejected the jammed bullet, shoved the magazine back into place, racked the slide again to cock the weapon, and squeezed off two rounds into the man's still-open mouth.

The man collapsed without a sound.

Colin lowered the pistol and looked around.

Holy shit!

What had he done?

He stuck the weapon back into his holster and looked out the window. No one was at the pumps. His wife was slumped in the seat, staring straight ahead. She had heard nothing. Thank God for loud radios.

He swallowed hard. He had to clean this mess up and get out. Fast.

He flipped the sign on the glass door so it read CLOSED and clicked the lock. He moved behind the counter, stepping carefully to avoid the blood, and pulled the wallets from the rear pockets of the men. He couldn't help but notice how ridiculous the first victim appeared. One lens in his little granny glasses was missing. Behind it was a red-black hole covered with sparkling shards of glass. Colin took the money from the wallets, then wiped the wallets with his gasoline-soaked handkerchief and dropped them on the floor. He scooped the bills from the cash register and put them in his inside coat pocket. With his handkerchief he wiped the countertop and the cash register drawer. He looked around. He wiped the telephone and the broken cash register display.

The security camera!

They had been changing the tape. He looked up. The shiny black eye of a video camera was staring at him from over the rear door. He quickly walked through the rear door and looked up. The VCR was in a locked metal box.

Colin pulled his pistol, took careful aim, and fired once. The bullet smashed the small lock. He pulled a milk crate forward and stood on it. With the handkerchief covering his hand he reached inside the VCR, pressed the cassette release button, and seized the tape. He stuck the tape inside his belt and reached up to wipe off the VCR. He wiped off the milk carton. As he went through the door he turned the dead bolt and wiped both handles.

He stopped. What else?

Keep it simple.

He knew from standing alongside homicide cops at dozens of crime scenes that the more a person tries to cover up, the more he reveals. The smarter he tries to be, the dumber he is. When the homicide cops come they study the scene and re-create the crime. Don't give them anything to work with. Point them in another direction.

Make the cops think this was a robbery. Nothing more. The perp shot the attendants, grabbed the money in the register and in their wallets, then snatched the videotape. In and out. Stranger to stranger. A clean job.

The cartridge casings.

He had forgotten the cartridge casings.

Quickly he returned to the back room where he stood in front of the VCR, then looked to his right and imagined the arc of the casing. He found it on the floor and dropped it into his pocket. Inside the store he began looking again. Two casings he found in a display of Twinkies. A third he found across the aisle in an open box of bubble gum. The fourth he could not find. Nor could he find the live round that was ejected when he cleared the malfunctioning weapon.

He had to get out before someone stopped.

He wiped the sign on the inside of the door and brushed the handkerchief over the lock. At the end of the counter a set of keys hung on a nail. He picked up the keys. One key fit the front door. With the handkerchief over his hand Colin opened the door, turned, and quickly locked it. He wrapped the keys in his handkerchief and walked swiftly, head down, eyes slicing up and down the road, toward his car.

For a moment he considered dropping the keys into the Dumpster at the edge of the concrete parking space. No. The cops would check there for evidence. On the way home he would toss the keys out the window.

Two cars passed the station as he walked across

the expanse of concrete. Neither driver appeared to notice him.

He rapped the car window. Hard.

His wife jumped, glared, and unlocked the door. He slid inside.

She turned down the radio. "Well, it took long enough. What were you . . . My God, what is that odor? Did you spill gas?"

"It sprayed on me." He turned toward her as another car drove down Cheshire Bridge.

She wrinkled her nose. "That smell." She pushed a button and the window slid down several inches. "You got it on your suit?"

"Yes." He slid his window down. All the way. "I'll take it to the cleaners tomorrow. You won't have to endure the odor long. We'll be home in two minutes."

She looked at him. "Are you okay?"

"I'm fine. Why?" The videocassette in the small of his back was uncomfortable. And the weight of the keys in his pocket was enormous. He pulled the handkerchief from his coat pocket and slid it under his leg. The Mercedes rolled smoothly under I-85 and gathered speed to catch the green light at Buford Highway.

"I don't know. You just seem . . ."

"What?" He turned and looked at his wife wondering if she suspected anything. Was he acting strange?

"I don't know. Jangled."

"I'm tired."

"Poor baby. You need a cup of coffee and a Sambuca?"

"Just Sambuca."

"Count the beans." She looked out the window. "God forbid you should have too many beans in the glass."

He did not answer. They were approaching a copse of trees that served as a buffer between two condominium projects on Lenox Road. He eased the handkerchief-wrapped keys from under his leg and held his arm out the window. Then, holding the handkerchief tightly, he flipped his hand over the top of the car, holding on to the handkerchief with thumb and forefinger and releasing the keys to be flung across the top of the car and down the hill into the trees.

She looked at him. "What are you doing?"

"I need fresh air. The smell of gas is making me nauseous." He balled the handkerchief up tightly, pulled his hand inside, and dropped the handkerchief between his feet.

"We're almost home," she said. "Thank God. I want to go to bed as soon as I walk in the door."

"That's okay. I can pour myself a Sambuca."

"Then your big night will be over."

He nodded and for a moment did not speak. Then he said, "Yes, my big night will be over."

2

If you believe the drum beaters and the horn tooters, Atlanta not only is an Olympic City but it is the cultural and industrial center of the Sun Belt and the Pride of the New South, a bright and shining Nineveh upon which God has bestowed special and abundant blessings. It is Holy Writ to say Atlanta is a blood-bought and glory-bound city; a city led by Archangels and peopled by the bold and the proud. And it is difficult to hear any other description of the city because a major portion of the population acts as a rah-rah brigade.

Nevertheless, there is another view. It comes from those who say if Atlanta could suck as well as it can blow that the Gulf of Mexico would be lapping at the city limits.

The second group may be onto something. Truth is that twenty years ago Atlanta was a special place. Today it is simply a violent cow town with a big airport.

And a big attitude.

One sign of the city's provincial nature is how it

withers early Sunday morning. As one week ends and another begins, bars and clubs close their doors. Bluestockings and conservative preachers have enough clout that officially no booze is sold from 2:00 A.M. Sunday until noon. The first few hours of the week in Atlanta are no different from the first few hours of the week in Birmingham or Chattanooga or Raleigh—it's Snooze City.

That's the reason C. R. Payne and a sergeant were the only two people working morning watch at the Homicide Squad; that and the fact it was the middle of the summer and three people were on vacation. Two others had called in sick. And one of those was Payne's partner, a senior investigator.

So when the telephone rang at 2:14 A.M. Sunday and the uniform on the other end said he had a double homicide, the sergeant looked around the empty squad room, smiled at Payne, and said, "You're up."

Payne took the phone and listened. He asked a few questions. He stood up while he talked to an I.D. tech and the medical examiner's office. Then he grabbed his coat and his notebook and walked rapidly out the front door.

"Hey, man, you gonna do okay," murmured one of the older black cops who worked in Assaults.

"Be cool, my brother," said another.

Payne nodded. Don't run, he told himself. The two victims aren't going anywhere. The crime scene is locked down. Yeah, be cool.

Payne opened the door of his unmarked car,

picked up the blue light from the floor, and slapped it on the roof. He crossed Ponce de Leon and raced up Barnett until he hit Virginia Avenue. He turned right and then a quick left on Highland. A few people were standing around wondering where to go this time of the morning. Must be tourists.

Payne was nervous.

Technically he was still in training. For the past two months, since he transferred from Assaults, he had been working homicides with an older partner, the guy who was breaking him in.

Payne swallowed. He was a twenty-nine-year-old black guy, the youngest and least-experienced cop in Homicide, and on his first solo assignment he draws a double pop.

"Hey, coach, I ain't got no head gear," he mumbled. "But send me in. I'm fresh."

That's the way it was in Homicide.

See some young guy in Assaults who's always hanging around homicide crime scenes. Asking questions. Talking to the old guys. They laugh and give him hell. Then there's an opening for a trainee on the morning watch. It's always the morning watch for new guys. To work days you not only have to be a *very* senior person, you also have to be able to caress the mayor's balls with one hand while lighting his cigars with the other. Even then your off days are some crap schedule like Tuesday and Thursday; never two consecutive days and never a weekend day. After maybe ten years your off days become Sunday and Thursday. To work days *and* have Saturday and Sunday off means you're approaching sainthood and on a first-name basis with the Almighty. That, or you have video of the mayor screwing a goat.

Anyway, get that kid in Assaults, give him a little training, and throw his ass into the pit. If he crawls out, fine. Welcome to Homicide, bro. Walk different, talk different, and be one of the Big Feet in the police department; a member of the aristocracy. But one mistake and that puppy is back in Assaults. Or in uniform directing traffic at the airport.

Payne gritted his teeth.

"They ain't sending my black ass back down the ladder," he said. "That ladder goes one way and that's straight up."

Payne rolled his shoulders and tilted his head to each side, loosening up his neck. He was 5 feet 11 inches and a muscular 190 pounds. Like the older homicide cops, he dressed well; middle-aged white-man well—black wing tips, dark suit, white shirt, dark tie, and dark suspenders. Some of the guys in Homicide wore hats to set them apart from other detectives. The people in SIS carried black brief-cases. But for C. R. Payne, his somber outfit was enough.

That was something Payne had learned at Emory University. He had pledged a white fraternity there, an act that caused other black students to ostracize him as "too white." He went to Emory rather than to a mostly black college because he had won a full scholarship and because he knew there was a big world beyond the university.

Like it or not, middle-aged white guys still run the universe. They go to schools like Emory. They belong to fraternities like the one Payne had pledged. And they dress like funeral directors. The more you are like them the less you frighten them. So dress like them and talk like them and act like them. Learn from them; learn where the buttons of power are located and learn how to press them. Those middle-aged white guys won't be around forever. And as Payne often reminded himself—I've got plans. The next dance is mine. Bet your sweet ass on that.

Payne turned left on Lenox Road and slowed for the sharp curve. As he approached Cheshire Bridge Road he slowed again. The Quicky Gas Station was at the junction. He swung left into the parking lot. Blue lights everywhere. Fire and Rescue was here. People from the funeral home—the body snatchers—were here.

A half-dozen uniform guys stood in the door of the gas station, jawing and swatting bugs. Several officers were inside.

Payne put on his coat and shrugged his shoulders. Too hot to wear a coat. But he was a homicide cop and homicide cops set the example. Every uniform cop wants to grow up and be a homicide cop. If he doesn't, he should be out selling shoes. Homicide cops are like Army rangers; they lead the way.

Payne reminded himself to walk slowly. Nothing was going to happen here until he made it happen. He picked up his leather-bound notebook and pulled his Mount Blanc pen from his pocket. Got to show these guys I'm not some porch monkey from the projects. I'm a graduate of Emory University, a detective, a damn good one, and I'm going to be all over this case. I am everything they all want to be.

"Who was first on the scene?" he asked a uniform.

Big guy steps forward. Beer gut. Pockmarked face. Eyes like million-year-old icebergs. These old officers are the meanest sons of bitches on earth. And tough. You could strike matches on their hearts. This one was fighting a grin. What the hell did he have to grin about?

"I found 'em," said the old head.

"Show me what you got."

Now Beer Gut was grinning openly.

"Something funny, Officer?"

"Yeah, you. What are you doing out so late by yourself?" Beer Gut looked over his shoulder at his grinning buddies. "Hey, guys. We got us a baby homicide investigator."

The uniforms laughed.

Even the black guys.

3

"Who's senior?" Payne asked.

Beer Gut pointed to a sergeant who was puffing on a cigar.

"Sergeant?"

The sergeant stared. White guy in his late forties. Whippet thin. Mustache that skirted regulations. Smoking a twenty-five-cent cigar. One look at his flat eyes and Payne knew the officer had a soul so empty it echoed.

"Yeah?"

"I'm Payne. Homicide." He pointed over his shoulder. "Ask your men to move out of the store, please."

"Payne, huh? Well, they named you right." He blew a cloud of cigar smoke toward Payne.

The young detective stepped aside to avoid the smoke.

"They're standing by in case the EMTs need assistance."

"They're getting a cheap thrill and they're contaminating my crime scene. I want them out. Now."

The sergeant knew the rules. "Okay, sonny." He turned toward the door. "Hey, you guys, get out of there," he shouted. "Homicide's here."

"Oooooooohhhh," said a young uniform in mock awe. He had been staring at the two bodies, planning the stories he would tell later sitting at the cop table in the back room at Manuel's Tavern: "You should'a seen it. Two of 'em. Lying on the floor. Both of 'em shot in the head. Blood *everywhere*. I mean *everywhere*." Then he would take another bite of his hamburger, wash it down with a long drink of beer, and say, "If I had gotten there a half hour earlier I'd have caught the perp. I'd a blown his shit away. Believe it. In a New York minute."

The officers stepped outside and stared at Payne.

Payne turned to Beer Gut.

"Tell me what you found when you got here."

Beer Gut had done this a hundred times. With no frills he laid out what he had found. He closed by saying, "Robbery, plain and simple. Some guy walks in, pops those two, and takes the money. Shot one of 'em in the headlight. You see his glasses?"

Payne stopped at the door. "Anything changed? This is exactly the way you found it?"

Beer Gut hesitated. "Two things. The door and the radio."

Payne looked at the glass door. Or what had been a glass door. He waited.

"I couldn't get in. I saw two bodies. They might

have still been alive. I nudged the door with the bumper of my police vehicle." For a moment Beer Gut almost grinned. "Smashed hell out of that door."

"And the radio?"

"When I arrived at the scene, the radio was so loud I couldn't have heard thunder. I hate rock music. I turned it off."

Payne nodded. He held up his hand, palm out. "Far enough. I'll take it from here."

Beer Gut's eyes narrowed. He glowered. "You don't want me to show you what I told you?"

"I'll take from here."

Beer Gut shrugged and turned away.

"Stick around in case I need you," Payne said over his shoulder.

"I got until eight a.m."

Payne stood in the door. He snapped on a pair of latex gloves, closed his eyes, and breathed deeply. The smell of fresh blood dominated the air. He wanted to *feel* the crime scene. The answers are always at the crime scene. This is where the perp demonstrates his work. Almost always he leaves something. If he doesn't, that in itself is a sign of his work.

"Can't see anything with your eyes shut," said a voice.

Payne opened his eyes. One of the EMTs; a woman about thirty. Blond. Overweight. "You got two victims here, Detective. One white male. One black male. Young guys. Behind the counter. Both of 'em DRT."

Payne stared. "DRT?"

"Yeah," she said, glad to use the old expression on probably the one guy in the police department who had not heard it. "Dead right there."

Payne smiled. "What happened?"

She shrugged. "Each one took it in the head. Perp was a good shooter. I'd say in the first one, and the medical examiner will have to make it official, the bullet crossed the midline."

"Crossed the midline. What does that mean?"

She stared at him for a moment. "It means his brain was fucked."

"Ahhhhh."

"Victims were dead when they hit the floor," she continued. "Both of them." She pointed. "Wallets there."

"You move 'em?"

She looked at him. Paramedics are not supposed to move a body. But sometimes they get carried away, like to practice their CPR, or just want to try a few heroics before pronouncing somebody dead.

"Took their vital signs. That's all."

"You through?"

"Yep." She turned for her partner. "Hey, can't do anything else here. Let's go."

Another woman stood up and came from behind the counter. Another overweight white woman with stringy blond hair. Why do so many fat women become EMTs? Is being a bleached blond a job requirement?

Payne walked behind the counter, stopped at the edge of the blood, and crouched. For a long time he stared at the two crumpled bodies. He opened his notebook.

White guy shot in the eye. Blew out the right lens of his glasses. No apparent entry wounds on the black guy. But blood had oozed from his mouth. Payne leaned closer. What appeared to be faint powder burns were around the eye of the first victim. The gun was within eighteen inches or two feet when the shooter pulled the trigger. Entry wound in the first guy and the lack of damage from hydrostatic pressure indicated a small-caliber weapon was used. The EMT was right. Good shooting.

Payne's brow wrinkled. The white guy's fingers on the right hand were bent at a peculiar angle. He leaned over and with his ballpoint gently nudged one of the fingers. Broken. Looked like three broken fingers. Odd. Could that have occurred as the guy collapsed? Maybe before death?

He made a note to discuss this with the medical examiner.

A half hour later the ID tech had videotaped the victims and the store from every angle.

"Go for prints everywhere," Payne said to the ID tech.

"Ummmmm." She had been doing this job when

the homicide cop was still drinking milk through a nipple.

Payne picked up the wallets and carefully pulled out the driver's licenses. He studied the faces on the cards.

He stood up and pushed the power button on the radio. Rock music blared. He pushed the button again, turning it off.

He stared at the bent cash register display. Perp must have tried to come across the counter at the victims. Why?

Payne tried the back door. Locked. He went to the front door and caught Beer Gut's eyes and motioned him forward.

"The owner here?"

"Yeah." Beer gut turned, looked, and pointed. "Indian guy. Over there leaning against the white Lincoln. He's busting a gut to get in here. You want him?"

"Yes."

"He says he had one employee. The white guy."

"Who's the black guy?"

Beer Gut shrugged. "He doesn't know. Maybe a customer." He took two steps and waved. The owner, short, lean, dressed in a blazer and khaki pants, very self-possessed, walked forward.

"I understand you're the owner."

"Yes. My name is Sadni Jansari." Lilting voice. Overpronunciation. Guy sure as hell ain't from around here.

Payne stuck out his hand. "Detective C. R.

Payne. Atlanta Homicide. How many people were working here tonight?"

"One."

"Know anything about him?"

Jansari shrugged. "An actor. He was . . ." Jansari held out his arm and wiggled his wrist. "How you say in America?"

"Gay?"

"Yes. Gay. He was gay."

"What's in the back room?"

"That is a storage room. A stockroom."

"You have a key?"

"Yes. But there is a key behind the counter. It hangs from a nail."

"I'll look."

"May I show you?"

"No, sir. If you don't mind. Stay outside until I've released my crime scene."

"Please. I need to go inside. This is my business. I must see what happened. This is not the first . . ."

"Yes?"

Jansari shrugged. "If you are a homicide policeman, you must remember. A man was shot here . . ."

Payne snapped his fingers. "Yes. I remember now. A customer was killed here several months ago."

"I try to make people forget. I have only just painted my store this week. Yesterday I finish. Today I open for business for the first time in three days." He looked up at Payne. "You think the man who did that came back?"

"Painted your business?"

"I paint the store inside and out. Make it like new."

Payne nodded. "I don't know if the individual involved in the first shooting returned. We'll look into it. Now if you'll wait here a moment, sir." He paused. "How much money is usually in the register?"

Jansari shrugged. "Never more than fifty dollars. For bills there is a safe with a slit in the top. I alone have the combination."

"The person who did this couldn't have gotten more than fifty dollars?"

"Probably less."

Payne nodded, reentered the store, and looked behind the counter. No key. Maybe it was in the attendant's pocket.

He walked back to Jansari. "Key is not there. Do you have another?"

Jansari hesitated one beat too long.

"If you'll give me the key, sir."

Jansari searched through his pockets and pulled out a key ring. He pulled off a brass key.

Payne opened the rear room. Before he went in he called the ID tech. "Back room, too."

"Ummmmmmm. In a minute."

Payne sniffed. A faint odor of gasoline.

A wooden crate that contained milk cartons was turned over. He looked up. The VCR for the security camera. The hasp was twisted. Shot off. The VCR was open. Damn. He looked around. There, against the back wall, a small ladder.

No tape in the VCR.

He leaned closer. The VCR smelled of gas.

Payne reviewed what he had. Two dead. Both shot at close range, both apparently shot by the same small-caliber weapon. One perpetrator? No bullets recovered. He would get those from the medical examiner. They would be deformed, perhaps too badly deformed for ballistics to do any good with them. One victim, the white guy, worked here. The black guy was maybe a customer who had been ordered behind the counter. The employee was gay. Could the black guy be another gay guy rather than a customer? Is that why he was shot in the mouth? Do a background on both guys. If the black was a customer, find out from family or friends where he was going or where he had been coming from. Check tag numbers of cars around the gas station. Cash register empty. Wallets empty. No tape in the security camera. Beer Gut was probably right. A robbery. Perp killed the victims and took the tape to conceal his identity.

Payne paused and gazed around the back room.

Cartridge casings? If the perp used a semiautomatic weapon there would be marks on the casings. Collect the casings. Then, once a suspect is identified, get a warrant to search for his pistol. A pistol owned by a suspect can be fired and the extractor marks on the casings compared. If they match—bingo.

Payne stood in front of the VCR, held his right hand out as if he were shooting at the lock, then looked to his right where he imagined the casing would have fallen. About there. He searched for five minutes but found nothing.

He went to the cash register and repeated the routine. He dropped to his hands and knees and ran a hand under the open displays of candy and gum and crackers. Nothing. He peered under several racks. Nothing. He stood up and looked atop the racks, probing gently between the bars of candy and packs of gum. He searched for fifteen minutes but found nothing.

Maybe the shooter used a revolver. Yeah, sure. Even high school kids carried large capacity semi-automatics—9mm, 10mm, even .45s. Who the hell carried a small-caliber pistol? They were women's guns. Could a woman have done this?

He turned to the ID tech. "You got anything?"

"It's what I didn't get that bothers me."

"What do you mean?"

"Countertop wiped clean. Door locks and knobs wiped clean. VCR wiped clean. Even the telephone wiped clean."

"Telephone?"

"You got it."

"You mean no prints?"

She shook her head. "I mean wiped clean. Somebody wanted to make sure we got nothing."

Payne waited.

"The perp used something soaked in gasoline to wipe everything down."

Payne's brow wrinkled. Gas on the telephone? From the hands of the attendant? Not likely. This is a self-service gas station and a convenience store. The attendant doesn't pump gas. He sits on his ass and sells lottery tickets.

The ID tech nodded. "*Everything* has been wiped down with gasoline."

Payne stared at the front counter. A robber doesn't wear gloves. All he touches is the money and he takes that with him. Why the hell would a perp take time to wipe down everything with gasoline?

He walked to the door and motioned for the sergeant. The uniform officers were still hanging around. A sure sign that this was another slow Sunday morning.

"Sergeant, I'd like to have crime scene tape put up. An outer perimeter from the gas pumps around the Dumpster to the rear of the station. Inner perimeter at the door."

He turned to the owner. "Mr. Jansari, I want your key to the front door."

"You need my key?"

"I'm going to board up the front door. Then I'm afraid I'm going to have to lock your station until I've finished examining everything. It may take a day or so."

Jansari threw his arms wide. "No no. This is my business. I must open in a few hours."

"Mr. Jansari, you won't be open for the next few days." Payne held out his hand.

"You can't close my business. You do not have such authority."

"This is a crime scene. Two people were killed. I do have that authority." He wiggled the fingers of his outstretched hand.

Reluctantly Jansari gave him a key.

"I hope it won't be long, sir," Payne said. "I know you're a businessman and you need to be open to do business."

"But can't I . . ."

"Mr. Jansari, I don't think you understand. I'm putting evidence tape across the front door. It is against the law for you to come back in here until I finish my investigation and release the crime scene. It is sealed until further notice."

"I will call your superiors."

"You have that right, sir."

As Jansari walked angrily toward his car, Payne looked around. He casually glanced at his car, then stopped in his tracks. He realized why the uniform officers were hanging around; why they suddenly were hooting in laughter.

Taped to the doors of his car—one on each side—was a set of training wheels.

4

Colin was sitting in his study drinking Sambuca when the phone rang.

His wife had gone to bed hours ago. He had poured Sambuca into a Waterford glass and gently dropped three carefully chosen coffee beans into the liqueur.

Then he sat down to think.

A few moments later he stood up and went to work.

He carefully wiped off the three cartridge casings he had picked up in the gas station and put them into a plastic bag. He would dispose of them later. The one remaining casing and the one live round he had not found were the only pieces of physical evidence left at the crime scene. He looked at the little .22-caliber pistol on the table and hoped he would not have to dispose of it. The Walther TPH was rare. The pistol had been imported into America for sale only to police officers. But some people such as Colin, who knew how to move around in the gray market, could occasionally find a

TPH—for a price. Cops paid maybe three hundred dollars for the gun when it was first imported. Then a mystique began growing around the weapon. And civilians, if they could get one at all, paid upward of a thousand dollars. In Atlanta or New York, a new out-of-the-box German model cost two thousand dollars, maybe three thousand. It was the most expensive of all .22-caliber pistols. And because there were so few imported, the price continued to climb.

The TPH was a great little weapon. Accurate. Relatively quiet. Very little recoil. Comfortable. And as smooth in its workings as a much larger pistol.

Colin used Stinger ammo in his TPH. He should have known better. Stingers are hot rounds that are longer than the recommended long rifle ammo. The extra length causes an occasional malfunction. But the rounds are so powerful that the occasional malfunction is worth it. Besides, Colin knew how to clear the weapon rapidly.

He looked at the weapon and smiled. Gun buffs sit around and talk big caliber. So do all the gun magazines. They think anything under a 10mm and you might as well be carrying a slingshot. Too few people understand that shot placement and penetration are far more important than caliber. You can use a .45-caliber and hit a guy in the arm and usually knock him down. But that's like using a sledgehammer to drive a tack. It forgoes accuracy for brute force. The little .22, if the bullets are placed accurately, is a devastating weapon, the weapon of an artist. And Colin considered himself an artist.

The TPH was Colin's dress pistol, the one he carried when he went to parties. At work he carried a SIG 9mm, a big and expensive weapon made in Switzerland with all the craftsmanship found in Swiss watches.

No, he did not want to even think about having to dispose of the TPH. But that was highly unlikely. If Homicide did not find his leavings he would be okay.

The money from the cash register and from the two wallets he took outside and incinerated in his gas barbecue grill. He did not want it. He had enough money.

He had been about to strip the tape from the videocassette and burn it when curiosity overcame him. He locked the door to his den, put the cassette into the VCR, sat back in his chair, and finished off the Sambuca. He crunched a coffee bean.

The overhead camera behind the counter had been carefully placed. The black and white pictures were contrasty and grainy, but the light in the store was very bright and he was easily identified. There he was, blond hair and erect carriage in a good profile, gesticulating, breaking the remote display on the cash register. He saw in painfully clear detail the attendant pick up the telephone. He saw himself lean over and break the attendant's fingers with the butt of his pistol. And then he fired rapidly.

When the pistol malfunctioned, he cleared it rapidly. Colin nodded in appreciation of his technique. Clearing Procedure Number Three: tilt the weapon to the side, remove the magazine, rack the slide to clear the jammed round, reinsert the magazine, rack the slide again, and fire. Good technique rapidly applied. Out of curiosity, he rewound the tape and timed how long it took for him to clear the weapon. Eight seconds. Not great. If he were really sharp he could have done it in six. But it was respectable.

The pistol barely jumped as it fired twice more.

Colin rewound the tape and watched it again.

He fixed another Sambuca, dropping in a coffee bean to replace the one he had eaten. He had to think this thing through.

Several drinks later he was still thinking. The Sambuca was not making him sleepy.

Maybe it was the coffee beans.

Maybe it was because he had killed two men.

He took off his horn-rimmed glasses, laid them on the table, and rubbed his eyes.

Nothing he could do about it now. It was over.

He could not be arrested. His mother would never understand. It would be the end of his job. His career as an author would end before it really began.

The telephone rang. He looked at his watch as he reached for the telephone.

"Hello."

"Mr. Biddle?"

"Yes."

"This is Detective C. R. Payne with the Atlanta Police Department. Homicide."

Colin froze. My God. How could they know so soon? He fought to make his voice calm and soft and sleepy, what a cop would expect at this hour of the morning.

"What can I do for you, Detective?"

"Mr. Biddle, I'm calling regarding a double homicide that occurred several hours ago."

Colin swallowed and waited a moment.

"Yes."

"Mr. Biddle, I'm sorry to call you so late. Or so early. Actually, it's five-ten. But I know from the older officers you like for us to call you when there's a big story. It will be daylight soon."

Colin slowly let out a long quiet sigh and closed his eyes in relief.

Payne. Payne. He didn't know the name.

"That's quite alright. You said your name was Payne. Forgive me, but it's early in the morning. Have we met?"

"Oh, no, sir. I'm the new man in Homicide. I just came out of Assaults."

"Okay. Well, it's good to meet you, even if it is on the telephone. Tell me about the homicides."

"Well, as I said, we've had a double homicide that I thought you might be interested in. It could be a good story."

Colin forced himself to perk up. "Where is it?"

"The Quicky Gas Station on Cheshire Bridge.

Just south of Happy Hermans. You know where that is?"

"Yes. There was a homicide there a few months back. I wrote about it."

"Yes, sir. I remember that. Tonight we had two victims. A white male who worked there and a black male. Both shot at close range."

Colin thought rapidly.

"Any witnesses?"

"No, sir. Actually, that's about all I have at this time. I'm still at my crime scene. The medical examiner just arrived. I'm about to begin searching my outer perimeter. In two or three hours I'll be back inside and search every inch of the store until I'm satisfied there is no evidence. I could be here all day."

"Found anything so far?"

"Nothing. But if anything is here, I'll find it. I may find clothes the perpetrator discarded or some other evidence in the Dumpster. The perp always leaves something. Always. You know that."

"You're right. Most of the time they do."

"You're welcome to come down. I'll give you the whole story."

Colin thought rapidly. He was in a dilemma. This was a great chance to go back and search for the cartridge casing and the live round. But he needed time before he returned to the place where he had killed two men. He had two or three hours before the detective began searching inside the store again. That was enough.

"Tell you what I think I'll do. I was up late last night. I just had a book come out and I was at an autograph party, you see. So I think I'll send Kitty O'Hara over. You know her?"

"I met her once. She won't remember me."

"She's good. She'll do a good job." Colin sighed. "I'd love to be there. And any other time I would dash over immediately. But my wife would never let me forget it if I left here this time of the morning. You know how that is."

"Well, sir, I'm not married anymore. But I remember how it was. I hear the older guys talking about the same thing when they get called out."

"Give me a few hours. Kitty can do the first story and then I'll take over and have a go at it. Now let me call her."

"Okay. As I said, I'll be canvassing my crime scene until I'm satisfied I've gotten everything I can. I'll be here all day."

"You're a good man. I can see why they promoted you to Homicide."

"Thank you, sir."

"Kitty will be there soon."

"Sorry again about calling you this time of the morning."

"Anytime. Homicides never happen at our convenience, do they, Detective Payne? Glad you called. I'm looking forward to seeing you later this morning."

"Good-bye, sir."

Payne hung up the phone. Most newspaper reporters were fawning butt-kissers, either that or mad dogs looking for somebody—anybody—to bite. But Biddle seemed to be a good guy. He was supposed to be a rich guy, too. He knew the chief and the mayor on a first-name basis. Biddle had mentioned his new book. My God, the guy knows all my bosses, is the best-known reporter in Atlanta, and he writes books. Payne nodded. It wouldn't hurt his chances for advancement to have the famous Mr. Colin Biddle interested in his case. Might get him a little attention.

Payne smiled and took off his jacket.

His career in Homicide was getting off to a faster start than he had planned.

5

Payne was bewildered.

He had returned to the inside of the convenience store where he was systematically removing stock from each shelf, stacking it carefully on the floor, and searching for shell casings. Even though he had found none, he did not believe the shooter had used a revolver. Revolvers are the safest of pistols. Idiot-proof. Point and shoot, that's all there is to it. But they are terribly outdated. No self-respecting robber would carry a wheel gun, not unless it was heavy metal like a .357. But where were the casings if the guy had used a semiautomatic?

Casings ejected from a small-caliber semiautomatic are thrown for a surprising distance and in an erratic pattern.

The medical examiner said each victim had been shot twice. When Payne had seen one victim shot in the eye and the other in the mouth, he had known the shooter was good. But two bullets fired so quickly the entry holes looked like one—this guy was a great shot. He had to have used a semiauto-

matic. Few people could have done this with a revolver. And four shots meant four casings. Four
casings would have sailed all over the store. So the
perp was a good shot. But was he also cool enough
and professional enough to pick up his spent
ammo? If so, this was not a garden-variety robbery.

He looked up when he heard the uniform at the
door call to him. Within an hour someone would
be here to board up the door so it could be locked.
Until then, the officer was keeping people away.

He grinned when he saw who was at the door.
No mistaking Kitty O'Hara. Her bleached blond
hair was a tangled haystack. Even from across the
store he knew she must have been out drinking last
night. Her eyes looked like two newly opened cans
of tomatoes and her face had the tired determina-
tion of a truck stop waitress after a double shift.
She wore a denim skirt as tight as it was short, and
it was very short.

Payne remembered what the older cops said
about Kitty: "You can tell how badly she needs a
story by how short her skirt is that day."

She must want this story badly.

In her right hand was a beer. The plastic collar
that once had held six beers—it now held two—
dangled from a little finger. A purse swung from
her left hand. Payne saw a notebook protruding
from the top. Judging by the heft of the purse, it
contained something else, something heavy. Payne
had heard she carried a chrome-plated .357 Magnum. He knew she had a permit.

He motioned at the uniform. "It's okay, Officer. Let her in."

Kitty sauntered in, eyes roaming all over the store.

"Morning, Miss O'Hara, Mr. Biddle said—"

"Kitty. Want a beer?" She hoisted the beers toward him and, with a sweeping glance, took in every detail of his dress. Great package. Navy suspenders against a crisp white shirt. Polished black wing tips. The buttoned sleeves gave her pause. The guy had been up all night and not only the cuffs but the plackets were buttoned. Another anal-retentive detail-oriented perfectionist. Forget this guy as a source.

He shook his head. "You drink beer this time of the morning?"

"Breakfast of champions. What's going on?"

"Mr. Biddle said—"

"Don't call that ass wipe 'mister.' "

He stared.

She shrugged. "Long night."

He nodded. "Anyway, he said you would be here. My name is C. R. Payne. We met once when I was in Assaults."

Her bleached eyebrows pulled together as she stared at his face. "I remember you. I was interviewing Amanda Jackson when she made lieutenant."

He nodded, pleased.

"Well, C. R. Payne, what's your first name?"

He paused. "Detective."

She laughed. "You, too, huh?"

His face was blank.

"You don't like your name any more than I do mine?"

"I like my name fine."

She shrugged. "Never mind. Can I come in?"

He stepped back. "Yes. You know not to touch anything, move anything, or step on anything. Stay in the middle of the aisles. And don't lean on anything."

He moved back into the store. "I'm looking for shell casings or bullet fragments. Come on back and I'll give you a rundown on what happened."

"Everyone else gone?"

"No one here but me and the evidence. And the evidence is still hiding."

"So what went down?" She took a long sip of beer and held it poised over a bare place on a shelf. "Okay if I put it here?"

He nodded.

She placed the beer on the shelf, slid the two cans off her finger and onto the shelf, and pulled out her notebook. "Mind if I take notes as we talk?"

"I haven't done this before. I know the older guys talk with Mr. Biddle all the time but—"

"Don't call him 'mister.' "

"Why don't you like him? He's written a book."

"He's a pompous shit heel, a dofus fuckhead. And his book wasn't worth killing a bunch of trees for. Now go ahead with what happened."

He stared. "You kiss your mama with that mouth?"

Kitty paused, then threw back her head and laughed. "Detective C. R. Payne, I think I like you."

"I bet you say that to every police officer. Now, let's do it this way. I'll walk you through it once without your taking notes. Then ask questions and I'll give it to you officially."

"If I want to use something you tell me the first time around, I'll ask about quoting you."

"Okay." He pointed to the counter. "At this point, here's what I know. Two victims. One black. One white. White guy worked here. The black guy might have been a customer, but I'm not sure at this time. Owner says the employee was gay. The black guy might have been gay also and hanging out. It's an apparent robbery. Perp comes in and shoots each victim twice. Head shots. Tightly grouped. They died instantly. Their wallets were on the floor. No money in them. Money taken from cash register. Looks like a robbery that went bad."

"Evidence? Eyewitnesses?"

He shook his head. "None of the above. But I'm not through searching my crime scene. A perp always leaves something. And there is always a witness. Always. Somebody saw this. Somebody was driving down Cheshire Bridge and looked over here and saw the car and maybe the perpetrator."

"But you don't know who?"

"Not yet. But they are out there. They might surface after your story."

"No evidence. No witnesses. You got jack shit."

He looked at her. "Where are you from?"

Her eyebrows rabbited upward. "Why?"

"Some of the expressions you use. Sounds as if you're from south Georgia."

"Southwest Georgia. Edison."

He grinned. "Albany."

She looked at him in disbelief. "Albany, Georgia?"

He nodded.

"That's only forty miles from Edison. We're neighbors. How old are you?"

"Twenty-nine."

"I'm the same age." She shook her head. "What the hell are you doing up here in Atlanta?"

He smiled ruefully. "Same thing you are. I wanted to get away from that place. If you grow up in southwest Georgia, Atlanta is another universe."

"You don't sound as if you're from southwest Georgia."

"Good."

She laughed, took another sip of beer, smacked her lips, and rolled her eyes upward. She plopped the empty beer can on the shelf and said, "Thank you, baby Jesus. I think I'm coming to life."

She pulled a pen from her pocket and tapped it against her teeth. "Okay, neighbor, let's do it again. Slower and more detail. Start with the names. Who were the victims?"

He looked at his notebook. "According to identification found on their bodies, the black male was one Alan Steadman, twenty-two, who resided at 666 Virginia Avenue, apartment four. Place of employment is unknown at this time. The employee, the white male, was a Kirk Kitteridge, twenty-three, who lived at—"

Kitty O'Hara gasped. Payne looked up. She was staring. Her lips trembled.

"What's the matter?"

She shook her head. "Nothing. Go ahead."

Payne recounted in official police language the details of the double homicide. Kitty asked numerous questions as she took notes. She stopped frequently to wipe her eyes.

Payne wondered what was going on. Reporters don't cry at crime scenes. Several times he asked if she were okay. Each time she shook her head and motioned for him to continue.

She looked around the store and pointed toward a shelf. "Is it okay if I get a package of Kleenex over there? I'll leave money on the counter."

He reached for his pocket. "Take my handkerchief."

"I don't want to use your clean handkerchief."

"It's okay."

She reached for the handkerchief. "I'll wash it and return it." She blew her nose and wiped her eyes. The handkerchief was clutched tightly.

She sighed and studied her notes. "I think that's

it. I'll go write this. If I need to ask you any more questions, what's your pager number?"

He gave it to her.

"And the number here?"

He looked at the telephone and gave her the number.

She closed her notebook. "Oh, God. I don't want to write this."

Payne waited.

She put the cap on her ballpoint and clasped the notebook. She wiped her eyes with the handkerchief and looked out the window at the dawn. It was going to be another hot day, another boiled blanket day, in Atlanta. Heat waves were beginning to shimmer from the street. She opened another beer and took a long drink. Then she leaned against the counter, rubbed the cold beer across her forehead, and sighed.

"His real name wasn't Kirk Kitteridge." Her voice was so soft he barely heard her.

Payne's eyes narrowed. "What?"

She looked up. "That was his professional name. He had it legally changed a few years ago when he decided to become an actor." She shook her head. "I knew he was working several jobs but I didn't know he was here."

"You knew him?"

She looked up at Payne. Tears streamed down her face.

"His real name was Charles O'Hara. He was my little brother."

6

Colin watched the video again.

He counted the shots fired and watched closely the trajectory of each shell casing until he was convinced he knew the location of the lost casing. He watched himself clearing the malfunctioned pistol after the second shot and followed the trajectory of the live round. He fixed both locations in his mind.

He stood up and smiled. Now he was ready to return to the convenience store. He ran his hand lovingly over the Plexiglas tower on his bookcase. The tower was formed by a ten-sided stack of slotted containers. Atop each stack was a date; the dates running from 1990 through 1999. Each of the slotted containers had twelve niches. Starting at the top, each niche was labeled with a small printed card containing the month of the year. Beside each month was a two-digit number. The numbers ran from fourteen to twenty with most of them hovering around sixteen or seventeen. Inside each niche was a matchbox-sized clear container. And inside each container was a tiny neatly clipped piece of newspaper that said "by Colin Biddle." On the rear of each clip was another number—the date of the month on which the article had been published.

This was Colin Biddle's collection of front-page bylines. "The Tower of Power" he called it. He had more front-page bylines than any other reporter at *The Atlanta Constitution.* The tower reminded him how good he was.

Colin gave the Plexiglas tower a final caress and left the room. He showered quickly and dressed in a pale blue shirt and khaki trousers. He stepped into a pair of brown Gucci loafers, the ones with the lugged soles that were made primarily for the European market, and then selected the Gucci blazer with the gold initialed buttons. The blazer was so blue it was almost black. As he walked quietly out the side door into the early-morning sun, he put on a pair of prescription Ray-Bans.

He drove his green Range Rover. And he wondered if that young cop—what was his name? Payne?—could have found an eyewitness who saw a Mercedes at the gas station this morning.

Kitty O'Hara was stepping into her Jeep when Colin drove into the parking lot at the Quicky Gas Station. He ignored her. He swallowed hard, covered with the emotion that always accompanies the first return visit to a place that engendered strong feelings or great emotions. Privately he considered the two victims just a couple of faggots, social detritus, the sort of societal losers who are turned into road kill by those who make the wheels turn.

Even so, he had killed two men. In an intellectual sense he had come to terms with that. But his emotions were another matter. He glanced at the pump where he had parked a few hours earlier, half expecting a pillar of cloud to arise from the ground as if to announce his presence as the killer. Or a great voice to boom from on high identifying him.

There was nothing.

Kitty O'Hara did not see him. She was facing the other direction and appeared to be wiping her eyes.

Colin stepped slowly from the Range Rover and looked around. He approached the yellow crime scene tape, walked under it, and sauntered toward the door of the gas station.

Inside, C. R. Payne looked up and recognized Colin. He watched the reporter with interest. The man had been at a party half the night celebrating his new book. Probably had a few drinks. Now he was strolling along in those expensive clothes, blond hair white-shining in the morning sun, as casually as if he were going shopping at some fancy store in Buckhead. The man had style. He was looking around, taking in the crime scene, filling his mind with details of where the shooting took place. A pro. Payne hoped his double homicide would wind up in the guy's next book.

Payne rubbed his hands in anticipation and walked toward the door. He opened it and held it wide.

"Morning, Mr. Biddle. I'm glad you could come down. I think this one will make a good story." He turned to his left and nodded toward Kitty's Jeep. "Kitty has been here for some time. She said she was going downtown to write the story." He stuck out his hand.

Colin smiled, a dazzling smile that made Payne feel as if they had known each other for years, then he reached out and shook hands. "Detective Payne, I believe. Delighted to see you."

Payne smiled. This guy was sharp. He had said "Detective Payne" and not "Officer Payne" as would so many people. Detectives don't like to be called "officer." That's what the uniforms are called. And that's why defense lawyers, in an effort to annoy detectives on the witness stand, sometimes call them "officer."

"You must have had a long night," Colin said. He looked toward Kitty's Jeep that was pulling out of the driveway.

"She will do the initial story. She's good, don't you think? But I shall do the follow-ups. Tell me what you have."

"Sure. Sure. Glad to. Come on in."

Payne held the boarded-up door wide, allowing Colin to precede him into the store. Colin walked a few paces, stopped, and looked around. He saw the stacks of goods on the floor where Payne had systematically removed them from the shelves and he realized that neither the casing nor the live round had been found. The casing was in or adjacent to the open carton of bubble gum on the top shelf and the live round was one aisle over. At the rate Payne was going he might find the live round in a few more minutes and the casing in maybe another half hour.

The detective had to be maneuvered so Colin could retrieve the evidence.

Colin squinted. "I'd forgotten how bright these lights are."

Payne looked at him curiously.

"I was in here several weeks ago. Maybe a month. Stopped to get gas."

Payne nodded.

"Haven't had time to do anything lately," Colin said. "I slept late yesterday, then ran some errands and took some clothes to the laundry. Yesterday afternoon I went over to Phipps and saw a movie made from one of Bill Diehl's books. I learn a lot from his stuff. Then I took a nap because I knew I would be up late at my book party. I didn't get up until it was time to dress for the party."

Colin looked up again at the lights. He squinted. He didn't know why he was talking so much.

"All the convenience stores are lit up this way," Payne said. "It's to deter robbers and to allow the surveillance cameras to get good pictures. Outside is even worse." He paused. "It didn't deter the shooter last night and if there are good pictures I don't know where they are. The shooter took the videotape with him."

"What?" Colin smiled in pretended disbelief. "The perpetrator knew enough to do that?"

"He was a dead shot and a cool customer—no pun intended."

Slowly and painstakingly, the detective briefed Colin on the case. The reporter did not interrupt; he only nodded occasionally. The detective finished and then said, "Kitty's brother was one of the victims."

Payne had provided a piece of information that rattled Colin. The newspaperman jumped and his eyes widened. "What? Her brother? What was he doing here?"

Payne nodded. "She informed me he was an actor. This night job was how he paid his rent. Nice kid from what she said. Very promising career ahead of him."

Colin shook his head in what Payne took to be sympathy for Kitty O'Hara.

Her brother. Kitty O'Hara had a fag brother? The black guy must have been his—whatever they call it—lover? Partner?

He realized the detective was staring at him, expecting him to say something.

Colin nodded as if deep in thought. "I'll certainly have to do the follow-up pieces now. Kitty can't write the story if her brother was a victim."

"I don't know. When she asked me to ID the victims, she kept on writing. Got all the information before she told me one of the victims was her brother." Payne shook his head in admiration. "Gutsy lady."

Colin smiled. Now Kitty O'Hara had a personal interest in the story. That was not good. He could have this inexperienced young officer chasing up blind alleys forever. But he did not want Kitty O'Hara involved. She was too close to her work. She had that single-minded, almost evangelical zeal sometimes found in a certain class of people; a type of zeal he had heard was once associated with the stereotypical old-time crusading newspaper reporters. Her persistence in following a story was legendary in the newsroom. Once, when she had taken a cab into a riot in the west side of Atlanta, the cabdriver stopped and ordered her out of the car. He refused to drive along the tumultuous streets. She had been covering a courthouse trial earlier and was dressed in a suit. While the cabby was shouting and trying to intimidate what he saw as another well-dressed Atlanta businesswoman, she reached into her purse, pulled out a shiny .357 Magnum, and stuck the barrel in his ear.

"Drive, you asshole, until I tell you to stop," she ordered.

The cabby drove.

When he told police what happened and described the woman who had hijacked his cab, the officer instantly recognized Kitty. He folded his notebook and tapped the cabby on the shoulder. "Buddy, you're lucky she didn't shoot you. If you ever see her again, you better do what she says."

Now Kitty would turn her persistence toward this case. Colin had to cut off every avenue as soon as possible. And he had to lull this young detective into a sense of comradeship.

"I thought you worked the morning watch."

Payne smiled. "I do. But until this thing is over, I'll be working morning, noon, and night."

Colin shook his head in sympathy.

"So tell me what you have."

As Payne talked him through what was known about the double homicide, Colin occasionally nodded thoughtfully. He appeared poised and interested. But his eyes darted frequently to the counter where he had stood and fired. He saw the head of the first victim—Kitty's brother—snap back from the impact of the two bullets and he saw the second victim sag bonelessly from the two shots into the open mouth.

He heard the rapid firing: *Snap! Snap!*

The dull *click.*

Then *snick-snick* as he cleared the weapon followed by *Snap! Snap!*

He smelled the blood.

He squinted. The lights in here were too bright.

"Find any physical evidence since we talked earlier?"

Payne slowly shook his head. "I've been checking my crime scene. I obtained the tag numbers of the three cars in the parking lot and ran a DMV check. Two belong to the victims. The third to a mechanic who works days. I will ask for a search warrant and then go through the apartments of the victims when I finish here. I should get a full report from the M.E. tomorrow. I don't expect much. The perp used a small-caliber weapon and the bullets almost certainly were so badly misshapen that the crime lab won't be able to get anything from them." Payne threw out his hands.

"Here at the crime scene I got nothing," he continued. He pointed at the shelves of goods. "I've been looking for shell casings."

"Find anything yet?" Colin's voice was carefully curious.

"No. Been through most of them. I'm taking every box or every item or every display from the shelf, looking through it and under it and behind it and then putting it back as it was. Nothing yet. If there's anything here, it will be either in the last few shelves on this aisle or in the next aisle. I've checked everything else. There was nothing in the back room. But I'm going to try again."

Colin smiled. "Then my timing is good. I could well be here if you find any evidence."

Payne nodded. "I'll go back to work, Mr. Biddle. If you have any questions, don't hesitate to ask."

Colin smiled that dazzling sunburst of a smile. "Well, thank you, Detective." He paused. "Say, do you mind if I call you by your first name?"

"Not at all. C.R. is my name."

Colin paused for a half second. Then he stuck out his hand. "You must call me Colin."

"Thanks, Colin."

Colin pulled a business card from his shirt pocket. It was a thick cream-colored card engraved only with Colin's name. With a pen he wrote his office and home telephone numbers on the card. He handed it to Payne. "You must forgive me. I'm not quite awake yet."

Payne looked at the card and slowly rubbed his fingers over it.

"Say, C.R., mind if I roam around a bit? Have a look at your crime scene? Just get a feel for the place? I won't touch anything."

"Go ahead."

Colin sauntered around the corner of the display rack, his eyes looking for the box where the missing casing had landed.

Payne dropped to his knees to continue searching through the boxes he had moved to the floor.

Colin found the box he was looking for. He stopped and casually rested his hand on the edge of the shelf.

"You're thinking of your next book, aren't you?"

Colin was startled. Not by the question, but by the sudden sound of Payne's voice just as he was putting his hand on the shelf.

"Oh, you know about my book?"

"Most of us in Homicide heard about it. Several guys have theirs. I think you gave them autographed copies?"

"I know almost everyone over there. You and I hadn't met at the time." His hand inched toward the box of bubble gum, his fingers quickly sneaked inside, groping, exploring.

"I'm buying your book in the next day or so."

Payne's muffled voice indicated he was still crouched on the floor.

"Don't do that. I've got some copies. I'll bring you one." Colin's hand roamed toward the end of the box, his fingers curling.

Nothing.

Wrong package. It must be the adjacent container, the box containing the chewing tobacco. His fingers began another rapid search.

"Will you sign it for me?"

"Of course. I'd be delighted. I'll put in something about our working together on a big case."

Then, in the bottom of the box, between two flat cans of tobacco, his fingers found the cartridge casing.

"I never had a signed book before."

Colin's fingers groped, trying to seize the casing without rattling the cans. It was small and light and awkward to handle. He pushed harder.

There, he had it.

Slowly he began to pull his hand from the box, the casing squeezed between his fingertips.

"It takes place here in Atlanta. You'll recognize a lot of the places and many of the characters."

Now the casing was out of the box. He slid his thumb forward for a better grip.

"Someone told me you used real names in the

book; that some of the police officers and people in Atlanta are named."

"Yes." Colin's voice was slow and casual as he slid his hand toward his coat pocket. "A lot of writers do that."

"Colin! You trying to sell that damn book in here?"

Colin was startled. He looked over his shoulder.

Kitty O'Hara was standing at the end of the aisle. She had seen him pocket the casing.

Payne was standing up staring at him over the shelf.

"Well, well, well," said the detective.

7

"Well, well, well," repeated Payne in his measured voice.

Kitty turned, almost reluctantly it seemed, toward Payne. Her eyes frequently shifted back to Colin.

Colin smiled. His hand was still tucked casually into the pocket of his blazer. He gripped the casing tightly.

"No, I'm not trying to sell my book, Kitty. Detective Payne was asking me about it." Colin waited, sure she had seen him put the casing into his pocket. Payne must have seen him also.

Why didn't the officer ask him about it?

"I'm glad you're here, Kitty," he said. "This is a grand story. It will help you maximize your career opportunities."

She wrinkled her lips. "Maximize my career opportunities? What the fuck does that mean?" Before he could answer, she continued. "You're standing there in your Jack Kennedy pose with your hand in your coat pocket. I thought you were about to say something at least as important as the Gettysburg Address."

Colin laughed.

She had not seen the cartridge casing.

"While you two are squabbling, you have overlooked an important development in this case," the detective said.

Colin turned toward Payne.

The detective's hand, clad in a rubber glove, held the live round. It was between his thumb and forefinger and the silver-colored casing sparkled in the light.

"Look at this. This tells the whole story."

The detective pulled the round closer to his face. "It's a Stinger round. He used a twenty-two. Can you believe that?"

"That's a big revelation?" Kitty asked.

Payne looked at her and then at Colin. "Okay, you two crime reporters. Based only on this live twenty-two-caliber round, what can you tell me about the perp?"

Colin looked at Kitty, hoping she would jump in. He thought quickly. Very little could be gleaned from the live round. It was the spent casing that was important, and he had found it. "It tells you he is very good," Colin said.

Instantly he regretted what he had said. Why give the detective ideas?

"What do you mean 'very good'?" Kitty asked. "You mean a professional?"

"Kitty. I thought you had gone to the office to write the story," Colin said.

"So did I," Payne said. He looked at Kitty. "You okay?"

"Yeah, I forgot my beer. I didn't want to leave it here. You'd think newspaper people go around contaminating crime scenes." She picked up the can of beer and the two empties and looked at Colin. "What do you mean 'very good'?" she repeated.

"Kitty, I'm sorry about your brother. I'll write the story if you're not up to it."

"I've written most of it in my head. I'll be okay. But tell me what you meant."

"When I was doing research on my book I read that the twenty-two is the weapon of choice for professional assassins."

Payne nodded in agreement. He held the live round higher. "Keep going. What else?" He looked at Kitty. He almost asked her what she thought and then he remembered her brother was a victim.

She swallowed and shrugged. "Actually, I'd agree with Colin. I don't know about professional assassins, but based on what you told me it had to be someone who was . . . who was a . . . good shot."

"Kitty, I was just so excited about finding this, for a moment I forgot." Payne was embarrassed.

She waved a hand in dismissal. "It's okay. I want to know what you think."

Attempting to be clinical and dispassionate, Payne held up the cartridge and said, "Here's what makes this so unusual." He looked at Colin. "I've read about the Israeli secret service and their little twenty-twos. I think they use Berettas. But those are pressed contact shots to the back of the head. They are an exception. People around here don't use twenty-twos. At least not in recent years. I've read over homicide reports of the past five years and I can tell you that the twenty-two is a weapon of the past. Even kids, I mean twelve- and fourteen-year-old gang bangers, use large-caliber weapons. Nines are the weapons of choice. Some of these people use forty-five-caliber pistols, forty-four mags, three fifty-sevens. Big stuff."

He shook his head and looked at the live round.

"I'll send this to the crime lab. Maybe it has microscopic scratches that will enable them to tell me the specific model weapon this came from."

Colin nodded. When his pistol malfunctioned, the round was caught at an angle in the breech. When he racked the slide back to clear the pistol, it had tossed the live round out before it was chambered. Could there be extractor marks? Could there be anything that would lead the ballistics experts at the crime lab to identify his weapon? He didn't think so.

The fact he had used Stinger ammo was not significant from an evidentiary standpoint. Anyone could walk into a hardware store or gun store and buy Stinger ammo by the case. But what was the detective driving at? What did he know?

Payne looked at Colin. "This cartridge tells me who did this."

Colin's eyebrows rose. His stomach churned. He waited.

"A black kid did it." Payne smiled.

Colin wanted to laugh in relief. "From one piece of common ammo you know a black kid did it?"

Payne shook his head as he slid the live round into an evidence bag. "The old guys talk about it all the time. A black kid comes into a store and pulls his weapon. To get the proprietor's attention, he jacks a round into the chamber. It's for effect. These kids believe it scares a victim to hear a gun racked. It would get my attention to hear a twelve-gauge racked, but a twenty-two?" He paused. "Dumb ass kids. But at least I know who to look for. He probably just walked in off the street and did it."

Colin was smiling broadly. "Now you have some physical evidence," he said. "You were right when you said earlier that a perpetrator always left something behind. Can Kitty use that in her story?"

"Not that I found a live round from a twenty-two-caliber pistol. You can say a small-caliber weapon was used and that physical evidence was found at the crime scene. But I want to hold back on this. Information that only the shooter has is important when we begin interviewing suspects."

The detective shook his head. "I can't get over this. A twenty-two used in a double homicide." He looked at Colin. "I hear that Kitty carries a three fifty-seven. Guys in Homicide tell me you have a permit to carry a weapon and that you know a lot about pistols. Guess you learned that from research on your book. But have you ever heard of a robber using a twenty-two? What do you carry?"

Colin had a split second of panic. "Usually a SIG. A nine-millimeter." He smiled. "To answer your other question, I'm certainly no expert. You know far more than I. But I thought there was a perception that the twenty-two is a common weapon among . . . among . . ."

"Among young blacks," Payne finished.

"Not just among young blacks. But among poorer people who use weapons. The Saturday Night Special is generally thought of as a twenty-two; a cheap twenty-two. Poor whites might use it as well as poor blacks. Some of that white trash over in Cabbagetown might use it."

"I told you both I'm new at this," Payne said. "This is my first case by myself. So my universe is somewhat small. But I can't remember any of the older guys at Homicide talking about any recent cases in which a twenty-two was used."

He paused. "I'm intrigued by this shooter. A black kid who is an expert shot with a woman's gun." Payne was talking more to himself than to the two reporters.

"The M.E. said each victim was shot twice. That means the shooter was very good. I mean *very* good. No one can be that lucky. And I only found the one live round when there should be four spent casings here. Maybe others are here and I haven't found them. But the guy took the videotape so I'm guessing he cleaned up the crime scene." Payne shook his head.

"This is confusing. I never heard of some crack head who had that much smarts or that much presence of mind."

He looked at Colin. "I wonder who this guy was. You write crime books. What do you think?"

Colin smiled and wiped a bead of perspiration from his hairline. "I think if I don't get back home my wife will be out looking for me."

He looked up. "And I think these lights are very bright."

8

Colin looked into the mirror. The mirror was framed with a wide purple band of cut glass. Quite contemporary. Colin had bought it in a craft shop in Maine in late spring. He tilted his head and smiled at his image. "I look like a true media professional," he murmured.

He wore a sand-colored suit from Henry Poole with a blue-and-white-striped shirt from Turnbull & Asser and a brightly painted silk tie from Jim Thompson. His gold cuff links, replicas of a vertebra from a rattlesnake, were from GoGo Ferguson on Cumberland Island. The shiny black wing tips were hand made by John Lobb in London.

Colin Biddle gleamed from head to toe and he felt great. Detective C. R. Payne was off chasing a nonexistent black kid as the perpetrator in the double homicide.

All was right with the world.

But when Colin picked up *The Atlanta Constitution* and saw Kitty's front-page story, his mood turned sour.

He was shaking his head in disgust when his wife walked into the breakfast room.

She looked out through the windows onto the broad backyard. "My flowers need water," she said.

He continued to shake his head.

"And my car has to go to the shop," she said. "I want that scratch repaired." Her thumbs moved rapidly as she pushed at her cuticles.

Colin's lips were pursed in displeasure.

She looked at him. "What's the matter with you? I heard you whistling in the bathroom. You never whistle. Now you look as if someone stole your rubber ducky."

He rattled the newspaper. "I'm going to have to take this story away from Kitty. She just doesn't get it."

"You mean she's not doing it the way you think it should be done."

Colin folded the paper so he could reread the front-page story. He placed the paper on the table, sipped his coffee, then jabbed a finger toward the paper. "She's writing this nonsense from that black detective about there always being a witness. Sometimes there are no witnesses. *Often* there are no witnesses. But she's convinced someone saw something and she's asking them to call her or call the detective."

"What's wrong with that?"

"She's soliciting news. She's supposed to report what happens, not try to make something happen. I don't do that in my stories." He wiggled his shoulders and said, almost to himself, "I'm a serious journalist."

His wife smiled, poured a cup of coffee, and sat down. She was wearing tennis whites. She stretched her long legs out from the table and admired them. Long and lovely and tan. Not that Colin noticed. Not that she wanted him to notice.

"We were so lucky the other night. That terrible incident must have happened not long after we left."

"Oh, it was an hour or so later." He pointed at the paper again. "I'm covering this story from now on."

"It couldn't have been an hour later. I was watching the news on TV in the bedroom and from what they said it was a half hour, maybe less."

"You believe TV news?" He snorted. "I was there. I talked to the detective. It was at least an hour later. Forget the melodrama." He shook his head and then froze as he read the last paragraph in Kitty's story. "My God. I can't believe they let her get away with this."

His wife reached for a banana. Banana and black coffee. That was her breakfast. That's what kept her slender. And being slender enabled her to keep the eye of the tennis pro at the club. She wanted to stay slender.

"I still think it happened just moments after we left."

"She's asking the fags to call her."

"They're gay."

"They're fags and she wants them to call her. She thinks someone in the fag community can tell her something about her brother or his . . . his black partner that might help the police."

Colin shook his head. He picked up the paper and rattled it. "This is *The Atlanta Constitution*, the most influential newspaper in the southeast, and she's trying to turn it into a bulletin board for a bunch of faggots."

"Temper, temper," she said sweetly. She raised her eyebrows and looked at him. "I'd say the most influential newspaper in Atlanta. Maybe Buckhead. No, *Creative Loafing* is the most important paper in Buckhead. Let's see . . . The *Constitution* is the most important newspaper"—she looked at him and then finished triumphantly—"within two blocks of the building where it is printed."

Creative Loafing is the alternative weekly in Atlanta. It is devoted almost entirely to entertainment news. That little jab hurt. Colin rustled the paper again. "I see you're your usual sparkling and scintillating personality."

"While you're eating, why don't you have a reality sandwich? The *Constitution* makes *USA Today* look like a serious newspaper."

"Not that tired old philosophy again. I've told you newspapers had to change. Besides, what makes you an expert?"

She smiled. "Well, to coin a phrase, I don't know much about newspapers but I know what I like.

And I know what you don't like. You don't like Kitty O'Hara."

"Neither do you. You think she's common."

His wife shrugged and took a bite of her banana. She chewed for a moment, swallowed, and nodded. "I think she's earthy. The two or three times I've met her she seemed very enthusiastic about what she does, very intense."

Colin stood up. "When she starts trying to make my paper an interactive device for every faggot in Atlanta, that's too intense. She's not writing any more on this story."

"Oh, the famous novelist is going to throw his weight around. For God's sake, what's so different about what she's doing and what the paper does all the time? *You* do stories like that. I've heard your lectures about how old journalism is no good and new journalism is no good and the only journalism that works today is the story that draws the reader into what is happening. Look at your newspaper. They list phone numbers and solicit reaction at the bottom of every story. Your newspaper is so touchy-feely and interactive I get nauseated reading it. The paper has no sense of purppose, no morality. But you must give it credit for one thing—it is trying to hold on to the ever-decreasing number of dimwits who read it."

"You're saying a double homicide can get solved by appealing to nonexistent witnesses and to faggots?"

"Tell me something."

Colin did not respond.

"Why are they faggots when you're at home and gay people when you're in public?"

Again, he did not answer.

"And how do you know there are no witnesses? Someone could have seen it. *We* were there and could have seen it. And the gay community is very closely knit. If Kitty's brother or his lover had an enemy, or if someone was really angry with one of them—maybe someone who was jealous—I don't know, but it could help. It could bring out evidence."

Colin bit his lip. His eyes narrowed. The detective thought the perpetrator might be a black kid. If attention were further diverted toward the gay community . . .

Perhaps he could help in that effort.

He looked at her and nodded, still thinking. "You know, you could be right."

"What?"

He leaned over and kissed the top of her head. "That is an idea worth pursuing. In fact, I shall go pursue it now. See you later."

He stood up and walked toward the door. When his Range Rover eased slowly down the driveway and into the street, she was still staring at the door.

9

"The tea-sipping son of a bitch did it," Kitty said. "He took the story away from me."

She picked up the pitcher and poured herself another beer. After a long drink, she leaned across the table. "Well, C. R. Payne, what do you have to say about that?"

Payne bit into the big hamburger that is the specialty of Manuel's Tavern and chewed, eyes on his plate as if thinking. Kitty's conversation had been jumping all over the place. He wondered how much beer she had drunk before he arrived.

"I remember what one of the old heads told me about newspaper reporters. He said reporters are like camels; they have to pee on somebody. He said it is not malicious, it is their way, the natural order of things. The sun rises in the east, winter follows spring, the moon waxes and wanes, and reporters pee on people."

Kitty stared. "I don't get the point."

"Try to avoid reporters. But if you must deal with one, invite him inside the tent so he will pee out. That's better than having him outside peeing in." Payne shrugged. "But you can never be sure he will pee out. The only thing you can be sure of is that a reporter will pee on someone."

"So you're saying my esteemed colleague pissed on me. Well, big whoop. What a fucking revelation that is. I mean I am sitting here dripping, and you, the philosopher king, come along and have a revelation that I have been pissed upon."

Kitty took another drink of beer. She reached into her purse. "That reminds me. Here is your handkerchief. Cleaned and ironed."

"Thanks." He did not want to ask how a conversation about camels and reporters had reminded her of the handkerchief. He folded the handkerchief and stuck it into his breast pocket.

"You trying to dress like Pisshead?"

He patted the handkerchief and returned to his hamburger. "What do you mean?"

She nodded toward the handkerchief. "He wears handkerchiefs in his breast pocket." She took a drink of beer. "Looks like a New Orleans pimp."

"He was wearing Gucci loafers, too." Payne shrugged. "I don't know how he does that."

"Does what?"

"Wears Guccis. Guccis were the second biggest disappointment of my life. I saved for months. Bought a pair." He shook his head. "Too narrow. Too tight. I never wear them anymore."

"What was the first?"

"First what?"

"First biggest disappointment in your life?"

"Perrier water. I'd heard of it. Seen the ads. So I bought a bottle." Again he shook his head. "One day I will learn not to want some things."

"Colin is a clothes horse and an Anglophile."

"There are worse things."

She made a raspberry. "He's a first-rate representative of a third-rate country. Who the hell wants to copy anything from England? Nation of usetabees."

"Don't equivocate, Kitty. Tell me how you really feel."

She held up her beer. "Do you know why reporters drink so much?"

"Enlighten me."

"Every one of us, including *moi*, have terminal cases of insecurity. We are worse than Sally Field about wanting people to like us. We're screwed-up flakes. It doesn't help when Colin waltzes in and takes over my story. And they let him."

"Can I order you a cup of coffee?"

"Colin in different." She paused. "I haven't figured out how yet. But he's different."

"How about that coffee?"

"Is your first name *Mother*?"

"Hey, you're my new friend from southwest Georgia."

"Are you married?"

"Your conversation does jump around."

"Well, are you?"

"Divorced."

She studied him. "For the same reasons most police officers get divorced?"

He stopped chewing and looked at her. He knew what she meant. Cops have one of the highest divorce rates of any group in the country. The reasons are usually drinking and womanizing. Cops drink their weight in booze about once a week. And when it comes to sex, cops cull nothing. A cop would screw a snake if someone would hold the head.

He shook his head. "No."

"Then why?"

"You always so personal?"

"Just asking questions."

He stared at his hamburger. "I have a schedule. I'm going to be a police officer a few more years and then I have other plans. Political plans. She didn't want to wait. She wanted me to resign now, forget my plans, and go into business." He shrugged. "I have my plans."

"So she walked."

He nodded.

"Well, C. R. Payne, have a drink of beer." She looked over her shoulder and caught the waiter's eye.

"Tommy." She waved.

The stocky young man walked to the table.

"Tommy, bring my friend a glass."

Tommy, who managed the tavern, looked at Payne.

Payne shook his head.

"He's working, Kitty. He doesn't want a beer."

Manuel's is the tavern of choice for newspaper people, politicians, Emory University faculty, plumbers, carpenters, and young women who know they will not be hassled if they come in alone. But it is especially a cop bar. For officers who are on duty and who come in for lunch or dinner and for officers who are off duty and who come in to drink. Uniforms, SWAT Team, Red Dogs, undercover officers, detectives; they all come to Manuel's. Tommy knew more cops than did Kitty.

"Well, I do, Mr. Innkeeper. My flagon is empty."

Tommy looked at her for a moment, then walked away. "Okay."

"Tommy has a good package," she said.

Payne looked at her, eyebrows raised.

She shrugged. "You guys are always commenting on a woman's breasts or her legs or her butt. Well, we can comment on your package."

Payne put his hamburger on the plate and leaned closer. "Does that mean what I think it means?"

"Hey, your package is your package."

Payne shook his head. "You talk worse than the women where I work."

"He took my story," Kitty said. She grabbed Payne's wrist and held tightly. "It was *my* story. *Mine*. And he took it. Just because he's Mr. King Shit."

"If that kinda stuff bothers you, you ought to work where I work."

"Well, I'm not used to it. I'm as good as he is. Better."

"He wrote a book."

"Hey, there are women preachers and three-legged dogs, but so what? So he wrote a book." She leaned back and stared at him. "That impresses you, doesn't it?"

Payne took another bite of his hamburger and nodded. "Yes," he said. "Yes it does."

"Well, C. R. Payne, he is living proof that you don't have to be a writer to publish a book." She leaned closer toward him. "I am from Edison, Georgia. You know Edison. You can pee from one side of that town to the other. When I was growing up, a big Saturday night for me was a possum and a six-pack. We didn't have anything. But we treated each other with honor and respect. You just don't do to a person what he did to me."

"A possum and a six-pack? Give me a break."

"What the hell were you raised on, C. R. Payne? Sugar titty and Moon Pie? Did you get treated this way?"

He stared at her. "I was a black kid in Albany, Georgia. How do you think I was treated?"

"What's C.R. stand for?"

He drank from his glass of water, put it down, and picked up his hamburger.

"Come on. What's your first name?"

"Okay." He sighed. "Since we're both from southwest Georgia, I'll tell you."

"What is it?"

He looked left and right. He leaned toward her. "Detective," he whispered.

She smiled and shook her head. "I can find out, you know. I have friends who will check your record and tell me."

"I doubt it."

"I have ways." Her smile broadened.

He stared. "You'd do that just to find out my name?"

"That's how I say hello. Hey, I'd fuck a venetian blind just to find out what time it is."

"You hung up on names because of yours?"

Her eyes narrowed. "What do you mean?"

He shrugged. "Kitty O'Hara. Some name for this town. I bet people call you Scarlett."

Her eyes narrowed and her lips tightened. She leaned forward and tapped him on the forearm. "Anybody calls me Scarlett, I steal their car, burn their house, and sow salt in their garden."

"You don't like Scarlett?"

Kitty snorted. "She didn't bang Rhet the first time she met him. Had him right there in the library and let him get away." She paused. "What the hell do you know about that book?"

Payne slipped into an exaggerated dialect. "Lawsy mercy, Miss Scarlett, I don't know nothing 'bout names."

Kitty stared in disbelief. "You read *Gone With the Wind*?"

"Black people do read, you know. I can also tie my own shoes."

"Come on, Payne. You know what I mean. Black people hate that book."

"You have to consider the time being written about. It's not like that today." He paused. "Well, most of the time."

Kitty took a long drink of beer and smiled. "Look at me, C. R. Payne. I wore a suit today. High heels. Panty hose. I even wore a goddamned bra. All to impress the editors and show them how professional I am and why I should stay on this story."

Tommy returned with a brimming pitcher of beer.

"Thanks, Tommy."

"You must not be going back to work today, Kitty."

"Tommy, I work all the time. Even when I am here, I am working. Even when I'm asleep, I am working. My brain never sleeps. I am bionic woman. Hear me roar."

She filled her glass. Slowly she shook her head. "My brother is dead. My little brother. But they don't see how that will make me work longer and harder to help find out who killed him. They think I will get emotional."

Tommy walked away.

Payne stopped chewing and looked at her. "You? Emotional? How could they believe such a thing?"

She stared at him. Her lips trembled. "My brother wanted to be an actor."

Payne nodded.

"His all-time favorite actor was Richard Dreyfuss. He saw every movie Richard Dreyfuss ever
made. His favorite was *Lost in Yonkers*." She
smiled, wiped one eye, and then shook her head.

"He thought Dreyfuss was so debonair, so sophisticated smooth in that role." She turned and
looked at Payne. "I thought he played a loser, a
second-rate crook who was always on the run."

Payne shrugged.

"But the character had a good heart," Kitty said.
"He gave a lot of money to his sister. I think that's
why my brother liked him. Because he had a good
heart. My brother saw that he was a kind man."

"You were close to your brother." Payne spoke
softly.

Kitty nodded, afraid to speak. She squeezed her
lips together to keep them from trembling.

"Maybe that's why they took you off this story.
Maybe they considered it a favor rather than
punishment."

Kitty's eyes hardened. "What if they jerked you
off this case? What if one of the senior homicide
detectives, one of the white guys, waltzed in and
decided he wanted this case? How would you feel?
Wouldn't you think it was racial?"

"Nobody will take this away from me! Not unless
I screw it up and I don't intend to do that!"

"Yeah, but what if they did?"

"It wouldn't necessarily be racial."

"Just because old Condescending Colon wrote a

book and is rich and wears nice clothes, you think . . ." She paused and then shrugged. "So would most people." She laughed and threw her arms wide. "All I know is, I want to find out who killed my little brother and they took the story away from me. I broke that story. It was all over page one this morning. Did you see it?"

He looked at her. His eyebrows arched.

"Of course you saw it. Your name was in it. Prominently. Spelled correctly. You looked good. You're a hero. Young detective on his first big case. That was my story."

Payne waited a moment. "Kitty, maybe you need to take some time off, get out of town, rest a bit. Where's your favorite place? Where do you go to unwind?"

"I spend a lot of weekends cavorting in the Wamsuttas."

"Wamsuttas? Are they like the Appalachians?"

"Yeah. But more fun."

Payne shrugged. "White folk."

She twisted her shoulders. "I've got to go to the ladies' room and take off this bra. It's killing me."

"Thank you for sharing that with me."

"Panty hose, too." She wiggled. "I'm wearing slacks from now on. To hell with those guys. So you got anything new?"

He looked at her. "Sure you want to hear it?"

She paused. "Yes."

"Look, we've got to have an understanding here. I have no problem giving you information. I trust you not to burn me. But your brother was a victim. And some of my information—"

"You think I can't handle it? You think I'm not professional? I know it's my brother. I know how he was killed. But I can separate my brother from my work. You saw the story. Did it look like I was having trouble?"

"No, it did not. I like how you emphasized the possibility of an eyewitness. And your idea about getting information out of the gay community, while I don't think it will work, is nevertheless a good idea. You did a good job."

"What do you mean it won't work?"

"The gay community is extremely closemouthed about stuff like that. In some ways they are their own worst enemy. They won't tell us anything about anything. Of course, if the case is not solved in the next five minutes they'll call a news conference and condemn the police force in general, and me, specifically, for being homophobic. They will have a news conference to say APD is part of a conspiracy to allow genocide in the gay community."

"They'll talk to me. He was my brother."

"They'll use you. But they won't talk to you."

"So tell me what you found."

"The medical examiner sent me a report this morning. Along with several misshapen hunks of lead. I wouldn't have known they were bullets unless he told me. He said the other two were so fragmented there's nothing but little pieces. So we got nothing from the bullets in the victims. I sent the live round out to the crime lab. When I talked to the guy he told me not to expect too much. Said an ejected Stinger round doesn't reveal much."

He paused.

"What else?"

He stared.

"Go ahead, tell me."

"Okay. Three fingers on your brother's . . . the first victim's hand were broken before he was shot. A hard-edged object—we don't know what—was used."

"*Before* he was shot?"

"Yes."

"What does that mean?"

"I don't know. Yet."

She sat back and thought for a minute. It did not make sense.

"So where are you?"

"A robbery. Apparently one perp. Used a twenty-two semiautomatic pistol. Excellent shot. One victim's hand broken. The remote display for the cash register was broken. I think the perp tried to come across the counter and get in the cash register."

Payne wiped his mouth and placed the napkin on the table. "There's one other thing."

She waited.

"Both victims were wearing watches. Your brother had on a nice ring."

Kitty nodded. "Daddy gave him that when he graduated from college."

"The black kid had on an expensive watch."

Kitty nodded in understanding. "The bad guy didn't take them."

Payne nodded. "But he took less than fifty dollars in cash. I don't know, but if your brother had to work there nights, I'm guessing he had very little money on him."

"He never had money. I gave him money every month."

"The perp left behind a ring and a watch that— even if he fenced them—would have brought more money than he got from the victims and the cash register."

"It doesn't make sense."

He stood up. "It brings me back to my theory about a whacked-out black kid doing the job, coming in there and racking back one for effect, shooting the two victims, then losing it. Just grabbing the money and running. Didn't even see the watches and ring." He paused. "Except he took time to wipe down everything and to take the videotape."

Payne paused. "I can't figure it out. I'm going back to the crime scene. The answer is always at the crime scene. Where you going?"

"I'm going to bourbon as soon as I finish this pitcher."

He stood up. "If they took you off the story, does that mean you won't be writing about it anymore?"

"No," she snapped. "I stay up-to-date on every open homicide even if I'm not working it. Colin might go off to research another book. The pecker head might die. God might decide she made a mistake putting that piece of shit on earth and she might call him home. So don't you hold out on me."

"Touchy, touchy. If you get any information from the gay community, let me know."

"Thanks, C. R. Payne." She grimaced. "Hey, I'm tired of calling you C. R. Payne. What's your name?"

Payne smiled. "See you." She watched him walk toward the door. God, he had broad shoulders.

Kitty pushed the pitcher away and waved her hand until she caught Tommy's eye.

"Bring me Jack black and his twin," she said. "I'm going to sit here with Jack and figure this out. We're going to have a private wake for my little brother and then I'm going to catch the son of a bitch who shot him."

"You want a double bourbon? How about something to eat?"

"I ate beer. The bourbon is dessert."

10

"**M**ajor Lloyd, this is the chief."

"Yes, ma'am."

Mickey Lloyd unconsciously straightened a bit in his chair at police headquarters and turned to look out the window on Decatur Street into the seedy run-down heart of Atlanta. At the upper echelons of the Atlanta Police Department the political riptides are as subtle as they are powerful. Mickey Lloyd had not risen to the rank of major without being able to read the tides and currents. He knew that when the chief called, addressed him by his rank, and identified herself simply as "the chief" that she was all business; that this was an official call and that it probably meant she was about to roll something downhill.

"I just received a call from the mayor's office."

"Yes, ma'am."

It was about to start rolling downhill.

"He called in regard to the double homicide on Cheshire Bridge Road early Sunday morning. The one at the gas station."

"I'm familiar with the case."

"The owner of the gas station, actually he owns a chain of gas stations, is a friend of the mayor. And a campaign contributor. The mayor said his friend had called him twice today."

"Yes, ma'am."

"He called about two things. The detective working the case . . . ?"

"C. R. Payne. Young officer out of Assaults. Good man. Fine detective."

Mickey Lloyd was legendary for his knowledge of the people and the cases under his command. He knew the details and the status of virtually every active case in Homicide. When a deputy chief or the chief asked about a case or about a personnel matter, Mickey Lloyd rarely had to check the records. He knew.

"Yes, well, apparently your young officer has not released the crime scene."

"As you know, Chief, that's normal procedure. The officer found a live round out there Sunday morning. Only physical evidence found thus far. He believes there may be additional evidence at the crime scene, evidence that might identify the perpetrator."

"The gentleman who owns the service station wants it released. He says the station was closed for a week after a homicide there several months back and that it took him some time to regain lost business. He wants to minimize that this time. He has asked the mayor to have the crime scene released so he can reopen. He said he was being treated like the KKK used to treat black people."

"That's a little strong. Not to mention incorrect. But I understand, Chief." He paused. "You said there were two things."

"The mayor's friend also expressed some concerns about his front door."

"Yes."

"He says someone drove a police car through his front door."

"The first uniform officer to arrive at the scene saw two bodies on the floor. At the time he didn't know if the victims were alive or dead. There was no time to call the emergency number posted at the store and have the owner come down and unlock the front door. The officer tried unsuccessfully to break the window at the lock. Motivated entirely by a desire to come to the aid and assistance of two citizens, he used the front bumper of his official vehicle." Major Lloyd paused. "He nudged the door. He didn't drive through it."

"Is that procedure?"

"Are officers trained to use their cars to break down doors? No, ma'am, they are not. But they are trained to improvise and adapt and to do whatever is necessary to protect the lives of civilians. He did the correct thing. I support him entirely."

"The constituent's concern is reimbursement. He expects the city to pay for his door."

"Doesn't he have insurance?"

"Yes, but there is a large deductible. He doesn't want this on his insurance record."

"I see."

"I'll inform the mayor of our conversation."

"Thank you, Chief. I am aware of the mayor's concerns regarding this constituent. The lieutenant in charge of Homicide will be so informed. The investigation is proceeding."

"Thank you, Major Lloyd."

Mickey Lloyd hung up the telephone but kept his hand on the receiver. He looked up at the pictures on the wall, pictures of him as a young man, as a SEAL in Vietnam sitting in the open door of a helicopter cradling an M-16. His face was smeared with camouflage paint. The picture had been taken moments before he took off for a raid in the Mekong Delta. He remembered as if it were yesterday the exhilaration of being a young lieutenant (j.g.) and leading men into combat. As a lieutenant he had responsibilities, but the fun and the excitement were greater than the responsibilities. Senior officers had much greater responsibility and none of the fun. Those senior officers envied him and many of them would have traded places with him. Just as today he envied the young detective— this C. R. Payne—who was out on the street working the double homicide.

He slowly pulled his hand away from the telephone and leaned back in his chair and smiled reflectively. His senior officers had covered his ass many times in the Mekong. And he always delivered for them. Every time.

There would be time later to roll things downhill; time to call the lieutenant in charge of Homicide and raise hell. But for now, let the young detective have his fun.

Oh, yeah. Too bad about that guy's door.

11

Colin stood up in his V-shaped workstation and looked out the window onto the rotting corpse of downtown Atlanta. Over the rooftops, two buildings away, was an enormous billboard covered with a picture of Reverend Ebenezer Cross, the charismatic black minister of the eight-thousand-member Holy Bethel AME Church. Reverend Cross had a stern look on his handsome face and was pointing an admonishing finger, so it seemed, straight at Colin. The caption on the billboard read: "Thou Shalt Not Kill."

Colin turned away from the window and looked around the newsroom. Some media critic from *Atlanta Magazine* had been through several months ago and written that the newsroom was like a warehouse of accountants or insurance underwriters. The writer had talked about the thick carpet that muffled sound, about the tops of heads bent over computer terminals, and about the five TV sets suspended from the ceiling that were the source of much of the newspaper's breaking news stories.

Colin sniffed. The writer was a former newspaperman crying over days that were long gone and would never return; he was crying over a time that perhaps never really existed except in the minds of white-haired old troglodytes. The Geezer Patrol, that is what Colin called them, that's what he called the old guys who hated the editor and who groused and moaned about the direction the paper had taken in recent years.

Colin didn't understand the Geezer Patrol. He was not as old as they, but he was older than many reporters and he understood the editor and understood the changes newspapers had to make in order to survive. He understood about short stories and no jumps and diversity and multicultural involvement and interactive stories about things that mattered to people. He didn't agree with the multiculturalism nonsense and the idiotic and ad nauseam coverage of the gay community. But he understood. He was a professional. That was the long and the short of it.

He turned and continued to peer around the newsroom, looking over the domain where he was a prince of the realm.

"Hey, famous writer, what's the buzz?"

Colin turned. The editor was standing at the edge of his work space, hand outstretched. "Congratulations on the book. Not a bad review. How long before you know how well it's selling?"

"Thanks very much indeed, Don. You know that is almost impossible to find out. I called Borders thinking they could get a computer readout from all their stores. But something's wrong. They indicate that only fifty books were sold last week."

"In the Atlanta stores?"

Colin nodded. "I know that's wrong." He did not add that he had bought ten of the books.

The editor nodded sympathetically. "I know it will sell a million copies."

"Thanks, Don. I really appreciate that."

"Need anything? I saw you looking around the news space."

"Well, as a matter of fact, I do. I'm trying to figure out how to get in touch with a gay person."

The editor looked at him as if waiting for more explanation.

"It's in connection with the double homicide." Colin shrugged dismissively and smiled. "Kitty O'Hara mentioned something about gays in her story. She and I had talked about that. I want to see if anything is there."

"You want any particular gay person?"

Colin shrugged. "I don't know. Just a gay person. Someone who knows that community. What do they think about the homicide? Did they know the victims? That sort of thing. A react from the gays."

"You know we have a number of gays on our staff."

Colin's eyes widened. "In the newsroom?"

"Yes." The editor scanned the room, mentally counting. "Two columnists, five reporters, and several editors among the men. We have almost that many lesbians among our women staffers." He paused. "Since this is in regard to the double homicide and one of the victims was black, you should also talk to members of the black gay and lesbian community."

"The black gay and lesbian community?"

"Yes. I'm trying to hire more. Diversity, you know. We need people who can report on that point of view, particularly the difficulties in being black and gay. Don't you agree?"

"Of course."

"The problems gays have announcing their commitments is very discouraging. We were the first major daily newspaper in the country to publish commitment notices."

"Commitment notices?"

"Yes, on Sunday. Along with the conventional wedding announcements."

"We do that?"

"Yes. I'm proud of that."

Colin recovered. "Well you should be. What sort of reaction have you gotten from the community? From the regular, the straight community?"

The editor shrugged. "About what you might expect in a conservative market like Atlanta. A lot of people just don't understand what we're trying to do."

Colin smiled ruefully. "I've been so busy on the book and I've been out of the office so much at the police station that a lot of things have missed my attention." He paused. "Who would you recommend that I talk with? Who best knows that community?"

The editor paused. "Oh, any of them would be glad to help you. They like for people to better understand what they're about."

Colin nodded. "Don, I am embarrassed. But I spend so much time away that I need your counsel."

The editor nodded. "You'll want to talk to a black gay man as well as a white gay man."

"Of course."

"You'll want a couple of spokespersons who are articulate and passionate in their concerns. Young gay men. The older ones are sometimes a bit conservative. Perhaps reporters who are members of Act Up?"

Colin paused. He had no idea what Act Up was. "Absolutely."

"Okay, here's who you talk to." The editor identified several people in the newsroom and pointed them out to Colin.

Colin smiled and stuck out his hand. "Thanks, Don."

"Anytime. Tell your mother I asked about her."

"I will."

The editor walked away.

Colin picked up his notebook and pulled a pen from his pocket. He took a deep breath and walked across the newsroom toward the young black gay man recommended by the editor.

12

Tommy stood over Kitty with a disapproving look. Her hair was disheveled and she had the lopsided smile of a puppy. The strap of a bra and more than a foot of panty hose dangled from her purse. The top two buttons of her blouse were unbuttoned.

"You're cut off, Kitty. I've called you a cab."

"I got one mother. I don't need another. I can drive."

She reached for her purse. Tommy beat her to it. He opened the purse and pulled her car keys out and dropped them into his pocket.

"Come by and get your keys tomorrow. The cab's on us." He leaned close. "And hide that gun. I can see it in your purse. You know you're not supposed to bring a gun into a bar."

"Another bourbon, Tommy my lad. I yearn to be in the arms of Jack black."

"I told you, you're cut off. The cab's outside. Let's go." He shook his head. "You're working on a double homicide. You need to get your rest."

She snorted. "Condescending Colon is working

on a double homicide. I'm working on . . . I'm working on . . . what the hell am I working on? My little brother is dead and what am I working on? I was raised on possum and sweet potatoes and what the hell am I working on?"

"You're making more sense than most newspaper people. But I still don't understand."

She drained the last drop of bourbon from her glass. "Tommy, did you know that bourbon is God's greatest gift to the world?"

"I run a bar."

"Tommy, only one thing tastes better than bourbon. And you don't find it in a bottle."

Tommy laughed. He leaned over and spoke softly. "Kitty, you've been coming in here a long time, you're a good customer and we like you. But you're drunk and people are beginning to notice. You don't need that. I want you to leave. If you don't do it on your own I'll have a couple of female employees carry you out. And if I have to cause a scene like that I won't let you come back."

She looked at him in amazement. "You'd bar me? I'm your best customer."

"Kitty."

"Okay," she mumbled, reaching for her jacket and purse. "I know. I'll thank you tomorrow." With some difficulty she stood up. She held on to the table for a moment. "Tommy, one more drink. I have to go to a funeral tomorrow."

"No more, Kitty. The cab is waiting."

They moved slowly toward the door.

"Is it a good cab?"

"For you, only the best."

She stopped. "I don't want one of these god-damned Atlanta cabs with shag carpet on the floor and chicken bones in the backseat and a driver who can't find his ass with a search warrant. I'm going home from my brother's wake and I want a good cab. With air-conditioning."

"This is a good cab."

"Where's the driver from? Nigeria? Ethiopia? Bangla-fucking-desh? Aren't there any cabdrivers from America? I want a driver who was born in Atlanta."

"He's a good driver. Local guy. White guy."

"I don't care what color he is. He can have polka dots on his ass. Just as long as he is from Atlanta and knows the city. Tommy, I only ride in cabs driven by people from Atlanta."

"You don't ride in cabs much, do you?"

"And it has to be air-conditioned."

"I promise."

"He knows the city?"

"Like his own backyard."

"Then I'll ride with him." She lurched out the back door into the parking lot. A cab was waiting. She threw her purse and her jacket inside. Then she carefully followed.

Tommy leaned toward the open window. "Kitty, give him your address."

"Up near Lenox Square. Go through Virginia Highlands and I'll show you."

Tommy gave the driver twenty dollars. "That should cover it. If not, let me know."

The driver nodded. He was a wizened scarecrow of a man.

"Good night, Kitty. Take care of yourself."

"Good night, Tommy my lad. I'll see you in the by and by."

Tommy laughed and waved.

Kitty fell backward as the cab drove away. Her dress rode high up her legs. The driver adjusted his rearview mirror.

"Where's the air-conditioning?"

"Broken. Sorry."

"Any cab I ride in has to be air-conditioned. How long has it been broken? Five years?"

"It stopped an hour ago. Haven't had time to fix it."

"Does any cab in this fucking city have air-conditioning? You ever been to London? You even know what a real cab looks like? This town has the lousiest cabs of any city in Amerca. Any city." She glared at the back of the driver's head. "I asked you if any cab in this city has air-conditioning."

"Yeah. Sure they do."

"Yeah, and I'm a fucking Chinese astronaut."

Kitty's dress rode higher. She unbuttoned another button on her blouse. It was hot. The night air provided little relief.

The cab drove up Highland, crossed Virginia, and turned left on Lenox Road.

Suddenly Kitty realized that the Quicky Gas Station was at the intersection where Lenox Road dumped into Cheshire Bridge. She decided to stop at the Dunk 'n Dine, have a cup of coffee, and then walk a block to the gas station to see if C. R. Payne was making any progress.

"Stop at the Dunk 'n Dine," she said. "I'll get out there."

"The fellow who paid the bill said to take you home."

Kitty's brow wrinkled. The guy takes a peek and gets carried away. Wants to ride around all night. He can't keep his eyes on the road.

She slid forward on the seat and tapped the driver on the shoulder. "I'm the passenger, asshole. I decide where I'm going. Now stop at the Dunk 'n Dine."

"I gotta do what the guy told me. Give me your home address, lady."

The cab was at the intersection of Lenox and Cheshire Bridge. She looked over her shoulder. An unmarked detective car was in front of the Quicky Gas Station. Payne was at work.

"Pull over."

"You said you lived near Lenox. I'll go up Lenox Road."

The driver accelerated rapidly into Cheshire Bridge Road, throwing Kitty back in the seat. Her bare legs flew upward. The cabdriver looked over his shoulder and grinned. He continued to occasionally look over his shoulder or in the rearview mirror as he drove rapidly under I-85 and up Lenox Road.

"Let me out."

"What's your address, lady?"

Kitty's eyes fell on her purse. She reached for the panty hose, wrapped her left hand around one end and her right around the other. Then she leaned forward and looped the panty hose around the cabdriver's neck. She put both feet in the back of the seat and leaned backward with all her weight.

The driver gagged and reached for the panty hose with his left hand and then his right. She jerked hard and the driver leaned back farther to keep from being strangled.

"Die you fucking pervert. Die," she shouted. She kicked at the back of his head with her left foot while her right foot pressed hard into the back of the seat. She pulled hard on the panty hose.

The cab began to weave erratically. On both sides of Lenox Road were condominium projects fronted by tall fences. Each project was separated by a buffer zone of trees.

The driver's eyes filled with panic. He gasped for air and tried desperately to keep the cab in the road.

"I'm gonna choke you like a goddamned chicken. I'll teach you to drive a cab with no air-conditioning. And don't look up the dresses of your passengers." She pushed harder on the seat with her feet and leaned backward. "You beady-eyed pervert."

Suddenly the driver slumped and the cab darted toward the trees on the right side of the road.

"Oh, shit," Kitty screamed, and dove for the floor.

The cab careened into a utility pole and slid through a clump of rhododendron bushes and into a copse of trees before slamming to an abrupt halt.

Kitty did not move for a long moment. She arose from the floor and looked around, then mumbled, "Toto, I don't know where we are. But this ain't it." She lurched from the cab, grabbing her jacket and purse. As she opened the door the driver was gagging.

She jerked at the panty hose around his neck, causing his head to bounce off the door. "God-damned kamikaze pilot. Now you're trying to steal my panty hose."

The driver weakly pulled at the panty hose and handed them out the window.

Her brows pulled together and she leaned toward him. "You awright?"

The driver coughed. He held his throat and gasped. "I'm calling the cops. You wrecked my cab."

"Go ahead." She opened her purse. "Where's my cell phone? I'll let you use my phone. When they get here I'll tell them you kidnapped me and would not let me out of the cab when I told you to. I'll charge you with false imprisonment. You'll lose your license."

Weakly the driver waved her away. "Just get away."

"I'll get away from you when you give me back that twenty bucks Tommy gave you. I'm returning it. You're a thief. And you don't have air-conditioning."

He looked at her and laughed.

A second later a chrome-plated .357 was pressing hard into his left nostril. The driver would have sworn the barrel had an opening the size of a garage. He stopped laughing and quickly dug into his pocket and handed her the twenty dollars.

Kitty smiled. "That's proof of why we poor defenseless women should carry guns."

She put the money into her purse and lurched away. "When you get that piece of shit cab repaired, tell them to work on the air-conditioning." She flung her purse over her shoulder and slowly began climbing the embankment. She slipped often.

"I think I may have had too much to drink," she mumbled as she lay facedown in the wet grass.

She pulled herself to her knees. There before her was something shiny. It was a key ring and it gleamed softly in the light from the streetlights. She tilted her head and looked closely. A chrome tag was attached to the keys. On it was written QUICKY GAS STATION and an address on Cheshire Bridge Road.

13

"You didn't touch anything?" Payne asked. He hunkered down in the wet grass, a flashlight in his hand, and stared at the key ring. He twisted his head to the side and read QUICKY GAS STATION on the key ring. "You were right."

Kitty glared. She lay where she had fallen, her head about eighteen inches down the hill from the keys. She had rolled over on her side to call him from her cell phone, then rolled back to stare drunkenly at the keys, watching them as if not sure they would remain where she found them. Her hair was rumpled, her skirt over her knees and her blouse unbuttoned. A rumpled pair of panty hose lay beside her.

"You were right," she mimicked. "Well, big whoop. Of course I was right. I can read."

"You're so touchy. Ever think of dropping that subscription to *Ms* magazine?"

"Haven't you asked me that before? There are times when you show every indication of being a real—"

"Did you touch anything?"

Her lips pursed into a drunken moue and she shook her head and slowly said, "Noooooo, Detective Payne, I didn't touch anything." She paused. "I'm not some rookie cop. I've probably . . . no, no probably about it. I've been on more homicides, more crime scenes than you have. I have more time in the bathroom at Homicide than you have in the office."

"You've also drunk more liquor than I have."

"I have to go to a funeral tomorrow and I must be prepared."

"You get drunk before you go to a funeral?"

"It's the Irish in my soul."

"It's the little girl in your soul."

"You're so goddamned tight your butt squeaks."

"I'm gonna wash your mouth out with soap and send you home without any dinner."

"Payne, tell me something."

He looked at her.

"Look at you. It's the middle of the night. You've probably been on the crime scene for ten or twelve hours, except for lunch, and look at you. You look like you got dressed five minutes ago. You are either the neatest man God ever made or you're made of plastic."

She put her hand in her disheveled hair and looked down at herself. "I look like I got dressed in a food processor."

She buttoned her blouse and pulled down her skirt. The panty hose she stuffed into her purse.

She looked around. "I've lost one of my shoes. That creepy cabdriver probably stole it. He's a pervert. He didn't have air-conditioning."

"So what's your point?"

"I look like hammered shit. I look like . . ." Her voice dwindled away.

He smiled. "White trash?"

She stared at him for a moment, then dropped her head. Her shoulders began shaking. She flipped over on her back and exploded with laughter. "White trash. Trash with flash. That's me. Payne, I'm gonna call the head of the NAACP and get you a lifetime membership."

"Already have one."

She looked at him. "You been wanting to say that ever since we met, haven't you?"

"Say what?"

"That I'm white trash. That's what you think, isn't it?"

"Don't be hard on yourself, Kitty. And don't forget where I'm from."

"Yeah, but you shook all that red clay off your shoes. You don't even talk like you're from the South. You don't have any accent. You speak better than I do. You got out and you got up." She paused. "I just got out."

Payne looked up the hill toward Lenox Road. A wrecker had arrived to pull the cab back onto the street. The cabdriver studiously avoided looking at Kitty.

"Kitty, this is the most incredible piece of luck

or coincidence or divine intervention or whatever you care to call it that I've ever heard of," Payne said. "You get drunk and are in a cab that runs off the road and you find keys from the gas station. The perp must have thrown them out."

Payne knew then the perpetrator had been in a car. The shooter had not been a pedestrian.

He stared at Kitty. "What in hell are you doing out this time of night?"

"I was coming to see you."

He raised his eyebrows.

"I've been at Manuel's since you left. Tommy threw me out. I was going to my apartment. But when the cab passed by the gas station I decided to get out and see what you might have found." She looked away. "The cabdriver didn't want to drop me off. We had a . . . we had a discussion. An animated discussion. And I . . ."

He held up his hands. "I don't want to know."

"He didn't have air-conditioning."

Payne shook his head.

"And he had a small package."

Payne smiled.

"This is my story, C. R. Payne. I'm writing about the keys. I won't say I found them." She smiled ruefully. "That opens up too many questions. You get the credit but I get the story."

"What about your boss?"

"You know, few people are perfect. But Colin is a perfect asshole. So if you're asking about the perfect one, he's not my boss. Besides, I'm here and he's not." She looked away. "I just happened to be going home and I saw your car and stopped and you told me what you had found."

Payne smiled.

"I'm worried about you," Kitty said. "You show entirely too much respect for that guy."

Payne shrugged. "He's an impressive person."

She snorted. "You need to get out more often."

"Not much of a story here tonight."

She tried to sit up, slipped, and tried again. A clump of blond hair fell across her face. "What do you mean?"

He shrugged. "All we have is a key ring."

"It shows where the perp lived. He was going home and threw the keys out. It wasn't some black crack head like you thought. It was someone who lives around here."

Payne smiled and shook his head patiently. "No, Kitty. Assuming these are the keys from the gas station, and I believe they are, it only shows what direction the perp drove away in after the shooting. Think about it. We're a half mile, a mile at most, from the crime scene. Straight up the road. All we can say is that he drove this way after the shooting."

"It was after one a.m. when it happened. Where do you think he was going if he wasn't going home?"

"I don't know. A bar in Buckhead, maybe."

She shook her head. "Too late. It was right before closing. He would have missed last call. You

don't go into a bar a few minutes before it closes."
She stopped and shrugged. "Well, most people
don't."

She looked away. Two weeks ago she had threatened to burn down a bar when the manager would
not let her in after last call.

"The geographic location of evidence can be
important. If we had found these keys down in
Carver Homes or in one of the other projects on
the south side, then it would have told us something. We'd have known the perp was from down
there. But not this time. All it tells us is that he
threw them out here after he left. He might live in
Marietta. This is simply the most expeditious way
to depart the crime scene. I still think it could have
been a black kid in a car."

"Why are you so determined to make the perp
a black kid?"

"I told you at the store."

Kitty glared. "Sometimes you sound like you're
reading from an instruction book."

"You did well, Kitty. We now have another piece
of physical evidence from the crime scene. We
know the perp came this way."

"And that's it? He came this way."

He nodded, turned on his flashlight, and pointed
it at the key ring. "Probably. There won't be any
prints. There are never any prints. Prints are only
in the movies."

"That's it? My big find. The big break in the

case. I risk my life to find this for you and that's it?"

He did not answer. He leaned closer to the keys. His eyes widened. He gently laid the light on the ground and took a plastic bag from his pocket. He pulled the Mont Blanc pen from his pocket, stuck it through the key ring, and slowly picked up the keys. The open plastic bag was under the keys.

"Kitty." His eyes were locked on the keys.

She watched as if hypnotized. "Yes."

"What do you see?"

"Is this a trick question?"

"What do you see?"

Through blurry eyes, she again looked at the key ring. "How many chances do I get?"

"Come on."

She leaned closer. Then she turned to look at him. "You tell me."

"Look at the ring that holds the key to the metal plate."

She shook her head. "Payne, I'm drunk. I couldn't find my ass with both hands and a flashlight. Tell me what I see."

"You found the key ring. Look closer."

She pulled closer and peered intently at the key ring. "The Rosetta Stone?"

"One more chance."

"The Elgin marbles. Shit, Payne, I don't see anything."

"In the ring. Caught in the ring."

"I don't . . ." She stopped and leaned closer.

"A hair." She looked up triumphantly. "The perp has white hair."

"That's not a hair."

"Then what . . . " She looked at Payne and then back at the key. "A fiber?"

"Bingo." Slowly Payne placed the key into the plastic evidence bag. He sealed the top and leaned closer to her. "Kitty."

"Yes."

"You can't write about this."

She stared. He was serious.

"You can write about the keys. You can say they may be from the crime scene. But you can't mention the fiber."

Kitty rolled on her back and wailed so loudly that the cabdriver and the crew of the wrecker heard her. The cabdriver nodded and said to the wrecker crew, "See. I told you she was crazy."

Three hours later an exhausted C. R. Payne walked into his small apartment off Ponce de Leon. He turned on the television and opened the refrigerator. A half loaf of stale bread, a diet Coke, and a small plate of tuna fish were all the refrigerator contained. He sighed and put everything on the table in the middle of the room.

A late-night movie was on television. The set appeared to have lights going off behind the screen. One second the screen would flash so brightly the characters would disappear. The next moment it was as if the movie had been shot by candlelight.

Payne sighed. One day he would get a new television. But it would not be until this case was solved. It was axiomatic at Homicide that unless a case was solved inside twenty-four hours, chances grew slimmer every day that it would be solved. This case was growing colder by the minute.

He wasn't going to have time to buy a television anytime soon.

Payne began spreading tuna on the stale bread. He opened the diet Coke. And for a long time he stared unseeing at the flickering movie.

14

Colin was up late.

His wife had been asleep for hours. But the door to his study was locked and the sound of the TV was turned down low. As the VCR rewound the tape he swirled his Sambuca, his eyes locked on the clear viscous liqueur and the remaining single coffee bean slowly going round and round in the Waterford glass. He pulled the glass to his nose and inhaled deeply the pungent scent of licorice.

He tensed when he thought he heard a sound in the hall. After a moment he realized it was nothing. His wife never awakened during the night. And tonight she had gone to bed particularly happy; her last words as she slammed the bedroom door were something about having the scratch on the trunk of her Mercedes repaired.

When he heard a soft *click* from the VCR he pressed the Play button, took another sip of Sambuca, and waited, eyes locked on the screen.

He saw himself enter the store, his gasoline-soaked arm held out away from his body and his face taut. He saw himself look around the store and he saw his mouth moving as he called out. Then from the lower right corner of the screen he saw the first attendant come forth. The second came onto the frame and moved behind the cash register to stop near his friend.

Their mouths moved silently. He never realized before how much body language revealed. He could sense his growing anger in his gestures, in the stiffness of his shoulders, in the cast of his head, and in the tightness of his mouth. It was all there.

Now he could sense something about the two attendants. They were not angry as he had thought that night. They faced the camera directly and he could see their eyes and their mouths and their expressions and their body language and he knew they were not mad. They were perhaps annoyed. But they were little more than kids. Both appeared to be in their mid-twenties. And while they had that petulant defensive air found in some gay people, they were not angry. He was the angry one. They were exasperated and they were camping it up, flaunting their sexuality, perhaps deliberately since he was a man in the store alone.

What the hell? They were still faggots and they had angered him.

Who would miss them? Two more of life's losers taken out early before AIDS killed them or before they infected others with their virus. Those people were so promiscuous they probably would have died within the next year or so. The world was divided between the sheep and the wolves. They were sheep.

The tape continued to roll.

He saw himself pull the pistol from his pocket and smash it across the fingers of the smirking attendant. Then the weapon was raised and two tiny puffs of smoke exploded from the barrel. He racked the slide back to clear the malfunction and there were two more tiny puffs of smoke.

He smiled in admiration of the Walther TPH. What clean lines the pistol had. The TPH, *taschen pistole mit hahn*—pocket pistol with handle—was one of the most coveted pistols ever brought into America. I looked like a small PPK. Double action with an excellent trigger pull and an easy takedown procedure.

He leaned forward, stopped the tape, rewound it for several seconds—by now he could almost stop the tape on the precise frame he wanted—and again punched the Play button. This time it was not the sweet little TPH that he watched, nor was it his professional technique in clearing the malfunction. This time he watched the expressions on the faces of the victims. The first one was taken by surprise and his only expression—it came a fraction of a second before the first shot—was a slight widening of his eyes.

But the second attendant not only widened his eyes, there was a flash of recognition in his eyes; recognition that his friend had been shot and that he was about to die. His hands came up to cover his eyes and blot out that fearful vision and his mouth opened in a wide "Nooooo" of denial. He was so shocked that in the eight seconds it took to clear the malfunction he remained transfixed—like a deer caught in the headlights—hands over his eyes and mouth open.

Colin rewound the tape, took another sip of Sambuca, and watched the tape again. This time he watched only the expressions on the faces of the two victims.

15

Payne sat in a back booth at the Majestic Diner on Ponce de Leon. He did not look up as Kitty plopped down heavily across from him. His eyes were locked on the front page of the newspaper.

"Hope you don't think it's rude that I didn't wait," he said. "But I have a big day and not much time."

"It's okay. Thanks for meeting me."

"Honey, whatcha gonna have?" said an overweight middle-aged waitress whose hair had been bleached to a sedgelike stiffness.

Kitty looked at Payne's orange juice, coffee, and dry whole wheat toast. She pointed. "The same."

The waitress looked at Kitty's eyes. "Honey, you look like you need more food than that."

"No, that will be fine."

The waitress nodded and turned and walked between the booths and the counter, her more than ample hips filling the aisle. She strode through the confined space with all the boldness of a battleship surging through a narrow channel. A man coming in the front door started down the aisle, saw her, and stopped and waited. She was a dreadnought and she owned this space.

Kitty watched Payne's eyes move rapidly over the paper. Until this morning she had not noticed how intelligent his eyes were. She looked away.

Payne folded the newspaper and placed it behind the covey of condiments huddled at the edge of the table. "What is the matter with your newspaper?" he asked

Kitty's eyebrows rose.

"That story by Biddle. He knows better than that. He's been around the police station longer than I have."

Kitty shrugged. "The newspaper is going through the biggest change in its history. Things are happening that I don't understand. I'm an old-fashioned reporter. Sometimes I think I'm the only one left."

"You don't write stories like Colin wrote this morning." He paused. "At least when you're writing, you don't."

Her eyes narrowed. "I did the story in yesterday's paper about your finding the keys. I left out the bit about the fiber if you noticed."

He nodded. "Back in the local news section." He tapped the newspaper. "But that stuff of Colin's is all over the front page."

She shrugged. "Personally, I don't like his story. I think he's way off base. But if I say that, they say I'm being emotional because of my brother."

Kitty looked up as the waitress slid her order across the table. "Thanks."

Payne sipped his coffee. "He's making this a homosexual thing; turning it all around the fact the victims were gay."

What he could not say to Kitty was that the two young men were just two more victims. They were not accomplished, not wealthy, not well known. So why were they worth so much space in the paper? Why was Colin trying to make them symbols of some kind?

He looked at her around the paper. "You asked for help from the gay community. I assume you got nothing."

"Not yet."

He took a sip of coffee. "Well, his story today is about Atlanta's gay community and all their paranoia—well, maybe not paranoia, but the usual stuff—about being persecuted and picked on and saying this double homicide was because they were gay. That's nonsense."

Payne paused a moment. "Unless he knows something I don't." He looked at Kitty. "Is he fishing or does he know something?"

Kitty paused.

"What's he up to, Kitty?"

"I don't know if he's fishing. But he left this morning for Key West. That's what I wanted to tell you."

Payne put his cup down and stared at Kitty.

"Key West, Florida?"

She nodded.

"For what?"

"Some kind of backgrounder about the gay community." She shrugged. "I don't know. I don't see any connection. But he's the man in the catbird seat down at the newspaper. Anything he writes gets in the paper. He is Mister Atlanta. Does anything he wants and the paper pays all his expenses. *Carpe per diem*, that's his motto."

She paused. "I couldn't believe it. They told me he interviewed some of the gay people in the newsroom and now he's gone to Key West."

"You don't have any idea what he's after?"

"Nope. But if it's anything about the gay community we will run it. Diversity rules. Multiculturalism reigns. Somebody comes out of the closet, we run it. If Condescending Colon says he can tie the gay community in Key West to an Atlanta homicide, then the paper will send him down there and they'll play his story on the front."

She smiled. "My brother used to laugh about how we handle news about the gay community. He loved it. But he thought we went way overboard. He said the gay community laughed at us and used us."

She paused and looked at Payne. Her voice softened. "Thanks for coming to the funeral. I saw you there."

"I'm sorry about your brother, Kitty."

She wondered for a moment if he was there because they were friends and it was her brother who had been killed or if he was there—as cops often are at a victim's funeral—in order to see who else was there. Often a perpetrator will attend his victim's funeral or stand outside watching the funeral. She decided she didn't want to know. She nodded and looked away.

After a second she squared her shoulders. "So what did you get from the crime lab?"

"First, talk to me about Key West. He's down there pursuing something he thinks is related to my homicides?"

"You have to understand something. Colin and I are fighting over this story. I wouldn't be covering it if I hadn't come up with that business about the key ring. He wants me off of it. So you need to know I'm not the most objective person in the world where the dickhead of the week is concerned."

Payne smiled. "I know that. But tell me if what he's doing is related to my homicides."

"*He* says it's related. That doesn't mean it is. The paper can tie a lot of things together that are not relevant from a law enforcement standpoint. You know that."

"Yeah, but I'm worried that I might be missing something."

Kitty snorted. "You'll find more at the crime scene than he will in Key West. Now tell me about the crime lab."

"Ballistics report won't be ready for another day or so. But the fiber guy called and said the fiber is linen." He paused and looked at her. "Not cotton. Not a cotton polymer blend. This is highly processed and bleached. Very white. No yellow tint or overtones. Good linen. Expensive."

"From what? Shirt? Handkerchief? Suit?"

"He doesn't know yet. But the point is . . ."

She interrupted. "What kind of shooter would be wearing expensive linen?"

"Exactly." He nodded. "The lab guy said linen is not common today. There are so many other materials out there. He said sometimes people use the word linen in a generic sense, like when they're talking about table linens. But this is real linen.'

"Does he know where it came from?"

"He guessed a handkerchief or a shirt. But it could have been a suit. He said that's not as important as the fact that expensive, one hundred percent, bleached, finely woven, and highly processed linen was found as contact evidence. He said linen is rarely found at a crime scene and that, in itself, tells us something."

"Tell you where it's from?"

"I did a little research. The best linen comes from Ireland or Belgium. But there is a difference in the products of those two countries. Belgian linen is more decorative, more lacy, more fancy. Most often found in tablecloths or napkins. Far more common and far more likely to be worn is Irish linen. Considering that and considering the context in which this fiber was found and considering other things, I'd guess it came from a handkerchief."

Payne sipped his coffee, then pushed the cup aside. "One other thing about that fiber. It was contaminated by gasoline."

"Gasoline?"

"Yes. Remember that the perp wiped down the telephone, cash register, the videotape box, and everything else he could find with gasoline? That's why I believe it was a handkerchief."

"You don't think this was a robbery, do you? You've dropped the idea about a black kid coming in and racking one back for effect." She was staring at him intently.

He did not answer.

"Why?"

"Look beyond the fact the money was taken from the victims and from the cash register. Look at what we got. Consider this."

As Payne began she sensed he was talking more to himself than to her. He was going over all the details again, probably for the hundredth time, trying to find something he had overlooked all those other times.

"A shooter goes into the station sometime between one and two a.m. presumably to buy gas. He wasn't there to buy a lottery ticket. The winner from last week had been announced only a couple of hours earlier and most people don't know who the winners are until they see it on TV or read the paper Sunday morning. So he goes inside and pulls out a little twenty-two-caliber, a pistol notoriously difficult to achieve any sort of accuracy with. Yet, he is an outstanding shot. Kills two victims, one of whom happens to be black and both of whom happen to be gay. When he left he dropped the keys into his pocket. He takes them out to toss them out the window and a single thread hooks into the key ring. That thread indicates he has expensive tastes. The crime must have been caught with the security camera because the perp took the tape. The crime scene was wiped clean with a gasoline-soaked cloth. Any cloth would have done it. The guy obviously knows forensics and he knows how we work. He knows what constitutes evidence and he understands the evidentiary chain. Why did he use a gasoline-soaked cloth? Did he go into the gas station carrying the cloth?"

Payne shook his head. "Crack heads spend money on clothes. But I never heard of a rock star who was that methodical. Maybe he saw a TV show or something. I don't know."

"I was thinking about that," she said. "I don't believe that whoever did this was black. Sure, crack heads buy nice clothes. But fancy linen? And a crack head who knows that much about forensics and takes the time to grab the videotape and wipe down the crime scene? Those guys would do a quick in and out. And they wouldn't carry a twenty-two. It would be something like my three fifty-seven."

He stared at her. "Keep going."

She shrugged. "I don't have a theory. Except about the gun. I think the shooter jammed his weapon. Twenty-two semiautomatics are notorious for jamming."

"Malfunctioning."

"What?"

"Malfunctioning. Not jamming. A jam has a precise meaning when applied to a gun. This doesn't fit. This was a malfunction."

"Okay. Twenty-two semiautomatics are notorious for malfunctions."

He nodded. "What else?"

"I don't think it had anything to do with the victims being gay. That was coincidental."

"You're right. And I don't think a gay guy was the shooter. Gays don't like guns. But if they get one, they almost always get a big one. Like most people who don't shoot a lot, they think the bigger the better. And another thing. Gay killings are notoriously irrational. If a gay person stabs someone, the victim might have forty or fifty stab wounds. We're talking real overkill. If a gay person had been the shooter and if there were a gay element to the shooting, the shooter would have emptied one magazine and maybe two. He wouldn't have been so cold and dispassionate, so clinical, so precise."

"What about the black victim? Think it was racial?"

"Just because a black guy happened to be a victim doesn't make it a racially motivated shooting."

Her brows pulled together. "You're not exactly a stereotypical African-American type."

"Why?"

"I just gave you a great opening to blame all this on some racial thing. You didn't even nibble."

"You expect me to do the Camel Walk, wear sunglasses, and run on CPT?"

"Now who's being sensitive?"

"I am not a hyphenated American. I'm an American. Period. This back to Africa stuff is silly. I went to the Million Man March but I don't hang with the brothers just to show what a good fellow I am. I know that white men run the world. I can't be whining about some lost civilization and go around talking about returning to Africa and blaming every mistake on racism if I expect to move ahead in the white man's world. I told you I have plans. Once I get in the door and move on up a bit, then I may get blacker. I may not. All want is to move in and move up."

"Growing up in southwest Georgia fucked you up as badly as it did me."

He shrugged.

Kitty paused. "You said most people who don't shoot a lot buy big guns?"

"Yes."

"What about people who shoot a lot? You said he was an expert shot. Would an expert have a twenty-two?"

Payne shook his head. "No. Shooters, even more than amateurs, go for heavy calibers. Cops who carry backup weapons rarely carry anything smaller than a thirty-eight or maybe a three-eighty."

"What if the perp was good? I mean, really good the way Colin was talking about?"

Payne stared. "You mean he was so good and so sure of himself that he could carry a twenty-two?"

"Maybe."

"But why did he shoot them? A guy wearing expensive linen doesn't shoot two guys for chump change."

"Your idol, Mr. Shitheel of the Week, thinks the fairies are restless. That's why he's tiptoeing around Key West."

Payne shook his head. "He must have a source who's feeding him." He looked at his watch. "I've got to get over to the crime scene."

"You've gone over it top to bottom and turned it inside out."

"Several times. But I'm overlooking something." He slid out of the booth and stood up.

"I'm overlooking something," he repeated. His eyes had a thousand-yard stare.

"Overlooking. Overlooking." He snapped his fingers.

Kitty knew he had suddenly had a realization about the case. "What the hell are you mumbling about?"

"That's it." He paused. "I wonder if . . ." He turned and walked rapidly toward the cash register.

Kitty threw her arms wide and shouted, "What is going on?"

"Talk to you later. Gotta run."

The battleship ripping down the narrow aisle saw him, kept coming, then paused when she noticed his eyes.

She stepped aside.

It was the first time in fifteen years she had moved aside for a customer.

16

The small sun-blasted airport in Key West is a remnant of the old and funky Florida Keys, one of the few remaining signs that the lower keys are America's Outback, that this is a backwater that sets its own rules and cares little for the opinions of the outside world. There is one runway and a small parking area for aircraft. The terminal building has peeling paint and the decrepit air of an old movie set. Except for the steady flow of airplanes, far more than one might expect for a small out-of-the-way place, everything seems to move as if it is under water. By midmorning the air is hot and humid and hazy and it envelopes new arrivals the second they exit an air-conditioned aircraft.

Tourists visiting for the first time step out onto the blistering tarmac, wait for their luggage, then walk rapidly toward the terminal. They are sopping with perspiration before they go through the narrow doors. The old hands proceed at a more leisurely pace. They saunter toward the terminal as if it doesn't really matter when they arrive. But they too are sopping with perspiration when they walk through the doors.

Colin laughed when he stepped from the little commuter airliner and saw the sign on the terminal—KEY WEST INTERNATIONAL AIRPORT. He waited as flight-line workers unloaded checked luggage from the rear of the aircraft and plopped it on the tarmac.

"They must have one flight a month to the Bahamas," he said to the casually dressed man behind him.

"Then it's an international airport, isn't it?" the man said as he brushed past and picked up his suitcase. Colin noticed several airport employees spoke to the man as he walked through the airport.

"It seems I've offended one of the locals," Colin mumbled to himself. "Oh, dear."

He picked up his black Tumi suitcase and checked the locks. All secure. The gun inside and the two magazines of ammo were safe.

He looked around. A banner hung over the entrance to the terminal that said, GAY ARTS FESTIVAL—JUNE 17–26. Beside it another banner said, WITH 30,000 GAYS AND LESBIANS HERE, ANYTHING CAN HAPPEN. Colin saw a sign in the parking lot that said, KEY WEST—GAY CAPITAL OF AMERICA. On the commuter flight from Miami he had read a promotional brochure that talked of something called Fantasy Fest in October; said to be the most exciting gay happening in the country.

Colin walked toward the terminal.

"I know I'm still in America," he said to himself. "Because I'm above the fruited plain."

17
_____

Buddy Anderson, the executive producer at WSB-TV, was more than a little wary as he walked across the lobby toward the tall black police officer.

"Detective Payne?" he asked, reaching out to shake hands. He avoided the detective's eyes. "The general manager said we're to help you any way we can."

"Thank you."

C. R. Payne looked at the producer. Guy was maybe thirty years old. Expensive suit. Crisp white shirt. Dark tie. Scuffy shoes. Those shoes had never been shined. You can tell a lot about a man by his shoes. Everything this guy had on was not only expensive, it was tasteful. But his shoes showed it was nothing but a uniform; it was all front, all facade.

He was obviously bright and ambitious or he wouldn't have such a big job at the biggest and best TV station in Atlanta. But his darting eyes and his body language revealed a man whose moral compass had not yet settled down to true north. "Your day in the barrel?"

Buddy shrugged. "General manager talks to the news director, news director talks to me, I talk to you." It was clear the guy would rather have a root canal without Novocain than talk with the cop.

"You understand what I want?"

Buddy motioned toward the stairs. He raised a cassette in his hand. "Tower cam tape from last Saturday night, early Sunday morning."

That's it."

Buddy nodded. "You're living right, Detective. It's only in the past few weeks we began leaving the camera on all night. Time-lapse tape of summer thunderstorms at night makes great video."

He pointed toward a small editing booth. "Have a seat. I'll set up the tape."

Payne walked into the room. It was the size of a closet with one wall of dark glass and the other three jammed floor-to-ceiling with electronic equipment and video screens.

"The general manager and I talked briefly but not about the technical aspects of this," Payne said. "Tell me about the tower cam's capabilities."

Buddy pressed a button, inserted the cassette, and looked at the detective. "Which one?"

"You have more than one?"

"We have a half dozen. They're all over town. Viewers usually know of the one down at the airport and the one on the tower outside." He paused. "I'm ready to roll tape."

"Just a moment. Why do you have a camera at the airport?"

"Actually, it's not at the airport. It's on top of a hotel down there. Maybe a quarter of a mile from the nearest runway. It stays pointed toward the airport. One day there is going to be one hell of an airplane crash and you guys will block traffic around the airport. With that camera, which is controlled from here in the satellite news center, we can get great video."

For a moment Payne digested the mysterious ways of television. "You mean you keep a camera down there because you think one day an airplane will crash?"

Buddy smiled. It was the slightly patronizing smile of a fast-burning TV guy talking to a man his age but a man whose career path had taken an altogether different course. In addition, Payne was a man whom, in most circumstances, Buddy would avoid. The technical aspects of television was an area, perhaps the only area, where Buddy could feel superior.

He raised a finger in correction. "We *know* one will crash. It's just a matter of time. We'll zoom in on that puppy, get people running from the crash— if anyone is running—we'll have video of them being carried if they're not. Smoke. Fire. Explosions. Squirting foam. The whole megillah. We'll get it all from a mile or so away. Fill your screen with close-ups. It will be incredible video. Incredible."

Payne nodded. "The camera is on top of a hotel

at the airport and you can control it from here? Pan it? Zoom it?"

"You got it."

"Tilt it up and down?"

"In a heartbeat. We can point it down and get the parking lot under the camera or we can point it up at almost a forty-five-degree angle. Everything in between. I don't know the numbers, but if we max out the zoom we can come in pretty tight from a mile or so away."

"How tight?"

"Your friends would recognize you."

"From two miles away?"

"Hey, it ain't a spy satellite that can get your tag number from outer space, but it's the same technology. Two miles is nothing."

"You said the camera stays pointed toward the airport. What about the one here?"

"The tower cam?"

Payne nodded.

"That one's different. Weather guys like to jerk off with this one. They keep it panning for time-lapse weather shots." He nodded toward the screen. "You want me to roll tape?"

Payne shook his head. Why was the guy so anxious to get this over with? It was more than being uncomfortable around a cop. Payne made a note to check out the producer's name in the computer, particularly with Narcotics and Vice.

"Not yet. I have a few more questions. You said the camera is on all the time?"

Buddy nodded. "It's like a computer or any kind of high-tech gizmo. Turning it on and off causes the insides to get hot. Expands and contracts. Expands and contracts. It's better to keep it up and running all the time. Turning and burning. Less wear and tear."

"Everything is taped?"

"That's why we have the tower cam." Buddy paused. "I don't know exactly what you're looking for, but if you find it, you understand you can't take the tape from the building?"

"Not a problem." Payne paused. He would deal with that later. "Does the camera pan around all night or does it stay aimed in one direction?"

"Depends. Sometimes the night people ignore it. Especially if there is no weather. It just hangs in there and points. But most of the time it is working. I guess they figure if they have to work nights, everything they control will work nights."

"What about the angle? I mean, is it shooting out over the tops of buildings, up at the sky, or pointed down?"

"Usually out over the tops of buildings. We want the weather stuff, but there has to be parts of the city people can recognize so they will have some perspective. Background. Bare-assed cloud shots won't cut it. Not good video."

"Over the tops of buildings?"

Buddy nodded. "If the camera is pointed south— toward downtown—you get tops of buildings. Same along Peachtree Street and up into Buckhead."

"What if it's pointed a little northeast of here?"

"Be specific."

"Up Cheshire Bridge."

Buddy rubbed his chin. He shrugged. "No tall buildings over that way. We're shooting from high up. Good video."

"How is the zoom set at night when the camera is . . . uh . . . turning and burning?"

Buddy shrugged. "Usually on the wide side. Again for perspective."

Payne nodded. "A hypothetical. Say the camera is on and panning three hundred and sixty degrees. During one or more of its rotations it catches something you want to see better. Do you have the capability to blow up the image?"

Buddy paused. He was intrigued. "We've never had any occasion to do that. But, yes, we can do computer enhancements."

"Would that be only on the videotape or could you make a hard copy? For instance, could you make a photograph of one frame from the tape?"

Buddy paused. Suddenly he was wary. "We have that capability. But we're not in the business of helping law enforcement. We're in the news business."

Payne looked at him. "Of course you are." He leaned back in the chair and smiled. "Roll tape."

18

Late in the afternoon Colin stopped at a tiny store-front on Duval Street and ordered a lemonade.

"It's very hot, don't you think?" asked a man who suddenly materialized at the window beside him.

Colin nodded but did not speak. He backed away two steps, making sure he stayed under the awning and out of the baking afternoon sun, and looked at the man's hand. Wedding ring. Hah! The guy had a wife. Behind him was another guy. He too was wearing a ring. They wore shorts, T-shirts, and boat shoes and were obviously together. He guessed that their wives were down the street shopping at Fast Buck Freddy's.

"Yes, it is. Extraordinarily hot," Colin said.

"You should get out of that suit," the man said.

He and his friend smiled as Colin opened his hands and said, "I'm working."

"Your lemonade, sir," said the waiter. Colin moved to the window, paid for the lemonade, and took a long drink.

"I'll have two of those," said the first man.

"I want a pink one," said his companion.

"One regular, one pink," said the first man to the young attendant in the window.

"What do you do that you're working down here?" the first man asked.

Colin paused, smiled, and said, "I'm a writer."

The first man's eyes widened. He turned to his friend. "He's a writer."

He turned back to Colin. "What do you write?"

"Well, I've just published a book. But right now I'm down here working on a newspaper piece. Homicide story out of Atlanta." He paused. "I'm a serious journalist."

The man nodded. "I can see that you are. When you say homicide, you mean . . . ?"

Colin took a sip of his lemonade. "Yes. Afraid so. Double homicide, matter of fact."

"If you're a newspaper person, there's a local newspaper you must read. It's called *Lips*. Wonderful newspaper. Just wonderful."

Colin looked at him. *"Lips?"*

"Oh, yes. A gay and lesbian newspaper. Just wonderful."

"One regular, one pink," interrupted the attendant as he pushed two lemonades through the window.

"Here, here's your pink one," said the first man, handing his friend a lemonade.

The two men laughed, leaned toward each other, and kissed. They nodded toward Colin. "Don't work too hard," the first man said. And they were off, walking down the street, holding hands, and sipping lemonade.

Colin stared after them, barely able to control his anger and disgust. They were wearing wedding rings, for God's sake, and kissing each other on the street.

Colin looked around. Not that anyone but him was paying attention. In this town you could perform an unnatural act with a donkey in the middle of Duval Street and no one would notice. Hemingway would twirl in his grave if he knew what had happened to his beloved Key West.

Oh, well, he mused. Faggots are better than the Afroed Americans. At least they keep their yards neat.

Colin's thin lips pinched together. He wanted a long cold shower and a good sleep. But first he wanted to sit quietly in an air-conditioned room and enjoy a bottle of champagne and a good meal.

Ten minutes later Colin was sitting at a table in the rear of a small French restaurant off Truman Avenue. He had interviewed more than a dozen people today and at the end of each interview when he asked about a restaurant for fine dining, this one was at the top of the list. It was known to the locals, but like most Key West restaurants, heavily depended on tourists. The difference was that this restaurant had something of a dress code, even if it was called "Key West casual." And it was quite expensive, a factor that kept away many tourists.

Colin was on an expense account so it did not matter.

His day had been lousy. He had been caught in two summer thunderstorms. In between the showers, the heat and humidity turned Key West into a sauna. Colin wore a tailored seersucker suit. Ever since his wife read *Sophie's Choice* she insisted on calling it his "cocksucker suit." It was so hot and humid that even the seersucker was damp and oppressive. Colin was drenched in perspiration.

And he was simmering in anger. Every person he had interviewed today was gay, and with every interview he had gotten more and more upset. Traffic on Duval Street was grid lock. The air conditioner in his car did not work and the rental agency did not have a replacement. The shower in his hotel room had roaches crawling through the drain. The manager—who was gay—dismissed his complaint with "Oh, that's just a palmetto bug."

And then the two married guys kissing each other. He realized they must be married to each other; one of those gay commitments the editor had talked about.

Colin had another sip of champagne and began composing leads in his head for the story he would write.

He wanted a lead with something about how Key West was a city that moved with the pace of a Burgundian snail and, like the snail, left a glistening trail. When the trail dried in the hot sun there was nothing left; the essence of Key West was in a shine that depleted in the light.

No. Too laborious.

He'd come up with something. Some inside kind of double entendre. To get it into the paper he might have to wrestle with Quasimodo, the slot man on the copy desk, but he would win. He wanted a joke that his friends would appreciate.

He drank a last sip of Dom Ruinart, his favorite champagne. He had bought a case several weeks earlier for about $80 per bottle. The restaurant listed the same champagne for $190 per bottle. Colin looked almost worshipfully at the empty glass.

Before he set the glass on the table the waiter was replenishing it. The waiter was very attentive, very professional, very sophisticated, and very gay. Colin nodded, careful not to smile.

The waiters here wore solid black; black shirts, black belts, black trousers, and black shoes.

Colin wondered why gay men looked good in anything they wore, were far more intellectual than most other segments of population, were sophisticated in their conversation, and were so very quick. If they didn't have such peculiar dietary habits they would be a delight to be around.

Colin smiled. He shifted in his seat to accommodate the pressure from the pistol in his belt. He'd have to remember that line when one of his friends asked him about Key West—Yes, it's a great town but it's filled with people who have peculiar dietary habits.

"Have you decided yet, sir?" asked the waiter. He had materialized out of nowhere at the moment Colin decided he was ready to order. Was the waiter telepathic in addition to being gay? Colin wondered if every waiter in Key West was gay. It was as bad as Atlanta. No, worse.

"If not, perhaps you would like for me to recommend a choice."

"Are there things on the menu you would not recommend?"

The waiter never missed a beat. "Yes, sir. Today the grilled eggplant is not up to our standard. And personally I could not recommend the lamb. But as for the remainder of the items, you'll be pleased with whatever you order."

Colin looked at the menu and nodded. "I've decided. For a starter I shall have the *saumon fume d'ecosse.*"

The waiter smiled and nodded in approval. "Excellent choice, sir. Our chef uses the classic garniture which I'm sure you'll enjoy."

"Then I shall have the *salade d'endive.*"

"We use fresh Belgian endive and it is topped with a roquefort, walnut, and herb vinaigrette. Splendid."

"As for the entree—do you have a house specialty?"

"The lobster is our signature dish, sir. We serve it flambéed in cognac with shrimp in saffron butter, mango, and basil. Everyone in Key West serves lobster. Ours is quite simply the best. You can't go wrong with our lobster."

"Then I'll have the lobster."

The waiter wrote down the order and stood with pen poised. "Anything else, sir?"

"Your food is very rich."

"Yes, sir, it is. Our chef, who owns the restaurant, was trained in the classic French fashion. We have no nouvelle cuisine. We have lots of butters and creams and sauces. Very rich indeed, as you point out." The waiter paused. "But we are also the best restaurant in Key West. You seem the sort of person who appreciates such things."

Colin did not respond.

"And your wine, sir?"

"I'll stick with the champagne."

"Excellent choices. You picked our best champagne."

Colin didn't speak. People would be ice skating on the lakes in hell before he needed a waiter to endorse his taste in champagne. He sat back and pulled out his notebook from an inside coat pocket and reviewed his notes. He had never interviewed so many gay men in his life. He had never seen so many same sex couples holding hands and kissing in public. Key West was a latter-day Sodom and Gomorrah. Sodom, anyway.

He smiled. Another good line. One with biblical authority.

Colin shook his head. It was early summer and

months before the height of the tourist season. What must the place be like in December or January?

He was halfway through his smoked Scottish salmon when he noticed a short black hair under a piece of the fish. His lips compressed. He pushed the plate aside.

"Are you finished, sir?" asked the waiter. The waiter had materialized again. He was like Casper the friendly ghost. Colin nodded without speaking.

"Was it not to your taste, sir?"

"It was fine." Colin waved a hand in dismissal. He was so angry he could not speak. A hair in Scottish salmon. In a restaurant like this. He picked up his glass of champagne and drained half the glass. His anger grew. This champagne should not be gulped. What was the matter with him?

His lobster was all and more than he expected. Flaky, moist, and suffused with an ethereal hint of saffron against a backdrop of basil and mango. It was easily the best lobster Colin had ever eaten. He chewed slowly, sipping champagne and trying to forget his day.

He was almost in a good mood by the time the waiter removed his plate.

"I see you have crème brûlée on your menu. How do you prepare it?"

The waiter smiled. "Our chef believes crème brûlée is perfection itself. It cannot be improved upon, even though some restaurants try to do so by placing a brownie or some concoction in the bottom of the container. We do it as we do all of our dishes, in the classic French fashion. Very simple. Very elegant."

"Do you heat the sugar at the last minute? It is hot when it comes to the table?"

The waiter's eyebrows rose a notch. "You know crème brûlée. Yes, sir. Naturally we must prepare the custard in advance. It is chilled. Just before it is served, the brown sugar is sprinkled lightly on top and then the ramekin is placed under the broiler. The sugar is hot when I put it on your plate."

"That's the only way to do it."

The waiter nodded and smiled. He held tight eye contact with Colin. "You're quite right, sir. That way you enjoy not only the"—the waiter held up his right hand and rubbed his thumb and forefinger together—"contrast in texture between the silky custard and the crunchy sugar, but you also have the juxtaposition in temperature with the cold custard and the hot hard sugar on top."

Colin nodded. "I'll have the crème brûlée. Cappuccino. And do you have Sambuca?"

"Of course, sir."

"On second thought, I'll change that. Since this is a French restaurant, I'll have a French brandy. Do you have Calvados?"

"Ahhhh." The waiter's eyes were locked with those of Colin. "A man who appreciates the very best. Yes, sir, we do."

Colin nodded.

"With your cappuccino or later?"

"With the cappuccino."

The crème brûlée was all the waiter had said it would be—cold silky perfection topped with hot crunchy sugar. Better even than in Le Cirque, where he had eaten several times when he went to New York to talk with his publisher.

Colin was in a good mood, in fact he was approaching a state of grace, when he saw another small black hair caught under the pale brown sugar and standing out boldly against the yellow custard. He froze, staring at the hair in disbelief. His body went rigid with anger.

A second later Casper was by his side.

Colin did not look up. He pointed with his spoon at the same time he rolled his lips around and probed with his tongue, wondering if he had eaten a hair.

"Someone in your kitchen has black hair," Colin said.

Casper pulled a cigarette lighter from his pocket, flicked it, and leaned forward. The hair poked out from the custard and rustled a bit in the breeze from the air conditioner.

Colin's voice was tight. "Look, I didn't say anything when I found a hair in my salmon. But two in one meal is intolerable.

The waiter's flame flicked quickly between Colin's long blond hair and the short black hair in the crème brûlée.

"It didn't come from me," Colin said. He was making an effort to control his voice.

"No, sir, it didn't. I am so sorry about this. There will be no charge for the salmon or the dessert. And your after-dinner drink is on the house." He picked up the offending plate.

"Forget the after-dinner drink and bring me my check."

"Yes, sir. Again, I'm very sorry. This doesn't happen in our restaurant."

"It did happen. Bring me the check."

A few moments later Colin walked out of the restaurant. It was dusk, that time of day when the government workers and many storekeepers have gone home; the lull as most people are inside getting ready to go out for dinner. The street was empty as Colin crossed, not bothering to walk down to the corner and cross with the light. He was walking toward the parking lot when he heard, "Excuse me, sir."

His hand slipped under his open jacket. From a narrow alley, inside a thick bower of oleander and hibiscus and bougainvillea, stepped the waiter.

Casper again.

"What do you want?"

Colin squinted. The waiter's black clothes made him almost invisible in the gathering dusk.

"I wanted to apologize again." Casper put his hand on Colin's arm. "If there's anything I can do to make it up to you . . ."

It was the hand on his arm that did it. Colin

exploded in rage. His hand snaked from his belt and emerged holding the Walther. The waiter saw the dim shape in Colin's hand and backed a half step into the trees and shrubs.

"No. No," he said.

Colin raised the pistol, pushed it toward Casper, coughed loudly, and fired two quick rounds into the waiter's open mouth. The waiter slumped to the ground and did not move.

Colin looked over his shoulder. No one was on the street. The trees had muffled the bark of the pistol. He crouched and waited a moment as he peered between the leaves.

What a stupid thing he had done.

Stupid.

Stupid.

Someone could have been walking along the street. Someone could have been in the parking lot on the corner.

He peeped through the leaves, looking in both directions. No one was in sight.

He looked down. It was too dark to see the cartridge casings. He would never find them. They were probably lodged somewhere in the tangled limbs and leaves of the oleander bush.

He slid the pistol back into his belt and walked down the sidewalk toward his rental car. He did not rush. He opened the door, slid inside, and quickly drove away.

As he turned down Whitehead Street toward his hotel, he shook his head and grimaced in anger.

If the police found the casings they would discover extractor marks, ejection marks, and firing pin marks.

Now he might have to get rid of his TPH.

He slammed his hand against the steering wheel.

19

Payne stared at the pictures on his desk. He pulled them farther apart, holding each by the white margin. He wanted no smudged fingerprints blurring these photographs.

Each was eight and a half by eleven and each was the high contrast that comes with photographs shot at night. Each had been a frame of tower cam tape. The first photograph was an overview of the Quicky Gas Station; it established the crime scene by showing the gas station, the front parking area near the gas pumps, and the overhang that protected customers in inclement weather. It also showed perhaps a hundred yards of Cheshire Bridge Road.

The second photograph was tighter. It showed the rear fender of a car under the overhang at the gas pumps. At the edge of the fender was the left rear leg of a man who was walking toward the right front door of the car. The man wore dark trousers and dark shoes. The owner had not been identified. The car was dark green, dark blue, or black. It had been identified as a late-model Mercedes, one of the larger top-end models.

Payne shook his head. The angle of the car and the angle of the camera were far enough apart that if either had shifted an inch, the license plates on the rear of the car would have been visible. Even so, he had a dark-colored late-model Mercedes and the leg of a person walking toward the front of the car.

Did the leg belong to a passenger or to the driver? If the driver, why was he walking toward the passenger seat?

The third photograph was of a man crossing the concrete parking apron toward the door of the convenience store. His arm was up and his face was obliterated by a white spot. The time lapse between the shot of the man's leg and the one of him entering the store indicated about four minutes had passed—time enough to pump a few gallons of gas. Why would someone in a Mercedes buy only a few gallons of gas? Why didn't he fill the tank?

The fourth photograph showed the man had pulled the glass door of the store open and was striding inside. The metal frame of the door obscured his face. The light at the front of the store was so bright that his head, even part of the door frame, washed out on the white light. All that could be determined was that it was a man in a dark suit. Payne could not even determine if the man was black or white.

The fifth photograph was of the same figure striding from the store toward the car. The man was one step out of the convenience store and, again, the lights were so bright that his head and features were lost in a white glare. It was as if a strobing burst of light obscured the head.

But the picture revealed several things: the man was carrying something in his hand, something white. One car and part of another could be seen traveling south on Cheshire Bridge Road. Someone had driven by as this guy was walking to his car. Payne squinted at the most visible car. It appeared to be one of those high-performance cars that fill Buckhead on Saturday nights. Someone in the car might have seen this guy walking across the open lot. A person in the car could be the unknown witness who often pops out of nowhere in a homicide investigation.

Payne wrinkled his lips in concentration and stared at what appeared to be a white container in the person's hand. What could the guy have bought in the store that would be a small white package?

He shook his head. The photographs were important, by far the biggest break in the case. The time hack on the videotape from which the photographs had been taken indicated that this man— whoever he was—had been in the store at the time the medical examiner estimated the homicides had occurred. And from the number of photographs of the gas station before the man departed, he was inside about eight minutes.

Why so long if all he had to do was pay for his gas?

It had to be the perp.

Payne felt a moment of chagrin that he had not tried to lift fingerprints off the handles of the gas pumps. They were used by numerous people and were covered by a film of gasoline so he wouldn't have gotten any prints. Nevertheless, it annoyed him that he had overlooked a possibility.

The next frame of tape showed that only one other car arrived at the gas station before the police car arrived. The tape showed that he simply drove under the overhang and drove out again. Maybe he didn't want to get out of his car and pump gas. Did he see something inside? He couldn't have. The first police officer on the scene saw only the feet of the victims and that was from the end of the store.

Could a pedestrian have walked inside and killed the two young men? Possibly. He could have gone in and out without being picked up by the tower cam. But that was unlikely considering the Mercedes was parked at the station about twelve minutes—some four minutes at the pump and eight minutes inside—during the crucial time frame.

The Mercedes belonged to the perp.

Payne looked at the pictures and shook his head. They revealed much. Payne had no doubt he was looking at the perpetrator. But who the hell was he? The pictures did not reveal enough to identify the person.

If the tower cam had rotated a half revolution faster or slower it would have shown the Mercedes entering or leaving the station. Or it would have revealed the man a few feet farther away from the station where he could have been identified. Or the car's license plates would have been visible.

And if the lights around the convenience store had not been so bright, or if the man had opened the door two seconds sooner or two seconds later, his face would have been visible. If the equipment at the TV station could have enhanced the photographs just a little bit more before they were developed as photographs.

Payne shook his head.

Close but no cigar.

He had a lot more than he had before. He smiled as he carefully placed the photographs into a large envelope. The producer at WSB-TV had been very helpful about developing the photographs from the tower cam tape, especially after Payne had pulled out his rap sheet about cocaine possession and said, "You didn't put these on your employment application here at WSB." It was a statement, not a question. It also was a guess. But he had been right. It was amazing how much the producer wanted to cooperate with him afterward.

Payne smiled. The media take, take, take. They never give anything. They take and take and then hide behind a combination of self-righteousness and the First Amendment. He shrugged. What he had done was one small step for the good guys.

Payne tapped the envelope and thought for a moment. The pictures were useless unless he could identify a suspect. He wondered if Colin had returned from Key West and, if so, what he had found. Did Colin know something that indicated the murders were connected to a squabble within the gay community? Payne didn't think much of that line of inquiry. But if the reporter had gone to Key West, he had to have a reason. It was worth pursuing. If the reporter had developed a lead within the gay community, a name, anything, maybe the pictures could be put to use. He needed a suspect.

Perhaps he could work a trade. He would show Colin the pictures—in absolute confidence, of course—and in return Colin would tell him everything about Key West and the gay connection.

He picked up Colin's card from the desk and dialed the number.

Payne turned off I-20 and drive about a half mile through a jumble of fast-food stores, gas stations, and schlock merchants before turning right on Panthersville Road. Almost immediately he was out in the countryside, passing a large nursing home and a mental institution backed by immense open fields.

Headquarters for the Georgia Bureau of Investigation was ahead on the right, a squat brick building far removed from any other buildings. He noticed surveillance cameras on the corners of the building as he crossed the parking lot and entered the lobby.

The cavernous sparsely furnished lobby divided the building roughly in half, with administration and investigations on the right and forensic sciences on the left. Forensics was further broken down by floor; pathology in the basement; fingerprints, handwriting analysis, and photography on the first floor; firearms, toxicology, trace evidence, and blood alcohol on the second; and drug identification and serology on the third.

Payne signed in with the receptionist and was sitting down to wait when the double doors on the left flew open and a big heavily muscled man with a broad smile walked toward him with hand outstretched.

"Detective Payne?"

"Yes." The two men shook hands.

"Good to meet you. I'm Kelly Fite, the chief firearms examiner. Come on back to the lab and I'll show you what we have."

The two men rode the elevator to the second floor, then walked down the hall to an office on the left. There Kelly Fite picked up a marked evidence bag containing a single 22-caliber cartridge. "I've got a written report for you. But would you like for me to go through what we found?"

"Please."

Fite shook his head. "Actually, we don't have much. We can give you some background and a few educated guesses. Of course, if you find the murder weapon, then we can make a match. But I doubt that will happen."

"Why not?"

Fite pulled the live round from the evidence bag and put it under a microscope. "You sit here and have a look," he said, pointing to a second set of eyepieces for the microscope.

Fite adjusted his microscope, then used a green arrow inside the microscope to point out what Payne should focus on. The arrow pointed to the lead tip of the projectile where a sharp indentation was apparent.

"See that. Cartridge jammed in an upward position. Here's where it caught at the edge of the chamber. Lead has a high coefficient of friction. This chambering mark is a good mark. It's enough to put him in jail if you identify a suspect and get his pistol."

Fite looked up when he noticed a middle-aged woman in a white lab coat had stopped at the door. He waved. "Peggy, have you got a minute?"

The woman in the lab coat smiled and nodded. She was very neat and meticulous in her appearance. Every hair was in place and her makeup was professional. The tan linen dress under the lab coat was smooth and unwrinkled.

"Of course, Kelly. What is it?"

"Say hello to C. R. Payne. New man in Atlanta Homicide. C. R. this is Peggy Haefele. She's in serology. Used to be with the FBI lab at Quantico, where she was their DNA expert."

She reached out to shake hands with Payne. "I'm from Atlanta," she explained. "I wanted to come home." She reached into the pocket of her lab coat and handed Payne a card. "If I can ever be of help."

"Thanks. Good to have met you."

She nodded and was off down the aisle.

Fite pointed at the evidence envelopes and looked up at Payne. "That's about all we got."

"No extraction marks?"

Fite shook his head. "Look in the microscope again."

Payne bent over the eyepieces and followed the green arrow as Fite moved it around. "The casing on a Stinger is cupronickel, which is a lot harder than brass. We have a few marks, but they're light because of the angle of the bullet and because the cupronickel is so hard. There are several marks on the very lip of the rim, but I don't have another bullet to compare them with so I don't know if they are significant. If he had actually chambered the round and then ejected it, the trace evidence would be different. Or if he had fired the round, then the ignition of the powder would have caused the casing to expand and we would have gotten markings from the chamber."

"Nothing off the pieces of bullet the medical examiner sent you?"

Fite shook his head again, almost reluctantly. "Your shooter is either very lucky or very good. First of all, Stingers weigh only thirty-two grains and they have a lot of power behind them. They're light and moving fast and they fall apart pretty quickly when they hit any sort of obstacle. The first victim was shot through his glasses. Glass deforms a bullet like you wouldn't believe. We didn't get enough from him to even confirm it was a twenty-two bullet that did it. Second guy, a little more. The bullets disintegrated when they hit his spinal column. We got enough from the base of one bullet to identify it as twenty-two-caliber. And a piece of rifling, just enough to tell it was to the right."

Payne's eyebrows rose in a question mark.

"Six lands and grooves with a right-hand twist— six right, we call it—is the most common rifling for twenty-two-caliber pistols. Almost all of them are like that."

"Did you talk to the M.E.?"

Fite nodded. "Small amounts of powder burns around the nose and eye of the first victim. A little stippling from unburned powder."

Payne nodded.

"Your shooter works close in."

"How close?"

"With most handguns I'd say around eighteen inches. But the Stinger is a hot load. It kicks out a lot of unburned powder. Could be two feet. Maybe a few inches more."

Payne thought for a moment. "So all we have is the chambering mark?"

Fite nodded.

"And all I have to do is find the shooter and get his gun?"

Fite paused.

"What is it?"

"This guy used a twenty-two-caliber pistol. He put two bullets in a guy's left eye and put two more in the second victim's mouth. Even at close range, that's good shooting. Very good. This mark on the live round indicates that somewhere in there he had a malfunction. But he still did some good shooting. So you have a shooter who carries a twenty-two and knows how to use it. You have to be very confident of your shooting ability to carry a twenty-two. The guy could be a gun nut, maybe a collector."

"So?"

"The guys knows he left a live round at the crime scene. If he knows half as much as I suspect he does about guns, he suspects you found it and brought it here."

Payne nodded. "If he knows that, he probably knows you might have found identifying marks on the round."

Fite nodded. "And I'm guessing he knows how to fix that."

"Fix it?"

"To change the chambering marks all he's got to do is stick a rat-tail file inside the chamber and move it around two or three times. He does that and it will change his gun so much that I can never testify his weapon was the one that made this mark on the round you found in the store."

"You couldn't identify it?"

Fite shook his head. "Nope. And if he really knows his stuff and he really wants to get cute, he could brush the file across the firing pin. It would then be entirely different from the firing pin that left marks on spent casings."

Payne thought for a moment. "It's going to be hard enough obtaining the guy's weapon. Let's keep this part quiet. I don't want him playing with a rat-tail file."

Bobby Rutherford was the slot man on the copy desk at *The Atlanta Constitution*. He worked the day shift. Bobby had finished all the course work for a Ph. D. at Emory University and lacked only writing his thesis. He was a small man, no more than five feet four inches tall, and quite slender. He was about fifty but his hair remained obsidian black. From a distance he would have looked almost boyish were it not for the large hump on his right shoulder. The hump was the reason he was a quiet man and the reason for the haunted pain in his eyes. Being short and reed-thin didn't bother him. But being extraordinarily bright and having to carry a large hump around took away the self-confidence that years ago might have prompted him to apply for a instructor's job at a university. It took away the self-confidence he needed to finish his thesis. It took away the self-confidence he needed to go out in the world and find a challenging job. It was the reason he hid himself on a copy desk where he corrected the grammar and syntax of his intellectual inferiors. And it gave him the haunted eyes.

Bobby looked up from the computer screen, took off his heavy dark-rimmed glasses, and rubbed his eyes.

"Would you read this, Marie?" he asked the woman at the next desk. "It's Colin Biddle's story out of Key West. It's in the slot queue."

"Sure." Marie had been on the copy desk for more than twenty years. She was slow and methodical and her eyes were filled with pain that went back many years. She had worked two jobs to put her husband through graduate school and the day he graduated he filed for divorce. Her dream in life had been to have children, but that dream had withered when she slipped alone into middle age. Now there was nothing but her job. And she did it right. She could take a story apart like no other copy editor. Reporters, the better reporters that is, always wanted her to edit their copy. She made them look good.

Marie read the story and shook her head. "Is this a joke?"

"I'm going to talk to him," Bobby said. "This is a major metropolitan newspaper. Even if he is Colin Biddle, he has to abide by the same standards as everyone else." He looked at Marie, waiting. Her judgment was always sound.

"I agree with you," she said. "But Colin does anything he wants." She paused. "You remember that we've lost several rounds with him."

"Not this time." Bobby looked across the newsroom, saw Colin at his computer, and sat down and quickly typed him a message. A few moments later Colin was standing by Bobby's computer.

"Hello, Quas. I understand you have a question about my copy."

Marie's head popped up sharply when she heard "Quas." But Bobby ignored the gibe and turned to the screen. "Yes, I do, Colin," he said in his soft voice.

"Well. What is it?"

"In a nutshell, it has no substance. It's inflammatory. It's misleading. I'm asking the city editor to pull it unless you rework it."

Colin stared at Bobby in disbelief. The corner of his mouth twitched. He could barely control his anger.

"You're not a reporter. You've never been a reporter. And you forget that not only am I the best reporter on this newspaper, I am the only real writer on this newspaper. You can pick up my novel if you doubt that."

Bobby nodded. "I understand all that, Colin. But it is not relevant. I'm talking about the Key West piece. You shouldn't be defensive. Everyone can have an off day."

Colin waggled a finger in Bobby's face. "Listen, Quas. Not only does it run, it runs exactly as I wrote it. You change one word without my approval and we'll go to war." He paused. His eyebrows raised. "Quas, you don't want to go to war with me."

Bobby nodded. "I'm going to the city editor with my thoughts. He may agree with you. If he does, fine. But I don't think the piece should run."

"You go to the city editor. You do that, Quas. And while you're going to the city editor, I'm going to the managing editor." Colin turned and stalked away. He entered the glass-enclosed assistant managing editor's office, closed the door, and began talking. He looked over his shoulder once and nodded his head toward the copy desk.

A few moments later he walked out, smiled toward Bobby, and returned to his desk.

20

Colin was watching the videotape. Over and over he had watched the segment where the first bullet shattered one lens of the attendant's glasses. The first two bullets were fired so quickly they seemed to hit Kitty's brother simultaneously. His head snapped back and his body hung bonelessly for a split second before slumping to the floor.

Colin realized again why he loaded his TPH with Stingers. The Stinger is an amazing round; one tenth of an inch longer than the long rifle cartridge with a reduced weight hollow-point bullet and a case full of slower burning powder. This results in a thirty percent increase in velocity and a twenty-five percent increase in energy over the standard long rifle cartridge. And it means extraordinary expansion of the hollow point and a near-perfect energy transfer when it impacts. Tissue damage inflicted by one of these hyper-velocity .22s is significantly greater than that inflicted by long rifle ammo.

Colin was watching the segment again when the

telephone rang. It was Payne. After the conversation he looked at his watch, took the tape out of the machine, and hid it behind a three-volume set of Samuel Pepys's *Diaries* on an upper shelf of his bookcase.

He opened a wooden door under the bookcases and looked into the area where his office supplies were stored. The space was taken up almost entirely with copies of *Street Smarts*. He pulled one out, opened it to the title page, and with a big smile wrote:

To my good friend, C.R.,
    A great detective who will solve many significant cases and who will—I hope—help me with future books.

                    With much respect,
Colin Biddle

Payne looked up in surprise at the man who opened the door. He had not expected to be greeted by a black man. For a frozen second the tableau existed. It was broken by the black man in the white jacket—the butler—who nodded and said, "Please come in . . . sir. I'll let Mr. Biddle know you are here." He pulled the door open wider and stepped aside. But he continued to stare at Payne.

Payne walked into the hall of the rambling two-story home on Tuxedo Road and looked around. The floor was a black-and-white checkerboard in what appeared to be marble. The ceilings were fourteen feet high and surrounded by three levels of elaborate scrolled trim.

"If you would have a seat in the living room," the butler said. He held his right hand out toward a room off the entrance hall and continued to glance surreptitiously at Payne.

At the entrance to the living room, Payne stopped. "Have we met, brother?" he asked.

"No, I don't think so. It's just that . . ."

"Yes?"

"You are the first black man who has come to this house as a guest."

"That so? Well, it happens that Mr. Biddle—Colin—is a friend of mine."

The butler nodded. He pointed to an enormous sofa covered in a heavy flowered silk. "May I get you something to drink?"

"A diet Coke would be fine."

"A diet Coke?"

"Yes, a diet Coke."

"Yes, sir."

As the butler slowly walked from the room, Payne looked around. The floor was covered in a large wine-red oriental carpet. The carpet was slightly worn—an antique that, if the size was any indication, must have cost upward of twenty thousand dollars.

The walls were of very dark wood—cherry, Payne guessed—and covered with paintings. Three small statues sat on marble pedestals along one wall. The paintings and statues were lit by recessed lights. A wooden chest, intricately carved with an elaborate seal of some kind, sat near the fireplace.

Payne shook his head in appreciation. This was the sort of house he would have one day. This was what living in America was all about.

He looked closely at every detail in the room. It was the room of someone who has traveled widely, a sophisticated room, a room exhibiting taste and—above all—wealth. Payne had seen houses like this in the movies.

On the far wall was a gold-covered three-dimensional piece of art. It was all the more noticeable because it was so different from everything else in the room.

Payne was walking across the room for a closer look when the butler returned. A glass of diet cola sat atop a linen on a silver tray. Payne reached for the drink. "Thank you."

The butler nodded. "Mr. Biddle knows you are here. He is finishing some things in his study and will be here in a moment."

Payne nodded.

"Is there anything else . . . sir?"

"No thanks."

"Very well." The butler turned and walked from the room.

Payne looked around again and then walked the length of the room toward the piece of art that had attracted his attention. It was of a crouched bare-breasted woman who had six arms. The three sets of arms jutted out from her body horizontal to the ground, then were vertical to her body until they reached her wrists. The wrists were turned parallel to the ground and the hands were curved in a graceful stylized manner that Payne faintly remembered from a college class in art history. He guessed the figure was Thai, a stylized Thai dancer.

But what he could not figure out was why everything on the figure was flat and one-dimensional but the large breasts were three-dimensional and of a curious texture, a texture different from the remainder of the crouched figure.

Payne drew closer.

This was one of those times when he realized that his Emory education had not lifted him completely out of southwest Georgia. There was so much he did not know. But his thirst to fill those gaps in his education was as great as his thirst to excel. He had to understand the mystery of the piece of art.

The breasts were definitely of a different texture and consistency than the painting. They didn't talk about this in his art history class. He looked around. No one was in the room. With a tentative finger he reached out and gently pushed at the nipple of the left breast. The nipple retreated under his finger. He pushed harder. The nipple retreated farther.

Payne removed his finger. The nipple stayed in retreat. Now he was staring at a woman with one large right breast and one large but concave left breast. Payne reached out with his right hand and surrounded the breast with a thumb and forefinger and squeezed gently. More of the breast rolled inward. Now the nipple protruded slightly but the remainder of the breast was flat.

Payne placed his drink on the carved chest, wiped his hands on his trousers, and pressed his flattened hands on either side of the errant breast. Then he slowly pressed his hands together, trying to push the breast to its former prominence.

The breast flattened even more.

Payne was alarmed. He also was embarrassed. If Colin saw this he would think Payne was a rube. And that Uncle Tom of a butler would make it even worse.

He had to do something. Anyone coming into the room would surely notice the Thai art.

Don't be intimidated, he told himself. Be cool. Improvise. Adapt.

Payne pulled the painting out from the wall and slid his hand up behind the frame, hoping to be able to press the breast forward from the inside. The backing on the frame prevented that.

If the expensive nature of everything else in the room was any indication, he had just flattened the breast of a very pricey piece of Thai art. He had to correct it before Colin arrived.

Again he spread flattened hands on either side of the breast and pushed toward the center. Nothing. The breast remained flat.

He backed up and stared at the painting. It was

obvious his hands could do nothing to restore the painting. There was only one thing left to do.

He stepped close to the painting, reached out with both hands to steady the frame, and tried to put his mouth over the nipple. If he could seize the nipple in his mouth and pull, he could resurrect the collapsed breast. It was the only way.

He had the nipple in his lips and then very gently in his teeth. With a small grunt of triumph he began to slowly move his head backward. He felt the breast beginning to move. His eyes focused down his nose and he watched as—with a distinctive *plop* sound—the nipple suddenly popped out to its former position.

Payne pulled out his handkerchief and brushed the nipple. Out of relief at his success he leaned forward and kissed the now fully erect breast.

"You beautiful thing," he whispered.

As he stood up he heard a cough. The butler was standing by Colin looking at Payne with distinct displeasure. Colin was smiling.

"Did you find her enjoyable?" he asked.

21

The waiter behind the bar at Otto's wore a tuxedo shirt and a black bow tie. He smiled and said, "Good evening, Mr. Biddle."

Payne got an "Evening, sir."

Payne had never been to Otto's, the quintessential Buckhead watering hole, and he looked around appreciatively at the dark walls, black ceilings, and the soft leather chairs in the main room. Nothing like this in Albany, Georgia.

"Good evening, Mr. Biddle. Your usual table?" asked a waiter.

Colin nodded and continued toward the rear of the bar, the waiter leading the way.

"How's the book doing?" the waiter asked over his shoulder.

"I have my copy," Payne said, holding the book Colin had given him earlier. "Autographed."

Colin laughed appreciatively. "Bit early to tell, Horace. But it looks good." He took a seat facing the front door.

"That's good, sir. You're our only famous writer. Are you working on another one?"

Colin smiled and adjusted his coat, pulling at the bottom so the collar did not rise over his shirt and so the shoulders would fit trimly and not bunch around his neck. He checked the handkerchief in his breast pocket. "Trying to. But I have a job, you know." Both Colin and the waiter laughed appreciatively.

"When they make a movie, who will play your part?" the waiter asked.

Colin laughed. "Oh, they can find any handsome young guy to play me. The real question is who will they get to play my friend C. R.?" He leaned over and clapped C. R. on the shoulder and with his other hand motioned for the waiter to come closer. The three men huddled over the table. "They were going to get Denzel Washington to play C.R., but they said Denzel's penis is too small. It looks as if C. R. might have to play himself."

The three men sat back and laughed.

The waiter looked at Colin. "Your usual, Mr. Biddle."

Colin nodded.

The waiter turned to Payne. "What may I bring you, sir?"

Payne paused. He was still writhing in embarrassment about being caught biting the breast on the Thai painting. He didn't want to make another social mistake of that magnitude. But what do rich folk drink in a place like this? He clasped both hands around the large envelope he was carrying and looked up at the waiter.

"The same."

"Two of The Macallan. Straight up?"

Colin nodded and the waiter disappeared. Then the newspaper reporter looked at Payne and, as if reading his mind, asked, "Been here before?"

"No. First time." Payne looked around, admiring the artful way the chairs were arranged. Dozens of little alcoves gave the appearance of dozens of little living rooms. Very cozy.

Colin nodded. "It's rather like a club for some of us. We don't have clubs in America as they do in England, you know. But this is close. Same people here all the time. Older crowd. It's a proper little bar. A single malt kind of place. Very inside-the-perimeter."

Payne wanted to add, "Very white," but he didn't. Except for the bartender he saw no black faces.

"I like it." Payne could not shake his embarrassment. What must this rich white guy think of him?

"I was glad you called, C.R. I was about to call you. Great minds in the same circles and all that."

"You were going to call me? About what?"

"By the way, what does C.R. stand for?"

Payne shrugged. "Nothing. Just initials."

Colin paused. Then he picked up on Payne's question. "Yes, I just returned from Key West. Fascinating town. Ever been there?"

Payne shook his head. "Were you working or playing?"

"Working." Colin smiled ruefully. "Strange place to work. We're talking about the gay capital of America. I found some things I thought might interest you."

"Here you are, gentlemen," the waiter said. He placed the two crystal glasses of scotch on the table and slid a bowl of salt-free pretzels between the two men.

"Thank you, Horace," Colin said. He picked up his glass and held it toward Payne. "May your first big case be a big success."

Payne smiled. "Thanks."

The two men clicked their glasses and each took a healthy sip of scotch.

Payne looked at the glass appreciatively. "So that's single malt scotch?"

"The best," Colin said. "Like it?"

"Very much." Payne tapped the large envelope he was carrying. "I've been making progress. Perhaps we can share some information. I wanted to bring you up-to-date on what I've found in the double homicide. Off the record, of course. And I thought you might tell me what you found here and in Key West."

Colin nodded. "Certainly." He hoped his suddenly rapidly beating heart did not give him away. He leaned forward. "Why don't you go first."

Payne nodded and paused as he gathered his thoughts. "Several things. First, the shooter is rich."

Colin's eyebrows raised. "Rich? How do you know that?"

"Did you know we found the keys taken from the service station?"

Colin shrugged. "I saw Kitty's story on that. The paper attached no significance to it. Which is why it was buried." He did not add that he suggested the story be held to six inches and buried in the back of the local news section.

"Attached to the keys was a fiber. Kitty didn't use that in her story."

Colin held up his hand. "Wait a minute. She knew about the fiber?"

"Of course. Didn't she tell you?"

"Go ahead."

Briefly Payne wondered why Kitty had not told Colin about the fiber. Oh, well. That was internal newspaper stuff.

"The crime lab determined that it was a bleached, highly processed fine grade of linen. Very expensive. I believe it came from the shooter's handkerchief."

Colin nodded and lifted his scotch. "Fascinating. Please continue." He wondered if his arm covered the linen handkerchief in his breast pocket.

"The shooter drives a Mercedes."

"What?" Colin could not contain his surprise. He jerked forward. Then, to cover himself, he asked, "May I use that?"

"No. As I said, everything we talk about is confidential. None of it can be used at this point. As me again after we catch the guy."

"How do you know he drives a Mercedes?"

Payne smiled, opened the envelope, pulled out the pictures, and began going through them.

"Here's the rear quarter panel of the car. It's been identified as a Mercedes. We think it is one of the big ones."

Colin almost panicked. The edge of the photo ended a half inch from the license plates of his wife's Mercedes. There, across the trunk, was something that looked like a ribbon of light. It was the deep scratch made when someone keyed the car while he was at the book party. Did Payne recognize the scratch for what it was? If Payne realized what he had, he could run a DMV check for every Mercedes in the Atlanta area. It would take a while—there must be thousands—but eventually he would find one with a scratch on the trunk.

And then he would have himself a strong suspect.

Did the police officer have a shot that showed the license plates? No. He couldn't have or this meeting would have never happened. Was the police officer playing with him? Colin had never had to exercise such self-control. "Who took these pictures?"

"Tower cam at WSB."

Colin stared at Payne. "Tower cam. You mean . . ."

Payne nodded, clearly pleased that he had so impressed Colin. "Yep. Weather camera on the tower at WSB. The idea just came to me that it over-looked the crime scene. I went over there and . . . it was a lucky shot. These are enhanced, of course."

"You got this photograph from a TV station? From a weather camera?" His mind was racing a thousand miles an hour. Whatever Payne had, he still did not know the identity of the shooter. But he was close. Too close.

Payne smiled. Maybe now Colin would forget about him biting the breast on the Thai painting. "Maybe you can use something like that in your next book. I thought using the tower cam was innovative."

Too innovative, Colin thought.

"How do you know this is the shooter's car?"

Payne dismissed the question with an impatient wave. "Time line on the video compared with time of the shooting. Between the estimated time of the shooting and the arrival of the uniform officer, this was the only car parked there. One drove through the lot but didn't stop."

"What else?"

Payne slid the next photograph into view. Colin's heart stopped. That was *him* walking into the store. His head and features were washed out by the light, but it was *him*. If his wife saw it, she would recognize him.

"Here is our shooter," Payne said with satisfaction. He sat back in his chair. "I can't ID him. I don't even know if he's black or white. All I know is he's the shooter and he's in a Mercedes."

"Hello, famous writer," boomed a big voice. "How you doing?"

Payne quickly slid the photographs into an envelope as he looked up. A man with unruly white hair and a bristly white mustache accompanied by a slender smiling woman was standing by the table. There were few places in the world that either the man or woman would not be recognized.

"Hello, Ted," Colin said as he stood up and reached out to shake hands. He kissed the woman on the cheek. "Jane." He pointed toward Payne. "I'd like for you to meet a good friend of mine, Detective C. R. Payne of the Atlanta police. Homicide Squad."

The man's eyes widened as Payne stood up and shook hands. "More research for another blockbuster, huh?" Payne nodded toward the woman. She shook his hand and smiled.

"Look, guys, I'd love to chat with you. But Detective Payne and I are right in the middle of—"

Ted held up his hands, palms out, and backed away a step. "I understand. I understand. This is work. Can't stand in the way of research for another big book. I'm reading your first one. I might have my movie people get in touch with you."

He smiled at his wife. "Jane's interested in it, too."

He slapped Colin on the back. "You're about to hit the big time, fella."

Colin laughed. "I hope so, Ted. By the way, I'm looking forward to seeing you at the party."

"We'll be there," Jane said.

"Good to have met you, Detective," Ted said. He waggled his finger at Payne. "Now don't be giving all your secrets to this man. They'll wind up in his next book."

Payne smiled as the two backed away, still waving, still smiling. They walked to the bar where they began talking to other customers and pointing at Colin. Payne sensed other customers staring at them.

Colin quickly sat down. "What else you got in there?"

Payne was staring after the couple. "You *know* them?" Payne fell back in his chair.

"They're old friends." Colin smiled. He nodded toward the large envelope. "Let's go back to work."

Payne looked at Ted and Jane. He could not get over this. Ted and Jane had stopped to talk with Colin. He had met Atlanta's most famous couple.

He shook his head, opened the envelope, and pulled out another photograph.

"According to the time line on the videotape, the shooter was inside about eight minutes. Too long if all he was doing was paying for gas. But about right if shooting two guys and then cleaning up the crime scene." He pointed. "Look at this. He's got something in his hand. Rich son of a bitch shoots two guys, then steals something from the store. Looks like a box of candy or something."

Colin leaned forward. He knew what it was. In the left hand of the man leaving the store, in *his* left hand, was a handkerchief. But it was folded over the key ring in such a way that the square edge protruded from his hand giving it the appearance of a small box. The bright lights around the store, the strobing effect of those lights on his hair, and the distortion that came with enhancement destroyed the depth perception.

In the lull, Payne overheard more of the bar conversation. "Writer . . . Atlanta police book . . . homicide detective . . . another book . . . Ted and Jane just stopped at his table."

Because he was listening to the conversation across the bar, Payne did not see the uncontrollable flush that momentarily surged up Colin's neck as he studied the picture of himself in the parking lot. Colin was almost afraid to look up. He was afraid Payne would suddenly recognize him in the pictures.

"What are you going to do with these?"

"Not much I can do unless I get a suspect. I was hoping you might have found something about the gay community that could be a lead; that could point me toward someone I might match the photos with. I don't have anything that will stand up in court. The guy's features are gone."

Payne looked around the restaurant and leaned closer to Colin. "I'm going to superior court tomorrow morning and get a court order to have WSB turn over their videotape to me. Then I'm taking it up to Oak Ridge, Tennessee, to their photo analyzers, get a better resolution and better enhancement. I talked to one of the vets in my office who said computers can wash out this white light and we can get a positive ID on this individual. WSB did the best enhancement they could. But the people at Oak Ridge can do a lot better. Then I might get you to run a picture of the guy in the paper and see if we can identify him." He tapped the photos. "I'm going to use these photos to nail the shooter."

Colin looked up. "What's at Oak Ridge?"

"Government labs. Best in the world at photo enhancement."

"Why wouldn't WSB give you the tape? They just pulled a few pictures off the tape and blew them up?"

Payne nodded. "Yeah and that was done as a . . . let us say as a personal under-the-table sort of favor. Guy there said I'd need a court order to get more."

Colin nodded. Someone, without the knowledge of top officials at WSB, had slipped the photographs to the officer. He made a mental note to make a phone call tonight when he got home.

"Gentlemen, another drink?" The waiter had returned.

Colin looked at Payne. Payne shook his head. "One's enough for me."

"No thanks, Horace. We're going out for dinner. Bring me a check, if you will."

"Certainly, Mr. Biddle."

Colin looked at Payne. "Let's go to dinner and talk some more. I want to hear more about your progress and then I'll tell you what I found in Key West."

Payne nodded.

"We're going over to The Bistro. Just a few blocks from here. Absolutely the finest restaurant in Atlanta. The owner is a friend of mine."

"I'm ready." Payne pushed the photos into the large envelope. He looked at Colin. "Wait until I tell you what I found about the murder weapon."

Colin had a feeling he was not going to enjoy dinner.

22

Buckhead, or the part of Buckhead that makes it famous as the location of Atlanta's trendiest bars and restaurants, is a small area of maybe five square blocks. But on a busy night, every inch of every one of those blocks is chockablock with well-dressed people—mostly young—shoaling about the streets, flashing their finery, and searching for the bar of the minute where they can do some serious relaxation.

It seemed to Payne as he rode through Buckhead that many of those people knew Colin Biddle.

Colin was constantly greeted by shouts and horn tootings as he drove down the street from Otto's, then turned around on East Paces Ferry and motored slowly back through the heart of Buckhead.

A flashing blue light suddenly appeared behind them and they heard the quick burp of a siren. Payne looked at Colin. "What'd you do?"

"Nothing that I know of." Colin looked in his rearview mirror as a police officer, wearing the white shirt of a senior police official, stepped from the driver's side of the car that had stopped them.

Colin rolled down the window. Payne's eyes widened as he looked over Colin's shoulder. They had been stopped by a major, one of the princes of the Atlanta Police Department.

The major slapped his hand on the roof of the Range Rover. "You know this piece of English garbage is blocking the road."

"What the hell are you doing out on the streets?" Colin asked. "You usually spend your shift sitting on your butt and telling other people what to do. Trying to earn your pay for a change?"

The major laughed. "Showing the flag. Showing the troops that their leader can still work the streets."

The two men laughed and shook hands.

"Fine-looking vehicle," the major said. "Every time I see it I try to figure out some way we can impound it for a while."

Colin patted the burnished wooden trim near the window. "Graham, I keep telling you that you can drive it anytime you want. All you have to do is say when."

Payne rolled his eyes. They had been stopped by a major whom Colin knew well enough to call by his first name.

"Too many people know this car," the major said. "You think I want people to think I'm some famous rich writer?"

Colin laughed. "How'd you like the book?"

The major shrugged. "Little dramatic. Not much to do with how it really is. Not deep at all. But what the hell? You got to tell a story."

"Sorry I asked," Colin said ruefully.

"You working on another one?"

"Making a few notes. Rolling around a few ideas. I'll start writing in the next day or so."

The major looked around Colin toward Payne. "Who's your friend? He looks familiar."

"I'm sorry, Graham. I thought you guys knew each other. C. R. Payne, Homicide, meet Major Graham Spurling, Zone Two commander."

The two men shook hands. "You're the new man in Homicide," the major said.

"Yes, sir."

"What are you doing riding around with the King of Buckhead?"

Colin interrupted. "I'm showing him how you live up here."

"You got a good guide," the major said to Payne.

"Yes, sir. I'm realizing that."

The major tapped Colin on the shoulder. "I've been reading your stories about the double homicide over on Cheshire Bridge. That's in Zone Two so it's my territory. You're doing a good job with that."

"Thanks, Graham. Detective Payne here is the lead detective on that case."

"Good luck on that, Detective. People in Zone Two like such things to be cleared up quickly."

"Thank you, sir. I'll do my best."

The major looked around. "Well, I have to get back out there and keep America safe. Fight some crime."

"We're going over to The Bistro. Take your dinner break and join us."

Payne looked straight ahead. Majors did not eat dinner with detectives, especially young detectives. Surely Colin knew that.

"Too high rent for me. Besides, I have to work. You two have fun." The major leaned lower to look across at Payne. "Detective, be careful about who you are seen with. This guy is a known pedophile."

Colin and Payne laughed.

"Graham, take care."

"You, too, Colin. Good to have met you, Detective."

"Yes, sir. Me, too."

As Colin drove away he turned to Payne. "I knew he wouldn't take off to join us. But I wanted to make the gesture."

Payne nodded.

A moment later Colin parked the Range Rover in front of The Bistro.

The Bistro is tucked away in a small shopping center in the heart of Buckhead. People who live two or three blocks away might not even know it is there. Jim Brown, the owner, if he is not too busy in the kitchen, can be found sitting atop a stool at the end of the bar, keeping a sharp eye on the dining room and nodding and speaking to his guests, most of whom are long-time customers. Brown spent ten years in Paris learning his profession. He prepares food with love and respect and if customers want it done some other way—such as ordering lamb well done—he will tell them to eat elsewhere. Rather than running off customers, his attitude has drawn them to him. They put themselves in his hands and they come back again and again to the elegant little restaurant.

"Hello, Hemingway," Brown said with a smile when Colin walked in trailed by Payne. "How's the book doing?"

Colin smiled. "Hello, Jim. It's doing well as far as I know." He turned toward Payne. "Jim, I want you to meet my friend, C. R. Payne, a detective with the homicide squad."

Jim shook hands. "You helping Colin with his next book?"

Payne smiled. "If I can."

"Jim can we have twenty-six?" Colin asked.

Jim looked over his shoulder. The single table in the corner was empty. "Of course." He caught a waiter's eye, pointed to Colin, raised two fingers, and pointed to the table.

Colin liked the table for two reasons: first, it was isolated and he could talk to Payne without fear of being overheard, and second, it was in such a position that everyone in the restaurant could see him. He knew that the waiters sometimes pointed him out to other customers as the crime reporter for *The Atlanta Constitution*. Jim was so blasé about such things that he wouldn't point out the President of the United States. But Colin had given several waiters advance copies of his book, and for the past few weeks, he had been pointed out as the author of the new crime novel about Atlanta.

Colin did not have much of an appetite. It was not the business about the fiber found with the keys. He would burn his linen handkerchiefs and order more from London. It was the pictures. They were extremely disturbing. But he had already planned how he would minimize their potential damage. All it would take was a phone call. And he knew what he would do about the scratch on the Mercedes.

Colin looked up as a waiter approached with two crystal glasses.

"These are on the house, Colin. You do still drink The Macallan, don't you?" Jim asked. "Or have you switched to champagne now that you're a big-shot writer?"

Colin laughed. "Thanks, Jim. Scotch is fine. My friend here is a scotch drinker also."

"I figured that. If he's running around with you, he must drink scotch."

Colin raised his glass and glanced at Payne. Perhaps he had underestimated the young police officer. Or perhaps it was luck. Whatever it was, he was about to nullify the detective's progress. The stories he had written and the stories he planned to write would cause great confusion to the detective. He downed the double shot of scotch in a single gulp.

Jim passed each of the men a menu.

"I recommend the vichyssoise," Colin said to Payne. "Best in town. The goat cheese salad is splendid. And for an entree, Jim does sea bass in a fashion you will find smashing. Absolutely smashing."

Payne nodded. "Sounds good to me."

Colin nodded at Jim. "Two."

He leaned over his empty glass and smiled at Payne. "I was going to tell you about Key West, but I've written a story that is coming out in the morning paper. The early edition will be out about ten. We can pick it up when we leave. So if you don't mind, let me get you a paper, you read the piece and then we can talk about it later in greater detail. You are the one with the big news tonight. Those pictures are incredible. Now I want you to tell me more. You've been making a lot of progress."

Payne shrugged and sipped his scotch. He wanted to talk about Key West. He thought that Payne did also. Now the rules had changed. But, hey, the guy knew Ted and Jane, was on a first-name basis with the zone commander, and seemed to know every other person in Buckhead. He would ride along. Besides, he couldn't get over the embarrassment about the Thai artwork.

He knew Colin was impressed with his work on the case. And that meant a great deal to him. He knew the reason it was important to him and the reason bothered him. But some things, especially from childhood, cannot be changed. Payne's only memory of his father was of a man who constantly ridiculed and denigrated and criticized. "You're sorry as gully dirt. You'll never amount to anything," his father had told him again and again. As a result, Payne did not take criticism well. Any criticism about his work tapped into his father telling him how sorry he was. Conversely, he needed praise from people who had accomplished much. And Colin was at the top of the heap. He needed Colin's praise.

He shrugged and looked across the table. "I'm not making enough progress to identify a suspect. There are lots of little pieces. But I can't tie it all together. Not yet, anyway. And the next few days are crucial." He smiled. "All of this would be an interesting case for your next book."

"How do you mean?"

"I mentioned going to a judge to get a court order for the videotape. But the car in the last photo, the one driving down Cheshire Bridge Road as the shooter was walking to his Mercedes, we are following up on that, too."

Colin's eyebrows pulled low. "What will you do?"

"I'm hoping you can help. Can you do a story hinting about the photographs without revealing any specifics, and say we are seeking the driver of a light-colored Acura that was driving south on Cheshire Bridge about one-fifteen or one-thirty

Sunday morning. We want to ask him what he saw."

Colin nodded. "I can do a story about that."

"It's a long shot. But possibly the driver saw something."

"What else do you have?"

"Let me run this by you. You have the background to appreciate it and maybe you can help."

Colin clasped the empty glass in both hands. "I'll try." Colin was working to keep a smile on his face. He did not want Payne to realize how preoccupied he was as he planned the things he must do in the next few days to thwart the officer's investigation.

"I've learned several things from the old guys at Homicide. One is that there is always a witness. Somebody saw something. The witness might not realize that what he saw was of significance, say he just saw a guy walking from the service station out to his car, but his description could break the case open. Somebody always sees something. In this case, maybe it was the camera." He shrugged and laughed. "Wouldn't it be something? To catch this guy with a weather camera?"

Colin nodded. "That would be something."

"I also believe the answer is at the crime scene. I'm overlooking something. It's there . . . if only . . ."

"If only . . . ?"

Payne shrugged. "If only the owner of the store would get off my case."

Colin leaned closer. "What do you mean?"

"Ahhh. He's a campaign contributor to the mayor. They're friends. He's complained about my holding on to the crime scene. He wants his store back. I can't blame him. He's a small businessman who wants his place of business. But it's my crime scene and I'm not through with it yet."

"You're still checking things there?"

"Every day. But I'm racing the clock. Any day I could be told to give the guy his store."

Colin nodded. "That's pressure."

Colin filed the information away. He would follow up with either a phone call to the mayor, suggesting, in confidence, of course, that it might be construed as racist for an Indian store owner to be deprived of his livelihood. Or he could send out word for the store owner to contact him and then he could do a story that would put public pressure on the mayor to release the store to the owner. No, a story in the paper would be better. He would call the store owner and interview him but make it look as if the store owner had called him.

"I've learned one other thing from the old-timers," Payne said.

"And that is?"

"To get inside a perp's head. I've talked about this case with some of the old guys. Called a retired FBI guy who did profiles for their Behavioral Science Unit. They told me two things that were fascinating. They said my perp knows a lot about police work and about forensics. That was obvious from the beginning. But they said he might be close to the police. He might be a police groupy hanging out in cop bars. He might have a job that brings him in frequent contact with the police."

Colin leaned back in his chair and laughed. "They told you all that? Based on what? On the crime scene and the perp's MO?"

Payne shrugged. "I know it sounds like witchcraft. But those guys know things. And it makes sense."

"What else?"

Payne paused. "The old guys couldn't give me any hard reasons for this; it was just based on their experience. It's sort of a gut feeling. But they said this guy will return to the crime scene. They said some perps are like dogs returning to their vomit, they will return to the crime scene." He threw his hands wide. "He might already have returned. I'm keeping my eyes open when I go there and I've asked people at several nearby restaurants to keep an eye on the place."

"Sounds as if you've got that one covered."

"I'm gonna get him, Colin. I'm gonna get him. I can feel it. He's mine." Payne laughed. "You know what the medical examiner said to me yesterday? I was talking to him and he said, 'I want to do the autopsy on the guy who did this when you catch him.'" Payne laughed again, a mirthless laugh. "He's going to be disappointed. This guy is coming in live. I'm taking him to court."

"I'm glad you're so enthusiastic."

Payne reached out and touched Colin's arm. "I didn't tell you the weirdest thing of all."

"What was that?"

"GBI crime lab thinks my perp could be a gun nut. They say even if I locate a perp and he has a twenty-two semiautomatic that he probably has altered it enough that no one will be able to testify it was the same weapon."

Colin's eyebrows raised. "How could he do that?"

"They got a chambering mark from the live round but they said the guy could take a rat-tail file and in two seconds change his twenty-two enough that there would be no comparisons."

"With a rat-tail file?"

Payne nodded. "Kelly Fite at the crime lab said all it would take to alter the pistol would be for the shooter to run a rat-tail file inside the opening of the chamber. Bingo. The weapon has new ballistics. No comparisons."

Payne shook his head. "That's just the good news. He said if this guy had dropped a spent casing at the crime scene and was really sharp that he could brush the file against the firing pin." Payne brushed the palms of his hands together twice, then held his hands wide. "Change it enough that technically or legally it would no longer be the same weapon."

Colin smiled. "I know you don't want that in a story."

"Not under any circumstances. Maybe you can use it in a book but not in the newspaper. I'm just talking to you."

Colin nodded. He looked up.

"Gentlemen." Jim stood beside the table, accompanying a waiter carrying two bowls of vichyssoise. He carried a bottle of wine. "Colin, I know you like this. So I took the liberty of bringing you a bottle on the house."

Colin tilted his head and looked at the label. A Corton Charlemagne. A 1990. A magnificent bottle of white burgundy. Wine purists might quarrel with his choice of a wine to go with fish, but the Corton Charlemagne was one of his favorites.

"Thanks, Jim."

"Drink more than that and you'll have to pay for it." He looked at the two plates. "You need anything, wave." He turned and walked back to his sentry post at the end of the bar.

Payne leaned over the bowl of thick vichyssoise and inhaled. He shook his head in delight. He was hungry. Perhaps that came from his excitement. Telling Colin about the photographs and talking about the case had somehow balanced the scales for Payne. He no longer felt any embarrassment about the Thai artwork. Someday, perhaps, when the case was solved, he would be able to tell his fellow detectives the story and they would laugh about it with him.

He looked at Colin. "I've never seen vichyssoise that smelled this good or was this thick. The texture is like silk. He must use heavy cream."

Colin nodded and slid his spoon through the soup. Suddenly he was very hungry. Tomorrow was going to be a big day.

23

As he exited the restaurant, Colin pulled two quarters from his pocket and dropped them into a newspaper vending machine by the door and pulled out two papers, one of which he handed to Payne. He took off his coat and draped it over his arm.

Payne saw Colin was wearing a pistol on his right hip. "You must have a special license."

A pistol toting permit specifically states the holder cannot carry a weapon into a sporting event or into a place that serves alcohol. Colin had been wearing the weapon all evening.

Colin smiled and shrugged. "Major Spurling is always kidding me about that. He said if I'm out with him some night and he really needs a backup that I won't be wearing it."

"The major knows you wear it into bars?"

"Yes." Colin pointed toward the newspaper he had given to Payne.

"Read that when you get home. I believe you'll find it interesting." Colin smiled. "It's not exactly in line with the thrust of your investigation." He paused. "To this point, that is." He nodded toward his Range Rover. "Come on, I'll take you back to the house. I've got a big day tomorrow."

He turned toward his car but Payne paused, dug into his pocket, and put another two quarters into the vending machine. He caught up with Colin as the reporter said, "What are you doing back there?"

Payne held up the newspaper. "Trying to read the paper but there's not enough light."

Colin stopped in his driveway to let Payne out. The officer's car was parked on the curb. Colin did not want to open the garage door and have the officer see the black Mercedes. Nor did he want his wife to meet Payne. Although he continued to minimize the incident, she had told several friends that they had stopped for gas that night at the place where two men were killed.

"Hope you don't mind if I don't invite you in for a drink," Colin said as he stopped. "But following this story is wearing me out."

Payne waved in dismissal. "Don't worry about it. I have to get up early and work on a warrant for the judge. Then back to the crime scene. I want to call the people up at Oak Ridge about the tape and somewhere in there I have to placate the store owner who wants his place of business released. Big one for me, too."

He held out his hand. "Colin, it was a nice evening. Thanks for dinner. The food at The Bistro was outstanding. When I can afford it I'll go back."

Colin smiled. "A very pleasant evening it was. We must do it again."

Payne stumbled as he alighted from the car. "It's so high off the ground," he said.

Colin nodded. "It happens to everyone the first time they ride in a Range Rover. Don't be embarrassed."

"Thanks again," Payne said.

"Good night." Colin waited and watched as Payne opened the door of his gray Plymouth. The front right fender was crumpled and when Payne turned on the lights, the front right beam pointed into the sky. The side of the car was scraped and dented. Colin smiled. Payne was far down the pecking order when it came to getting a city car to take home.

Payne waved as he drove away. Colin waited until the officer rounded the corner before he reached over the sun visor and pressed a button that raised the garage door.

Payne walked into his small apartment, loosened his tie, and turned on the light over the kitchen table. He tossed the thick envelope stuffed with the crime scene pictures onto the table, turned on the television, and shook his head as if to clear the slight buzz from the scotch and the wine. When the television came on, he shook his head again. The screen went from almost dark to a washed-out whiteness. Soon he would be forced to buy a new TV. He unfolded the paper, looked at the front page, and sat down to read. Colin's story was on the front, above the fold in a box. The headline read, CONSPIRACY TO KILL GAYS REVEALED.

What conspiracy?

The words "An Analysis" appeared over Colin's byline.

KEY WEST—Here in this self-described "Gay Capital of America" may lie the secret to recent homicides of two gay men in Atlanta.

The two men were shot and killed last Sunday during the early-morning robbery of a convenience store on Cheshire Bridge Road.

Numerous interviews here with gay activists reveal a widespread belief that militant conservatives have begun a nationwide campaign to kill gay men.

"It's genocide," said Thad, a gay man who works at a well-known department store on Duval Street. He did not want his last name used because "They might come after me."

The large openly gay community here, which consists of gay men and women from along the Eastern Seaboard, believes that conservatives in Washington, perhaps unknowingly, have created a strong and militant backlash against gays and lesbians across America.

The Atlanta incident is the hottest topic of discussion in this hot and steamy town that dangles like a lavaliere at the western tip of the Florida Keys.

"We know all about Atlanta," said Burt, a waiter at a popular raw bar.

"It's another example of the right-wingers going out and killing gay men. Those two Atlanta men were killed simply because of their sexual persuasion. They were executed."

"It's going to be happening all across this country. The same thing that happened to African-Americans in the sixties and the same thing that has happened to Jews throughout their history is happening to gays and lesbians in the nineties," said Carl, the muscular manager of a water sports concession at Smathers Beach.

"But we're not going to wait on a conservative congress for action like the African-Americans did," he added. "We're forming the gay-lesbian equivalent of the Jewish Defense League and we're going after those peckerwoods."

The Jewish Defense League is a secret organization that over the years has taken sometimes violent action against those it believed to be anti-Semitic. It is on the FBI's list of terrorist organizations.

"Whoever killed those two Atlanta men better not make bail," said Dickie, the editor of a gay newspaper here. "Because if he gets out on bail we are targeting him. We are fighting back. Atlanta will be our first battleground."

Key West is the largest town in Monroe County, Florida, and has the highest incidence of AIDS in Florida and the tenth highest in America.

Payne read the article again.

Then he stared at the newspaper for a long time.

"Judge, this is Colin Biddle. I do hope you'll forgive me for calling you so late but I think it's important."

"Hello, Colin. It's all right. How's that book of yours doing?"

"Fine, Judge, thank you for asking. I'm hoping it might catch fire and take off."

"Well, I wouldn't be surprised if it did. You've always been talented. I told your mama that thirty years ago. I told her you would grow up and amount to something. Next time you come in my office I want you to sign my copy. I bought one yesterday."

"Thank you, Judge, that's gratifying, particularly coming from you. I'll be honored to sign it for you."

"Tell me what's on your mind. I'm sitting here having a brandy before I go to bed."

Colin swirled his Sambuca and watched the three coffee beans cluster in the middle of the glass.

"Judge, I know this is a bit unusual, but I'm calling you more as an old family friend than as a newspaperman. I trust our conversation will remain confidential."

"Son, I have more confidential conversations in a day that most people do in a lifetime."

"I'm following the story about the double homicide; the one out on Cheshire Bridge, and have come across some disturbing information of something that is about to happen."

"Yes."

"Judge, the police are coming to you tomorrow morning to ask for a court order that will force WSB television to turn over videotapes that then will be given to the U.S. military for enhancement and interpretation."

The judge paused. Now he understood why Colin wanted to keep this conversation confidential. "Go on," he said softly. He took another sip of brandy.

"Judge, this disturbs me for two reasons. First, if granted, this could be seen by the newspaper as a First Amendment issue. And you know how rabid we are on that subject."

"I do. And your second reason for concern is the posse comitatus aspect."

"Yes, sir, it is. I don't believe the U.S. military has any business participating in civilian law enforcement. In my layman's opinion, that's a dangerous precedent."

"Well, the drug wars have loosened up considerably the concern about posse comitatus."

"Yes, sir, you're right." He left unspoken that the case involved had nothing to do with drugs.

There was a long pause. "What you're trying not to say is that your newspaper would have a good time jumping on me if I granted this."

Colin paused. The truth was that the newspaper didn't really care about this sort of story anymore. But the judge was of the old school and he remembered when the Atlanta newspapers were a great moral force, a force to be reckoned with by any politician who might have even thought of stepping outside arbitrary and rigid newspaper-imposed lines of probity and rectitude.

"Judge, you've known the papers longer than I have. They can be cheeky."

There was a pause as the judge remembered other days. And when he spoke it was as if he were talking to himself. "They would write their scathing little self-righteous editorials and make my family and friends think I was one step away from being a traitor to this country. They would paint me as a moral bankrupt."

Colin did not answer.

"Next year is an election year," the judge said.

"Yes, sir."

Another pause. Now the judge's voice was stronger. "Colin, I'm glad you brought this to my attention. As I haven't seen the city's petition, I can't speak to the merits, if any, of their case. But since you came to me in confidence I'll reply in confidence and say I don't think your newspaper will have to work itself into a lather of indignation over this one."

"Yes, sir."

"Now, son, I want you to come by my office tomorrow. I want you to sign that book of yours that I went out and bought."

"I'll be there."

"And tell your mama I said hello."

"I will. Thank you, Judge."

"Good night, son."

"Good night, sir."

The judge stared at the telephone for a moment. He took a healthy drink of brandy, leaned back, stared unseeing at his bookcase, and said to himself, "I'm glad there is one person left down at that goddamned newspaper who has some maturity and judgment."

Payne looked up. His head was buried in his hands as he tried to sort through the meaning of the story about the gay revolution. It was happenstance and nothing more that the two homicide victims were gay men.

What was Colin doing? His story would be picked up by radio and television and become a media mantra. Even the national press would pick up on the story of a conspiracy involving gays and lesbians, especially if the original piece were done by someone as respected as Colin Biddle. And when the lieutenant read the paper or heard the story on television and came to him, what could he say? He knew nothing of any conspiracy.

Was Colin that far ahead of him in investigating the homicides?

With a weary sigh he opened the large envelope on the table and spread out the photographs. Perhaps he had missed something. Slowly and one by one he went through the pictures.

He was going through the pictures for the third time when he saw something that made him pause.

The picture showing the rear of the Mercedes had a streak of light across the trunk.

Or was it a streak of light? It was too long and too straight. Besides, it was not consistent with the other patterns of light in the picture. Usually, the light was manifest in little splotches or bursts of white—not in long straight lines.

It was a mark of some kind.

Payne smiled. Tomorrow he would call DMV and get a computer printout of every late-model dark Mercedes in the metropolitan area. There were thousands so he would need help. Then he would get on the phone and start calling repair shops.

24

Payne walked in stiff-legged anger down the court-house steps, the city attorney a step behind. The city attorney seized his elbow as they reached the street.

"Don't take it personally, Detective. Our case was solid. We demonstrated the need for judicial relief and he refused us. End of story."

Payne shook his head. He looked at the lawyer, a man almost twice his age who had been the city attorney's representative with the police department through every mayor's administration of the past three decades. "This is not a First Amendment issue. I could have ID'd the shooter with that tape."

"You're going to have to do it some other way."

Payne laughed. "You see the morning paper?"

"Yes."

"According to *The Atlanta Constitution* this case is about a big conspiracy to kill gays. I've got a national conspiracy on my hands here. The shooter could be some homophobe." Payne shook his head. "Not too many million of those out there."

"So is the reporter ahead of you? He embarrass you?"

Payne looked at the traffic clogging the intersection by the courthouse. "I don't know. I thought when I first read the story he was big-time wrong; that he had gone off on a tangent and didn't know what he was talking about. But when I was getting dressed this morning, every local TV station had picked up his story for their morning news. Driving in, that's all I heard on the radio. The talk show hosts are running wild." Payne shrugged. "I have a lot of respect for the newspaper guy. All the detectives do. He's our friend. But this thing is about to get out of hand."

Payne paused. He looked at the lawyer. "You've worked with the police for a lot of years. What do you think?"

"I think the judge denied a good petition. I think you have to solve a double homicide. And I think I have to get back to my office." The lawyer shook hands, nodded, and walked away.

"Thanks," Payne muttered. "Big help." He looked up and down the street, then turned toward the parking lot a block away. He would return to the crime scene and begin again.

Ahead of him a small truck stopped and a man jumped out and began loading the newspaper vending boxes at the corner. Payne glanced idly at the front page, then stopped, dug into his pocket, and said, "Let me have one of those."

"Hot off the press," the vendor said. He pocketed the two quarters and hopped into his truck.

Payne looked at the front page of the first edition of *The Atlanta Journal,* the afternoon sister paper of the *Constitution*. A headline jumped out at him.

Atlanta Police Racist,
Says Local Merchant

The story was written by Colin Biddle.

An Atlanta businessman says police have "taken my place of business away from me and won't return it.

"The city's racist policies are depriving me of my right to make a living. My family is suffering," says Sadni Jansari, owner of the Quicky Gas Station on Cheshire Bridge Road.

After two men were killed during a robbery at the store last Monday morning, Atlanta police sealed the building.

"They told me to stay away," Mr. Jansari said in a call to complain. "They said they would arrest me if I went into my store. This is America. How can they act like the Ku Klux Klan?"

"That is a crime scene and we are actively investigating the case," said a police spokesman.

Police Chief Beverly Harvard was not available for a response. But a spokesman for the mayor's office said the mayor was aware of the case. "He has called the chief to inquire about this matter," said the spokesperson. "And if there is no resolution within the next few days, he will take action."

Payne could read no more. Ku Klux Klan? What kind of nonsense was that? The Indian was accusing him—a black man—of being a racist. The only time he had talked to Jansari was that night at the crime scene. And then it was all business. The guy was an idiot.

And why hadn't Colin called him on this story? Today or tomorrow the lieutenant would tell him to release the crime scene, that Jansari's store had to be returned. He angrily folded the paper and was about to march away when he noticed that the story Colin had written for the morning paper was also on the front page. Two front-page stories on the same day about his homicide case; stories that, while they did not mention him by name, nevertheless burned him badly. And the judge had denied his motion to subpoena tower cam tapes from WSB.

This was not a good day.

He looked at his watch again. No time for lunch. If he was going to have his crime scene taken away, every available moment would be spent there going over the store again and again, looking for the evidence he knew was there.

*   *   *

The telephone in the convenience store was ringing when Payne unlocked the boarded-up door and walked inside.

He picked up the phone. "Yes," he said impatiently.

"C. R. Payne?" said a woman's voice.

"Yes."

"Kitty O'Hara. I need to talk to you."

"I don't have time to talk with another newspaper reporter. You people have burned me enough for one day."

"I saw where your hero crapped on you. Meet me this afternoon. It's important."

"I'm too busy. The only reason I've talked with you this long is because your brother was a victim. You said you read the paper. You know they're about to take my crime scene. I have to get what I can while I can. Now get off this line."

"There's been another homicide. Another gay man."

Payne's eyes widened. For a moment he could not speak. He looked around the store and out on the street. "What are you talking about? There's been nothing on the radio. I haven't heard anything at the office."

"It wasn't in Atlanta. But it was the same shooter."

"Kitty, stick to your newspaper job. Let me be the detective."

"He was shot with a twenty-two-caliber pistol at close range. You want to hear about it?"

Payne stared at the street, not seeing passing cars. His investigation was still at square one after a week.

"Okay."

"I have to make a few phone calls first. Meet me at the Clermont Lounge at six-thirty and I'll show you what I have."

"The Clermont Lounge? Are you out of your mind?"

"Six-thirty."

Click.

Payne stared at the phone. He slammed the receiver down.

Reporters.

He remembered something one of the old police officers once said: There's only one thing lower than whale crap. And that's a newspaper reporter.

Colin carefully clipped the two front-page bylines from the paper, used scissors to trim the edges of the clippings, and then wrote the date on the back. He placed them inside the "June" compartment in his Tower of Power.

Two front-page bylines in one day. Doubles. Not bad. Numbers nineteen and twenty for June. He was approaching his record of twenty-two front-page bylines in a single month. He could break the record in the next week.

Not only could he break the record, but if he planned the stories right he could have three bylines on the front page. Triplicates. It would take maybe a week. Perhaps next Sunday when the paper was far and away the biggest of the week.

Trips.

On a Sunday.

He smiled and patted the Tower of Power.

Colin was in his study waiting for the butler to bring him his midmorning cup of tea when she swept briskly through the open door.

"It was open so I came in," she said.

Colin smiled.

"I'm off to the club for my tennis lesson and I can't find my keys. Do you know where they are?"

Colin nodded. "I have them. You'll be glad to hear I'm taking your car in this morning to have the scratch repaired. Why don't you take my car." He handed her the keys to the Range Rover.

She took the keys, then folded her arms across her breasts, one hip outthrust. She raised her eyebrows and stared at him in disbelief. "Well. I think I'll write an essay, declare a national holiday, and march in the streets."

"I'm sorry I waited so long. But it will get done today. I'll have to leave it there a few days. They're providing a loner."

"Are you working here today or are you going to the office?"

"Here. I'm planning a couple of articles for the paper and I'm beginning work on the new book. Actually, I'm rather excited about it."

"Jolly well peachy keen and all that." She paused

and looked away. "I'm having a tennis lesson and then playing a couple of games with some girl-friends. We'll be in the clubhouse for a while afterward. So I won't be home until sometime this afternoon."

He waved a hand in airy dismissal. "Fine." He looked up as the butler entered. "Ah, there's my tea. Thank you."

She waited until the butler left. "I have some things in the trunk. Would you take them out before you take the car to the shop?"

"Of course. I was going to check on that in just a moment. As soon as I finish my tea."

She turned and, with long tanned legs flashing, walked out the back door into the garage. As she backed the Range Rover toward the street, she looked at the house and mumbled to herself, "What an insufferable son of a bitch. Every time I look at him I want to mash his face in."

Colin walked to the kitchen window and watched until the Range Rover disappeared around the corner. He took his cup of tea back to his desk and sat down and drank it leisurely, a faint smile on his face.

When he had finished he walked out the back door, backed the big black Mercedes from the garage, and then turned it around in the driveway as if he were backing toward the kitchen door. He twisted the wheel slightly, causing the car to swerve from the driveway. When he was sure the car was aimed at the corner of the serpentine brick wall around the patio, Colin pressed the accelerator. The powerful motor emitted a throaty roar. Colin braced himself.

The Mercedes hit the retaining wall with a shriek of metal against brick. The trunk punched through the serpentine wall and caused bricks to tumble across the trunk and rear fender.

Colin stepped from the car and examined the damage. Not quite enough.

He slid back into the driver's seat, changed into a forward gear, and drove forward about twenty feet. He stopped, shifted into reverse, looked at the rearview mirror, and accelerated rapidly. He moved the steering wheel slightly to the left.

Again he hit the wall with a tremendous crash.

He opened the door and walked to the rear of the car just as the butler hastily ran out the back door.

The two men examined the rear of the car. One rear fender was crumpled. The trunk was crushed almost beyond recognition.

The butler shook his head in dismay and looked at Colin.

"I seem to have panicked there for a moment," Colin said.

Several hours later Colin strode purposefully into his study, crossed the room, and reached behind the second bookshelf from the top, behind the C. S. Lewis collection, and pulled out the Walther TPH. He hefted it, staring at the sculptured little pistol with both affection and dismay. He had no choice in what he was about to do.

He walked into the kitchen and looked out the window. The butler was overseeing a construction crew at work on rebuilding the serpentine wall.

Colin looked under the sink and peered into the three cigar boxes he laughingly referred to as his "workrooms" and ran his fingers among the jumble of odds and ends. The second box contained what he sought: several files. One of the files had a regular file on one end while the other end was a rat-tail file. Colin picked it up.

Two paper towels were placed atop the kitchen table. Then Colin thumbed the magazine release switch on the butt of the TPH and pulled out the full clip of Stinger ammunition. He thumbed the safety to the Off position, then slowly pulled the slide toward the rear until the cartridge in the chamber popped out. He picked up the cartridge and placed it near the magazine. He pulled the slide back several times to make sure the weapon was empty.

Holding the pistol in his right hand, he used his middle finger to push the trigger guard down, thereby unlocking the slide. With his left hand, he pushed the slide up and toward the rear until it disengaged. Then he carefully lifted the slide, holding it tightly and not allowing the slide return spring to kick it from his hand.

Now, with the parts of the pistol before him, he was ready to go to work.

The designer lamp over the kitchen table he

pulled low so he could see into the darkened recesses of the disassembled weapon. The pistol was so small he did not have much room to work.

Cupping the frame and barrel assembly in his left hand, he twisted it until the light shone into the chamber. Very gently he inserted the rat-tail file—no more than a quarter of an inch—and burred it around the edges of the chamber. Twice he rotated the file around the chamber. Then he eased the file another quarter of an inch into the opening and rotated it twice around the circumference.

Now, from a ballistics standpoint, he had a virginal chamber. It could not be matched with chamber marks on any casing found in Atlanta. Or Key West.

He tilted the pistol toward the vertical and placed the file at about a thirty-degree angle to the chamber, then slowly moved the file forward a fraction of an inch. He did this several times from different positions around the end of the chamber.

Now the entry port to the chamber was like new. If anyone used his weapon and caused a deliberate malfunction and the soft lead nose of the bullet caught on the edge of the chamber, the mark made would not compare with the live round the police found in Atlanta.

He placed the file on the paper towels and turned over the upper part of the pistol—the slide mechanism—and looked for the firing pin assembly. From a pad near the telephone he picked up a ballpoint pen and used the pointed end to depress the firing pin. It was spring-loaded, so he had to turn the slide vertical and cup both the slide and the pen in his left hand to hold the firing pin fully forward. Very carefully he eased the tip of the rat-tail file forward until it brushed the end of the firing pin. Again. A third time.

Now, any test firing of his weapon by the police would yield firing pin marks entirely different from those found on the casings he left in Key West.

He knew he might have gone considerably further than evidence found by the police dictated. For instance, the Atlanta police did not even know about Key West. But Colin believed he could not be too careful. And it was a game to him to stay so far ahead of the police that no matter what they did or what they found, it would do them no good. And as of now there was nothing the police could do, no ballistics test they could perform, that would tie his Walther to any crime scene. If the police by some bizarre stroke of luck did come to suspect him and obtained a warrant and asked him to produce his .22-caliber pistol, he would do so. It would yield them nothing.

But such a turn of events would yield him something very important.

It would let him know he was a suspect.

Colin smiled as he wiped off the pistol in a cloth dampened with gun oil.

He decided to put the .22 back into the original presentation box and leave it atop the desk in his study.

25

Colin slumped in the leather chair in his study and stared at the flickering television screen. Even though his wife was out of the house—she was at the club taking a tennis lesson—he had lowered the blinds and locked both the outside door and the door to his study. The remote control for the VCR was in his left hand. His right hand cradled the Walther.

He had watched the tape so many times that he knew every move he made and every move the two dead men made and he could pantomime each person's actions, everything from the second he walked into the store until he disappeared from the screen into the back room. It was all there. He saw his back stiffen, saw himself smashing the mosquito against the wall and then breaking the remote cash register display. He saw himself breaking the attendant's fingers with the butt of the pistol and he saw the puffs of smoke as he fired the Walther.

The choking intensity he felt the first time he had watched had not diminished. Not in the slightest.

As the tape began again, he placed the remote control on the table and began mouthing the dialogue of those on the screen. He raised the Walther in perfect synchronization with the movements on-screen and mouthed "Pow! Pow!" as tiny puffs of smoke appeared on the videotape. He raised his left hand to cover the barrel of the little .22-caliber pistol and racked it back, again in perfect synchronization with the on-screen movements, and again mouthed "Pow! Pow!"

Colin picked up the remote control and stabbed at the Pause button, freezing the tape as the second man's head was knocked back by the force of the two bullets in his mouth and catching him in that slumping split second before gravity took over and he dropped like a sack of salt.

For a moment the on-screen Colin froze, looked over the counter as if in disbelief, and then gathered himself and began acting like a professional. Colin nodded in satisfaction. Not even a blue-blooded Brit could have been as calm and rational under stress as he had been that night.

He watched until the tape ended and then he pressed the Rewind button.

He stared at the Walther. In another time and in another place he would have cut three notches into the butt. He moved his hand up and down, feeling the weight and heft and balance of the Walther. He turned it sideways to admire the profile.

"Fewer than two thousand of these things in the

country and I've got one," he said softly. "Mine is in mint condition."

He nodded and whispered, "And it has killed three men."

He sighed deeply and stared at the blank TV screen, thinking now about the man in Key West. If only that fag had not followed him from the restaurant. He knew what the guy really wanted. God knows, he had experienced it enough. It came with the territory; with his blond hair and young face and his expensive clothes. They were always smiling at him and looking at his groin even when he was with his wife and even when his wedding ring was in plain sight. What the hell, did they think he had a wife as camouflage?

With a sharp *click* the humming of the VCR stopped. The darkened room was silent.

Colin sighed deeply and stared at the floor.

What was he going to do?

He had diverted the homicide investigation here in Atlanta. Nothing to it, really. Not when you work for a newspaper. Besides, the young cop was so inexperienced and so deferential and so gauche. Colin smiled as he remembered the tumble of embarrassed explanation when he walked into the room and Payne had his mouth over the breast of the Thai figure.

As for Key West, well, that was Key West. Enough faggots were dying there that no one would notice. If they weren't dying of AIDS, they were fighting and stabbing and shooting each other in their jealous rages. He had covered enough homicides in the fag community to know how irrational and violent they were.

His victim was just another dead gay man in Key West.

Big deal.

And the story he had done from Key West would force Payne's investigation into the gay community. Already Colin had received calls from three national newspapers whose reporters wanted to do stories about a major conspiracy against gay men and women. The detective would have to go up that blind alley.

In addition, the reporters who had called all expressed curiosity about his book and his coverage of the homicides. He realized that *he* was about to become a story. And he resolved to hasten it along with a call to a friend at *Creative Loafing*.

Colin pointed the remote control toward the TV. But before he could press the button he heard a noise. Someone was knocking at his study door.

He jumped up and moved toward the TV set.

"Who is it?" he shouted over his shoulder. Quickly he removed the tape and slid it behind a row of books. The TPH he returned to the presentation box on his desk.

"Who do you think it is?" demanded his wife. "What are you doing in there with the door locked?"

"Just a minute," Colin said. He looked around

the room. Then he picked up a notebook lying on the desk and walked to the door.

"Sorry, I didn't realize it was locked."

His wife stared at him quizzically. Her white tennis clothes made her tan appear even darker than it was. It also made her legs look about as long and racy as those of a thoroughbred. Her brow furrowed and the thumb of her left hand ritualistically pushed back the cuticles of each finger.

"I was going over some notes."

She looked over his shoulder and then back at him. She snorted in disbelief. "Don't wave that notebook at me and tell me you're working. Do I look like the village idiot? Why are you sitting in a darkened room?"

"I was thinking."

"That'll be the day." She looked over his shoulder again and tried to brush past him. But he would not move. "This is my study," he said quietly.

"Oh. The sanctum sanctorum. The private little jerk-off room. Nevermore shall anyone be admitted." She paused and stared. "What are you doing?"

"I told you, I was thinking. Planning my next step in this homicide investigation. You know how busy I've been on that. And outlining parts of my next book. I've come up with a title. It will be called *Splatter* and will be about—"

"Colin, you've been acting weird ever since you started on that story. Turn it over to Kitty and go to work on the next book. Maybe it will be bigger than this one."

"I have to do both. The double homicide is my story."

"You are jumpy and preoccupied and you're acting stranger than usual."

"You know how writers are."

"Yes, I do. Writers are ass wipes. No woman in her right mind would spend more than five minutes with a writer. By the way, weird writer is an oxymoron. You're all a bunch of paranoid pricks."

"Nice alliteration. But it's not an oxymoron. Perhaps, 'redundant' is the world you're groping for. And you should drop the profanity. You know I dislike that."

"Fuck what you dislike. Fuck you and the horse you rode in on."

Colin nodded. He pursed his lips and looked at the floor. Then he looked into his wife's eyes. "Your tennis lesson didn't go well? The pro found problems with your technique?"

Her eyes widened. Then she recovered. "Don't try to change the subject. Writers are the Evil Empire. Writers are the enemies of society. You people have lives that are like runaway garbage trucks. Whatever falls out you call news. But the rest of us know it for what it is."

"Still angry about the serpentine wall?"

"What about my car?"

"It will be repaired better than new. You have the loaner until then."

"I can't believe you backed my car into that wall."

He shrugged.

She glared at him and flounced down the hall. Then she turned and over her shoulder said, "Your book is in the basement and every miracle in the Old Testament won't change that."

A moment later Colin heard the bathroom door slam.

"We'll see," he said softly.

26

The dancer known as Flamenco was atop the three-foot-by-eight-foot dance floor behind the bar. She had split two paper matches and then stuck the shafts of the matches into her mouth until they were soaked with saliva. Each Y-shaped shaft she gently pulled apart and stuck over the nipple of a large breast. As "Ring of Fire" blasted from the jukebox, Flamenco lit the matches and slowly began gyrating until her breasts—crowned by fire and rotating in opposite directions—were slicing large pendulous circles through the air.

Above was her face; wet of lip and flat of eye. Below was a stomach of Falstaffian dimension.

In between were the counterrotating fire-tipped breasts.

That was the sight that greeted Payne when he walked into the Clermont Lounge on Ponce de Leon. He stopped in his tracks.

A second later he sensed Kitty beside him. "So whatta you think, Payne?"

"She should have learned to type."

Kitty laughed. "Come on, I saved you a place at the bar."

Payne crawled onto a stool in the center of the horseshoe bar. Behind the bar was a narrow walkway for the waitress. And behind her was a platform around the edges of which were several dozen bottles of liquor. The tiny dance floor where nude dancers worked was toward the rear of the platform. The dancers picked their music from the blaring jukebox by the door, put in a quarter, then walked around behind the bar to climb onto the stage. A salty musky odor that seemed to come from somewhere in the back of the large room fought with the smell of stale beer.

Dancers in various stages of undress were leaning on the corner of the bar.

"I'd pay some of them to keep their clothes on," Payne said.

"Hey, be nice. These are my friends. Good people."

"I don't want to be critical of your friends. But I see one who is uglier than Yassir Arafat, one older than my grandmother, and one bigger than Santa Claus." Payne looked around the bar again. "Is this a gimmie hat convention?"

Twelve of the fifteen men seated at the bar wore gimmie hats. They were rawboned good old boys, construction workers from up in the north Georgia mountains or from small towns around the South, from places where women did not dance naked on a stage. And they stared at Flamenco as if she were a nubile twenty-year-old.

Kitty shrugged. "I don't know. Checked out a few. They had good packages but that was all."

"I feel like Eddie Murphy in *48 Hours,* the scene where he went into the country music bar."

"I feel at home here. We used to call these places 'fighting and fucking bars.' "

"No wonder you got out of southwest Georgia. Black people go in bars like this in Albany they get killed. And they deserve it because they are crazy. I'm half-crazy to be in here with you. Now tell me what you found out that's so important."

The waitress stopped in front of Payne. She was lost somewhere in her forties, had an explosion of blond hair and the largest, perkiest breasts Payne had ever seen. She hoisted her breasts as if not sure they were attached properly, twisted, shrugged her shoulders, and said, "What'll you have, honey?" Her voice sounded as if someone had filed her vocal cords with sandpaper.

"Diet Coke."

She put her hands on her hips and stared. "Diet Coke? You a po-lice?"

"Relax, Gloria," Kitty said. "He's my friend. This is C.R."

"Well he sure ain't no newspaper person. Not if he's drinking a diet fucking cola."

"You got that right," Payne said.

Gloria smiled. "Honey, welcome to the new and improved imperial Clermont Lounge. This is the biggest collection of movers and shakers in Atlanta. If you're Kitty's friend, I'll serve you anything you want."

Kitty leaned closer. "Gloria used to be Grover."

Payne stared at Kitty and then at Gloria and then at Kitty. The light slowly came on. "Grover? You mean . . . ?"

Kitty nodded. "Had the operation about four years ago. Fantastic boob job. Hormones kicked in. And she wears that padded underwear that gives her a great butt."

Gloria pushed a Coke across the bar. Then she turned around, looked over her shoulder, and patted her shapely rump. "Honey, I got tired of being a man." She turned around and hoisted her breasts again. "But I still haven't got used to these breasties. I was a man when I ordered them. Now I can't sleep on my stomach."

"Do most men know about . . . ?" Payne asked.

Gloria shook her head and laughed. "No. Men are so stupid. They just go straight for the cookies. And that's okay with me. I want them to fuck me all day and all night. I just love for them to fuck me like a Snickers bar."

She blew an air kiss to Payne, waved her hands over her head, and danced down the bar saying over and over, "Fuck me like a Snickers bar."

Payne shook his head. "What planet is this?"

Kitty elbowed Payne. "Hey, I can't call you C.R. in here. What's your first name?"

"Detective."

"You never lighten up, do you?"

"I don't remember."

Payne jumped as someone wrapped her arms around him and he felt two breasts pressing into his back. He moved away and looked over his shoulder. Standing there smiling at him was a nude black woman with a glued-down head of blond hair. Payne was thunderstruck to look down and see she also had a thicket of blond public hair that glowed in the dark.

"Baby, my name is Opium."

"Opium?"

She grinned and pointed. "The golden triangle."

Payne laughed.

Opium squeezed his leg. "I'm about to dance. But I want to tell you how much I like seeing a good-looking young black man in here. I'm dedicating my dance to you, baby."

Payne looked at Kitty and then back toward Opium. "That's very nice of you."

Opium moved closer to Payne. He backed up against the bar. She leaned over and rubbed her breasts across his chest and smiled. "Baby, I can crush beer cans with these."

"I believe you."

She gave him an arch smile. "Without using my hands."

"Okay."

"Baby, these little white boys that come in here love to eat my blond . . . you know. I let them do it because it's fun. But once in a while when I need some old-time religion, when I have the need for some down-home industrial-strength screwing, I go out and find me a young black man like you." She thrust her hips. "And I know that my redeemer liveth."

She tilted her head back and roared with laughter.

Then, her eyes locked with Payne, she nodded toward Kitty. "This little white girl—and she's my friend so it's okay to tell me the truth—she giving you any?"

"What kind of a question is that?" Payne was embarrassed.

Opium smiled. "You must not have tried. 'Cause I can tell by looking at her that she's ready to give it up if you ask. But, baby, you don't have to ask me. I'm asking you."

Opium lowered her head and smiled seductively and moved toward Payne.

He leaned over and whispered in her ear.

She backed up a half step. "You shitting me?"

He opened his coat. His badge was on his belt and behind the badge was his pistol.

Opium looked at Kitty. "I bet his love log is as big as his gun." She pinched Payne on the cheek. "I got to dance in a minute, baby. Soon as Simone is through. You wait for me. You keep your eyes on what you can have anytime you want it."

Behind the bar, Simone stepped on stage and began moving to a song called "Sex Drive." Simone was Hispanic, about thirty, and had a lithe body. Her outfit consisted of a pair of red high heels.

Gloria stopped in front of Payne and nodded toward the dancer. "Look at Simone. Nice young girl with firm breasties. She's got two kids. Can you believe that?" She moved down the bar to another customer.

Payne wiped his brow and nodded. "I can understand how it happened." He shook his head. "Kitty, I got things to do. Tell me what you got."

"You know I don't have a hell of a lot to do these days? Just day-to-day stuff since Condescending Colon bumped me off the homicide."

"Skip the background."

"You need the background."

Payne stared at her impatiently.

"I was going through the wire copy this morning when I found it."

"Translation."

"The wire copy. Stories from other parts of the country sent to us on AP, *The New York Times* wire, *Wall Street Journal* wire, the . . ."

"I get the picture."

"The story was on AP. On the regional wire. That's a wrap-up of news stories from every state in the southeast."

"Hey, buddy." Someone was poking Payne in the shoulder.

He turned. One of the gimmie hats was standing there with an unlighted cigarette dangling from the corner of his mouth. The guy wore jeans, a sleeveless tee-shirt, and had dirty hair down to his shoulders.

"You got a match?"

Payne locked eyes with the gimmie hat. "Not since Superman died."

The good old boy stared at him a moment, thought about it, grinned, and moved on.

Opium stepped slowly onto the small stage, her eyes on Payne. Now that she was across the room and in a soft pool of light, Payne saw that Opium's body was even more luscious than it had seemed a moment ago. She was about thirty-five and her rock-hard body was that of an athlete. But it was the enormous thatch of blond pubic hair that was her greatest attraction. The gimmie hat crowd lining the bar was transfixed.

Kitty leaned closer to Payne. "She washes it in a special dye and they use some kind of unusual lightbulbs for her act." She grinned at Payne. "Makes it glow in the dark. Drives men crazy."

Payne pulled a five-dollar bill from his pocket and leaned across the bar.

"Thanks, baby," Opium said. She pursed her lips in a moue toward Payne. "Remember what I told you."

"Now you're marked as a big spender," Kitty said.

Payne was about to answer when he saw Simone, still wearing nothing but red shoes, amble toward a booth in the darkened back corner of the bar. One of the gimmie hats sat in the booth. Simone slid into the seat next to the wide-eyed construction worker. She moved closer and Payne could see from the movement of her shoulders that her hands were moving. The gimmie hat tilted his head back and presented his glazed eyes to the ceiling. His mouth lolled open.

"Are they doing what I think they're doing?" Payne asked.

Kitty shrugged. "You don't want to walk around back there. Your shoes will stick to the floor."

Payne looked at her.

Kitty nodded. "They are violating a half-dozen Georgia ordinances." She shrugged. "At least she's not on the street. And that guy is getting his testosterone level lowered. He could be out stealing hubcaps."

Payne nodded toward a curtained alcove in the corner. A woman's head was peering through the curtain. "What's that?"

"That's where the dancers change clothes. That's Headlight peeping through the curtain."

"Headlight?"

"Yeah. She doesn't dance until after midnight."

"Why?"

Kitty shrugged. "She had a mastectomy."

Payne turned and stared at Kitty in disbelief.

"She's still got one," Kitty said. "That's why they call her Headlight. By the time she comes out to dance, everyone is drunk and seeing double anyway. Most men never notice."

Payne was about to respond when his pager

sounded. He looked down at the display and grimaced. "Lieutenant's calling." He looked around.
A pay phone was on the opposite wall. "Too much
noise in here. I have to go find a phone."

"Want to use my cell phone?"

"No. The office is two blocks away. I'll go see
what he wants." He stood up. "You were at the
regional wire part. You got about ten seconds to
tell me your latest vision. Then I'm outta here."

Kitty pulled her stool closer. "Sex" was still
booming out of the jukebox at decibels approximat-
ing those of a 747 beginning its takeoff roll: *Sex
drive, sex drive. Get outta this car and under my
wheel."*

Three stools down, a good old boy looked up
into the bosky universe Opium presented to him,
grinned, and said, "Ever need that thing trimmed,
you let me know."

His buddies almost fell off their stools laughing.

One of the other dancers waiting to come on-
stage was at the bar acting as a cheerleader for
Opium. "Get it, girl," she said. "Go, baby girl."

Kitty leaned close to Payne, her lips brushing his
ear. "A gay guy was killed in Key West the other
day. Shot twice at close range."

Payne pulled away and stared at her.

"Shot with a twenty-two," she added.

"They got a shooter?"

Kitty shook her head. She handed Payne a piece
of paper. "They got jack shit. Here's the name and

number of the Key West homicide officer handling the case."

"A gay man was killed in Key West with a twenty-two? That's what you had to tell me?"

Kitty pulled back, stared at him a moment, then leaned closer. "Colin was in Key West when it happened."

"Sex drive. Sex drive. Get outta this car and under my wheel."

"Who?"

"Colin Biddle. Your hero."

Payne was exasperated. "I know you don't like the guy. But—"

"He was *there*."

"Does he own a twenty-two?"

Kitty shrugged. "He collects guns. He carries a gun."

"Does he own a twenty-two?"

"He has to."

Payne stood up. "Kitty, watch my lips." Payne spoke slowly and distinctly. "Do you know if—"

"No, dammit. I don't know. But he does."

Flamenco was standing at the edge of the stage, carefully splitting two matches and wetting them with saliva.

Gloria nodded toward Flamenco. "I don't know what kinda dance that is, but it ain't no minuet." She looked at Kitty. "You remember the minuet?"

"Honey, I don't even remember the ones I screwed."

Payne wadded up the piece of paper Kitty had

given him and dropped it on the floor. He turned and walked out.

The jukebox blared out the opening lines of "Ring of Fire." Flemenco lit her matches and began twirling.

27

Lieutenant Christian J. Carter looked up at Payne. Carter was a big heavyset man with a neatly trimmed beard and a palpable air of martyrdom.

"I've always liked you, Detective Payne," the lieutenant said. Slowly he stood up and walked around to the front of the desk. He sat on the corner and motioned for Payne to sit down in one of the straight-backed chairs.

Just like the management books say, Payne thought. Get out from behind the desk and act like one of the boys. But at the same time sit up high on the desk so you can look down at me.

The lieutenant had become famous a year earlier when a TV reporter showed up on a crime scene and asked him if a homicide was drug-related. The lieutenant nodded, pointed to the ground a few feet from the body, and said, "They killed him here." Then he pointed to where the body was located and said, "They drug him over here. Yep. It's drug-related."

The lieutenant nodded and repeated, "Yes. I've always liked you."

He looked at Payne. "You came up out of Albany, Georgia. Cracker country. I came out of the projects here in Atlanta and it was rough for me. But it was even rougher for you."

Payne did not answer.

"You get your paperwork in on time," the lieutenant continued. "You work hard. You are ambitious. You dress sharp." The lieutenant paused and Payne knew he was saving the important reason for last. "And you don't use profanity. I've always admired you for that."

The lieutenant rubbed his hands together and smiled.

Payne knew not to respond to anything the lieutenant said; not until the lieutenant asked him a direct question. The lieutenant was making a speech and didn't want any interruptions. That was why he had left the door to his office open. He wanted everyone in the department to hear him when he chewed someone out.

"I brought you up out of Assaults and put you here in Homicide because I knew you could cut the mustard." The lieutenant pursed his lips, raised his eyebrows, and looked upward as if seeking divine inspiration. He was beginning to raise his voice.

"Homicide is the elite of the police department. Now I had hoped you would set an example, show some of these smart-ass white boys around this office what a talented young black man could do."

Payne was getting a free ride on the black guilt train.

"You are an Emory graduate. You went to a fine school. I had to work my way through night school down at Georgia State."

The lieutenant shook his head in mock disbelief.

"Now you making me look bad."

The lieutenant paused. He leaned down until he was eyeball to eyeball with Payne and then slowly, loudly, and emphatically enough for everyone in the squad room to hear, he said, "And that ain't good."

He continued to stare. But the slight tilt of his head and raised eyebrows indicated a response was called for.

"I'm doing my best, Lieutenant. Things are starting to fall into place. I'm pursuing a good lead with the DMV. In another few days I'll have . . ."

The lieutenant stood up and returned to his chair behind the desk. He pointed a bony Baptist finger toward Payne and said, "What have you got? I'll tell you what you got. You got nothing." He held his hand in the air. "No. Wait. I'm wrong. You do have something. You have one of the mayor's friends calling complaining about this department. Detective Payne, do I need that in my life? No, I don't need that in my life."

"Sir, if—"

"Quiet."

He paused. "You know what else you got? You got the mayor calling the chief and the chief calling

Major Lloyd and Major Lloyd calling me. About an hour ago Major Lloyd chewed me out royally. You have not lived, young detective, until you have been chewed out by Major Mickey Lloyd. And when he ended his chewing out, do you know what he said to me, young detective?"

Payne shook his head.

"He said recess is over. That's what he said to me: Recess is over. Do you know what that means?"

"Lieutenant, another few days and—"

"It means this department has had enough of your playing around. It means you got to go to work, young detective."

"Another few days and—"

"Another few days? I'll tell you what you'll have in another few days. Unless you return that individual's place of business to him and unless you arrest somebody you're going to have a job in Assaults. If you are lucky. That's what you'll have in another few days."

Payne had all he could take. He had tried to hold his temper. But every time the lieutenant opened his mouth, Payne heard his father criticizing and denigrating him. He stood up.

"You want me to arrest someone or you want me to solve the case?"

"What?"

"I said do you want—"

"I heard what you said. Get your smart mouth out of here. The clock is ticking. It's gonna be my way or the highway. Right now, I'm thinking the highway. Because I don't think you can hack it up here in Homicide. And I'm thinking you're going back to Assaults."

Payne nodded. "Lieutenant, I had hoped for your support on this. But with or without your support I'll do my job. I want another week."

"You got two days."

Payne stared at the lieutenant. "I want a week."

"One more thing, young Detective Payne. You'd be well advised to spend more time trying to solve this case and less time hanging out with that white newspaper reporter. Drinking and eating with him in Buckhead ain't doing your business any good."

The lieutenant smiled benevolently.

"You can't learn everything you need to know at Emory."

He pointed toward the door. "Now get out of here."

Payne crossed the squad room toward his small office at the rear of the building.

Carl Lee, the homicide cop they called "Big City," and his buddy Kenny Snow, known as "The Rev," intercepted him in the middle of the squad room.

Carl Lee was wiry and a sharp dresser, a man whose eyes flashed like summer thunderstorms. He was jovial and so well mannered that some people mistakenly judged him as diffident. That is, until they saw his eyes. His eyes burned as if fueled by mysterious substances. Kenny Snow was older and wore a mocking smile. His favorite pastime was watching the television sermons of Ebenezer Cross, a black minister who preached hellfire and damnation at Holy Bethel AME Church on Atlanta's southside.

Big City and The Rev were two of the most experienced homicide cops in Atlanta. When these two hooked their elbows through Payne's arm and guided him into their office, he looked from one to the other in surprise.

"What are you guys doing?"

"We're kidnapping your black ass," The Rev said.

"No profanity in the squad room," the lieutenant said. He had followed Payne out of the office and was watching.

"Fucking right," Carl said under his breath.

"Eat shit, you big bastard," The Rev muttered.

Carl looked over his shoulder toward the lieutenant, "Yes, sir. We just wanted to talk to Detective Payne." The two men walked Payne into their office.

"Relax, Payne," The Rev said. "Just listen to what a couple of old white guys have to tell you." He closed the door.

Payne warily eyed the two older cops. He was looking at a combined total of more than a half century of police work, most of it in Homicide. Big City had also been on the SWAT team and had trained as a sniper down at Fort Benning. And he was the only detective in Homicide who was a qualified EMT.

These two guys knew things.

"The Rev and I, along with everyone else on this side of Atlanta, couldn't help but overhear that endearing conversation you had with the lieutenant," Big City said. He had a grin a yard wide.

"Yeah, well, he's the lieutenant."

Payne knew these two detectives more by reputation than as friends. Two years ago they were interrogating a suspect in the bubble—the tiny interview room at the end of the hall—and the guy was stonewalling them. He was guilty as sin. He had been caught in the act. But he refused to admit his complicity and he refused to sign a statement. He thought he was a hard case.

Then The Rev turned to Big City, cocked his head as if listening to a distant sound, and very solemnly intoned, "It is time for the rabbit."

"Are you sure?" Big City asked.

The Rev nodded solemnly. "Mister Jesus says the rabbit wants to talk to this asshole."

The suspect looked from one to the other and laughed. "Rabbit? What the hell you two talking about?"

Big City left the room. A few minutes later a figure wearing a pink rabbit suit hopped into the room and without a word began pounding on the suspect. The rabbit had long ears, a wide grin, and little holes through which gleamed a set of eyes lit by peculiar inner fires. The rabbit snarled and growled and pummeled hell out of the suspect. It went on until the suspect agreed to sign a confession.

The Rev looked at the rabbit and said, "Mister Jesus is never wrong."

During his trial, the suspect recanted. "The police beat me up and made me confess," he told the judge.

"Who beat you up?" the judge asked.

The guy looked away, took a deep breath, and said, "It was a rabbit. It hopped into the room and beat me up."

The judge leaned across the bench. "A rabbit?"

"A pink rabbit. A big one."

Even the judge laughed.

The confession stood up and the guy went to jail.

When it came to creative law enforcement, The Rev and Big City were masters of the game.

And now The Rev was leaning toward Payne. "In all that crap the lieutenant gave you, there was only one thing that made any sense."

"And what was that?"

"When he told you to stay away from that newspaper guy."

Payne was exasperated. "Every one of you guys talks to him. All the time. Every case."

Big City nodded. "Yes. But we know how to control that puppy."

"That's for another day," The Rev interrupted. "We don't want to give you too much the first time.

And right now we got more important things to talk to you about."

"That's right," Big City said. He looked at Payne. "You know that you are about to be a shit sandwich?"

"That is, unless you let us guide you through the valley of the shadow," The Rev said. "We can give you the keys to the kingdom."

"You gonna be such a star the lieutenant will put your picture on his wall," Big City said.

Payne smiled. "You guys are full of it."

Big City nodded in agreement. "It was all that dope I smoked in the sixties."

"Just listen for one minute," The Rev said. "If we heard correctly, your basic problem is that some citizen, a friend of the mayor's, is calling him and he's calling the chief and dah de dah de dah. Right?"

Payne nodded. "The owner of the convenience store wants it back. Wants me to release my crime scene and I'm not ready. The answer is there. I know it."

"What else does he want?"

"What do you mean?"

"What else does the store owner want? He must want something. Everybody does."

Payne shrugged.

Big City shook his head in mock resignation. "I don't know about young police officers today." He looked at the Rev. "Shall I tell him?"

"Tell him."

Big City threw his hands wide. "This bozo had a homicide at his store earlier. Now he's got two more. He's afraid of losing business. He's afraid of crime. He wants peace of mind." He leaned toward Payne. "You can give him that."

"I can?"

"You can. Call him. Tell him you need a week. Tell him if he can give you a week that you can do a big favor for him."

"Why do I get the feeling you guys have already worked this out?" Payne paused. "Okay, what can I do for him?"

The Rev shrugged. "About every other police officer in this town either has a security company or works an extra job at a security company. Most of them owe us favors. We can get a free eight-hour shift from a bunch of guys."

"Call the store owner," Big City said. "Tell him you can provide free security, a uniform officer, Friday and Saturday nights for the next two months. He won't turn that down."

"You guys can deliver?"

Big City looked at The Rev and then at Payne. "Does the pope wear a beanie?"

28

Payne shook his head in bewilderment when he read Colin's story in the morning paper. The front-page story said Atlanta police were looking for someone who might have been driving along Cheshire Bridge Road in a bright-colored Altima the night of the double homicide. It wasn't an Altima. Payne remembered pointing to the picture of the car and saying, "a light colored Acura." Colin must have misunderstood.

He switched on the television. Every station in town had picked up Colin's story and honked out the news that police were looking for a bright-colored Altima. Payne called several stations and asked for a correction. The news director at each station refused; they said they would stand by the story they had picked up from the morning paper. They said the changes Payne wanted were trivial and insignificant.

Payne reread Colin's story. Part of the article said newspapers all over the country were following up on the idea of a national conspiracy to kill gay men and women. Atlanta, the piece said, was only one city in which gay people had been killed in recent weeks and thus it was a bellwether about the extreme edge of the national antigay conspiracy.

Lieutenant Carter in Homicide was quoted as saying his department was working with the intelligence unit to determine if anything were known about such a conspiracy.

Payne shook his head. It would roll downhill later today.

The article then listed cities where acts of violence had occurred recently against gay men and women.

Payne wondered why Colin's story did not mention the homicide in Key West.

Colin sat in his locked study watching the videotape, mouthing the conversation of the three people on the screen as if dubbing the dialogue in a silent movie. The Walther was in his right hand.

"Pow. Pow."

He raised the pistol, gripped the top with his left hand, and smoothly racked the slide back.

"Snick. Snick."

He pointed the pistol again.

"Pow. Pow."

His voice and his sound effects for the pistol were perfectly synchronized with the on-screen action.

He punched the Rewind button on the remote control and then stared at the pistol, testing different grips, holding it first in his right hand and then his left and then the right. When the videotape ended, he did not press the Play button. Instead he continued to fondle the pistol, turning it over and over, racking the slide back, then slowly easing the hammer down.

He ran his left hand over the grip of the pistol. After a long moment he decided what he must do. He gently laid the Walther on his desk. He unlocked his study and walked into the kitchen where he rummaged under the sink.

Back in his study he picked up the pistol carefully in his left hand and shifted it until it was gripped tightly by the barrel. He did not want to do this on the frame or on the magazine. He wanted to do this so he could see his work when he held the pistol in his right hand. He angled the file so he could apply the sharp edge to the left side of the grip.

Slowly, back and forth, he pulled and pushed the file until three notches were cut into the grip.

Almost reverently he placed the Walther in the presentation box. After staring at the little pistol for a long moment, he slowly closed the lid.

Colin paced his office for a few moments. He pulled the drapes aside and gazed out the window, seeing nothing. Then he sat at his cherry desk, fingers resting lightly on the keyboard of his computer. He brought up the file containing the outline of his new book and stared at the screen until the screen saver flashed—big green letters on a pink background admonishing him: "Go Back To Work. Now!" He tapped a key to bring back the file, erased a sentence, and started writing.

A few moment later the screen saver was flogging him again.

It was difficult to concentrate on fiction when real life was threatening.

He stood up, walked around the desk, and opened the presentation box. The Walther gleamed dully in the overhead light. For a long moment he stared at the pistol. It was loaded, a full clip with one in the chamber. Every two weeks—on the first of the month and the fifteenth—he unloaded the clip, reloaded the bullets into another clip, and slid the new clip into the pistol. Rotating the clips insured that the spring remained strong and that the bullets would feed smoothly when he fired the weapon.

Colin picked up the pistol, held it close to his face, and stared at the three notches he had cut into the grip. After a long moment he walked across the room to the VCR and pressed the Play button. Slowly he walked to his chair. By now he could pantomime every frame of the tape without looking at the screen. And do it with perfect timing.

His eyes closed and he fell into the sequence.

"Pow. Pow."

With his eyes still closed, he raised the Walther and made a motion as if racking the slide back. "Snick. Snick."

"Pow. Pow."

He opened his eyes a split second before the tape ended.

Then he placed the pistol in his lap, closed his eyes, lay back, and sighed.

If only there were a tape of Key West.

29

Creative Loafing was first to pick up on the evolving saga of Colin Biddle. When "The Loaf" hit the streets, there on the front page was a story about life imitating art; a story of how Atlanta's best-known police reporter had written a crime novel and was now leading the innovative coverage of the double homicide that had traumatized the city's gay community. Colin Biddle had uncovered a national conspiracy to kill gay people. He had made the two Atlanta gay men symbols of that conspiracy.

WSB-TV carried the story one step farther. A wrinkle-browed newsreader from the most prominent television station in Atlanta weighed in with a news story about this scion of Old Atlanta and his book and his coverage of the double homicide but then added a kicker that all of this might become fodder for Colin's next book. Colin was properly evasive on that point.

After the interview he had gone home and stopped in the kitchen where he looked into the mirror, the one with the border of purple cut glass, and he smiled and straightened his tie and said, "Old son, you are becoming a personality."

A friend of Colin's mother called the managing editor of *The Wall Street Journal* who called the Atlanta bureau. The next day, in a remarkably fast turnaround of what was in truth a feature story, there was a story on the front page of the *Journal* about the heroic reporter in Atlanta.

Early the next morning Colin was in the WSB-TV studio to shoot a live interview with *Good Morning America.*

Mel Berger, his agent at the William Morris Agency, called that afternoon to say the publisher of *Street Smarts* had called. Bookstores all over the country were clamoring for Colin's book. Another press run of fifty thousand was under way. The publisher expected to go into still another press run by the end of the week. And then, if the flood gates opened, there was no limit to what the book could do.

The chief of the Atlanta bureau of *Time* called for an interview. "They're thinking about putting you on the cover," he said.

Every Oxford bookstore in Atlanta sold out of *Street Smarts* that day. So did Barnes & Noble and Borders and Waldenbooks. All the book stores were screaming at Ingram, the book distributor, to deliver thousands of books.

Colin's book was about to become a runaway best-seller.

Within a week, ten days at the outside, Colin Biddle would be riding the wild wave.

Payne was eating dry whole wheat toast, drinking orange juice, and wondering what he was overlooking in the double homicide when he heard Colin's name mentioned on television. He looked up at his flickering TV set and there was Colin dressed in a beautifully fitted navy suit, a blue-and-white-striped shirt, and a blue tie with small white polka dots; a bold but—as Colin would say—absolutely smashing outfit.

Payne's eyes widened.

The reporter on *Good Morning America* was talking about Colin's book and about the double homicide in Atlanta.

Payne watched. Colin was outlining his conspiracy theory about gays. The woman interviewing him from New York was lapping it up. A plot out of Atlanta to kill gays fulfills all the stereotypes of the South and New York will suck it up like a shop vac snarfing roach carcasses.

After a moment, Payne put down his spoon. He stopped listening and began watching.

Colin was very fair. His long hair was very blond. The combination, combined with the troubles in Payne's TV set, was causing enormous contrasts on the screen. Colin's skin appeared washed out. But even more striking, his hair was so blond that occasionally, when he turned his head to a certain position and the lights were full upon him, there was a strobing effect.

The TV flickered from an almost white screen to almost black.

Payne's eyes grew wider.

Colin held up one hand to make a point. At that moment his head disappeared in the light. All that was visible on-screen was a silhouette with an up-raised hand.

Payne stood up so rapidly he knocked over the table.

30

Payne jumped up from the table, spilling his coffee, and ran across the room. With his eyes still on the television, he ripped open the envelope containing the tower cam pictures and hastily fanned the pictures out across the countertop.

His eyes raced back and forth between the pictures and the flickering, strobing television screen.

His face contorted in bewilderment and confusion.

It *couldn't* be.

The camera shifted angles. Now Colin was seen from the side. He lifted his hand to make a point. It was the same motion caught by the tower cam. His hand blocked his face at the moment the TV screen whitened. Again, his head disappeared in the light.

There was no doubt.

Colin Biddle was the man in the tower cam photos.

Colin Biddle was the shooter in the double homicide.

Payne swept the pictures off the counter onto

the floor and stared with growing anger at the television set.

He had been duped. Not only had he been duped, but he had kept Colin abreast of every step in his investigation.

He had violated a fundamental rule in police work: never ignore the obvious.

And he had violated another, albeit unwritten, rule: never tell anyone except another police officer everything you know about a case.

He had told the *perpetrator*.

He dropped his head and closed his eyes and bit his lip. Slowly he shook his head from side to side.

The past few days raced through his memory like a videotape on fast forward. Colin Biddle at his fresh crime scene. The guy could have pocketed evidence. The linen fabric tossed out between the convenience store and Colin's house. Colin wore linen handkerchiefs in his breast pocket. Colin's knowledge of evidence and the evidentiary chain and forensics and investigative techniques was broader—maybe even deeper—than that of many cops. He was a gun nut, a good shot, and a police groupie.

Payne shook his head back and forth in disbelief.

He picked up the tower cam photos from the floor. His eyes fell on the scratch across the trunk of the Mercedes. Colin had probably recognized it as a scratch and not as a burst of light the moment he saw it. This must be his wife's car.

What had Colin done to disguise the scratch so

it could not be traced to him? Did he have it repaired in another city?

Payne made a mental note to check on the Mercedes tomorrow morning.

That night he and Colin went to dinner he had told the reporter what the GBI said about altering the murder weapon. Now, if Colin owned a .22-caliber semiautomatic pistol, and Payne was sure that he did, it could have been altered.

He had told Colin about his plans to ask a judge for a court order releasing the videotapes at WSB-TV and the next morning the judge had denied his petition. Did Colin have anything to do with that?

Payne trembled in anger and self-disgust. He had telegraphed every move he made to the guy he was searching for. He had even called Colin and invited him to the crime scene just hours after Colin had killed those two young men. He had given away every possible bit of evidence to the person guilty of the crime.

He lifted his head. "I'm a cop. I'm a cop," he shouted.

Colin could not be identified by the tower cam pictures. They would never be admitted into evidence. And Payne couldn't bring his temperamental TV set into a courtroom and replay a tape of Colin's interview on *Good Morning America*.

There was no evidence against Colin that would stand up in a court of law. The Mercedes was, at best, a long shot. His gut told him that Colin had done something to cover those tracks.

He had nothing.

Wait.

What about the homicide officer in Key West? The one Kitty had mentioned. The police officer investigating the killing of the gay man who had been shot at close range with a .22-caliber pistol.

"I threw his name and number away," Payne said aloud.

"Doesn't matter. That's a small department and this is a recent homicide. Somebody there can tell me who's working the case."

He picked up the telephone, chatted a moment, and said, "I'm standing by."

About fifteen minutes later his phone rang. "This is Detective Richard Diaz. Key West Homicide. Understand you want to talk to me."

"Yes, I do. Thanks for returning my call so quickly. I'm investigating a double homicide that occurred here in Atlanta. I think there are some similarities between my case and the homicide you are investigating. Maybe we can help each other."

"I don't have much. Waiter at local restaurant was shot twice with a twenty-two. We found the cartridge casings."

Payne took a deep breath. "Where was he shot?"

Diaz paused. "We haven't let that out. We're saying he was shot at close range. But I can tell you he took two in the mouth."

Payne closed his eyes and nodded. "Stinger ammo?"

"We haven't released that either. How'd you know it was Stingers?"

"That's what my boy used. You get any ballistics off the bullets?"

"No. They hit the victim's front teeth. Pretty badly mangled."

"What about from the casings?"

"Yeah, got some good marks. Extractor marks. Ejection marks. Firing pin mark. You got a gun I can match them with?"

"Officer Diaz, are—?"

"Richard. My name's Richard."

"Thanks, Richard. My name is C.R. Are you fellows on BulletProof or BrassCatcher?"

BulletProof is a computer program coordinated by the Bureau of Alcohol Tobacco & Firearms and used by law enforcement agencies to contain a database and to transmit information about bullets used in felonies. The lands and grooves on bullets are photographed by a laser-focused camera and the information is converted into a bar code that can be transmitted by modems. BrassCatcher is a similar program but it is concerned with transmitting two pieces of information from shell casings: firing pin impressions and breech face marks.

"Neither."

"Who is the closest law enforcement agency that has it?"

"Miami. But they use DrugFire."

DrugFire is the FBI system of bullet identification. It is not compatible with BulletProof or Brass-

Catcher and, in fact, is inferior to those systems. A number of states turned down entreaties by the FBI to participate in DrugFire and make it the national standard. BulletProof and BrassCatcher instead became the standard.

"Richard, I don't want to break the chain of evidence. My suspect is very sharp. Can you FedEx the evidence to the GBI crime lab here in Atlanta?"

"I'll have to get it okayed by my chief. I know Kelly Fite, I've heard him lecture at seminars and I know his reputation. He's the best firearms man in the country."

"Can you do it today?"

"Chief's down the hall. You want to hold on?"

"Yes."

Four minutes later Diaz was back on the phone. "C.R., you there?"

"Yes."

"My chief says he's glad for any help that we can get. The casings, plus my report, and crime scene photographs, will go out FedEx today. Can you alert Agent Fite?"

"You don't know how much I appreciate this. Please thank your chief. I got one more thing."

"What's that?"

Payne picked up his autographed copy of Colin's book. He looked at Colin's photo on the back cover. "I'm going to fax you a photograph. Could you take it to the restaurant where the waiter worked and see if anyone saw this guy that night. Maybe he was there."

Diaz gave him the fax number. "This guy from Atlanta?"

"He is. Very prominent. I have to ask you to keep this quiet. But I can tell you that if I clear up my homicides here, it will clear up yours also."

"We won't say anything. But there's an Atlanta newspaper person who's onto this. She's called several times."

"Kitty O'Hara?"

"You know her?"

"She's okay. Don't worry about her."

"Okay, partner. Good luck."

"Kitty, this is Don. Do you have a minute?"

Kitty paused. The editor had never called her at home. In fact, he was rarely seen by most reporters. He was painfully shy, almost reclusive. When a reporter got on the elevator with him, the editor did not make small talk. He studied his shoes.

She had heard that he hobnobbed with Colin and a few columnists; that he had them over to his house at Christmas. But the editor rarely ventured from his office at the newspaper. His managing editor carried out his wishes.

Now the editor was on the phone.

"Sure, Don. What is it?"

"I understand you don't want to do the story on Colin."

"That's right. I don't think I can do a good job."

"You know him as well as any reporter on the paper plus you work the same beat. You are both police reporters. I think you would do a good job."

"Don, why is a story even necessary?"

"Surely you can see that. In the last few days he's ben on two national television programs. Local TV. *Time* is doing a piece on him. There are several other national pieces in the works. Half the media outlets in the country have done stories on him and his book and the double homicide he is covering." Don paused. "With some occasional help from you."

"Yeah," she said wryly. "I think I broke the story."

"It's embarrassing that all these other people have done stories, yet the paper he works for has done nothing. We should have been first. Now I need a first-rate piece and it has to be done quickly. I want it in the paper in two days. And I want you to do it."

"Don, I don't like the guy. I can't be fair." She couldn't tell the editor she thought Colin was both homophobic and racist.

"You're a professional. You'll do a fair and straightforward job." He paused. "We're playing catch-up on this one. So run it long and get stuff no one else has had."

Kitty sighed. She had tried. She had to do the piece or put her job at risk. If you're a reporter, you report. Personal feelings must be put aside.

She'd always believed that, now she had a chance to prove it.

"Okay, I'll call him and get started."

"I knew I could depend on you. And, Kitty . . ."

"Yes."

"We're putting it on the front." He hung up.

Kitty stared at the phone. "Well, big fucking whoop. I have to write about Ass Wipe to get a front-page byline."

31

Kitty was hunkered down scratching Stiffy, her long-haired cat. Stiffy was about twelve; she wasn't sure as she had gotten him at the pound. But he was so old that sometimes he couldn't control his claws. He would be walking across the carpet and his claws would slide out and he couldn't retract them. He would lock himself into the carpet and stand there for several minutes rocking back and forth like a jerky old movie. Then the synapses would connect, the machinery would get the message, the claws would retract, and he would proceed in his imperial fashion, calm and unperturbed, never showing the slightest sign that something hadn't worked for a moment.

She waited as he rocked back and forth.

The phone rang.

Still scratching Stiffy, she leaned closer and whispered, "Probably Don Martin calling to tell me I have to refer to him as Saint Colin." She gave Stiffy a final scratch, stood up, and walked across the room to catch the phone before her answering machine cut in.

"On the other hand, maybe he's come to his senses and decided not to do the piece on Colin," she said.

"Hello. You don't want me to do it."

Pause. "Do what?"

"Who is this?" She spun around, barely noticing that Stiffy had begun to move across the room.

"C. R. Payne."

"Shit, C.R. Fuck. Why did you walk out so fast the other day?"

"What kind of way to answer the telephone is that? You got the nastiest mouth of anyone I ever heard."

"That was my well-mannered and courteous telephone persona. You should hear me when I'm pissed. You calling to ask me to dinner and apologize?"

"If I did, I'd take you to some place a lot better than where you took me. Clermont Lounge. Sheeeesh. I had to have my suit cleaned."

"C.R., I'm about to walk out the door on the highest journalistic mission since John Peter Zenger said the king of England was a dork. My marching orders come from the honcho supremo himselfo. So what's happening?"

"I need a favor. It's got to be in confidence. You can't use any of it now. But in a day or so it could be one of the biggest stories you've done in a long time."

Even though Kitty was in her apartment and no one but the cat was there, she looked around as if afraid someone might overhear her. That is the nature of reporters.

"I get an exclusive?"

"Yes."

"It's about the double homicide?"

Payne sighed. There was no way to shade or disguise what he wanted. She would know what he was after almost from the minute he opened his mouth.

"Will you be talking to Colin soon?"

Her eyes widened. She bent over and twirled around in a circle, wrapping the telephone cord around her and pulling the phone from the table. The noise was so loud Payne jerked the phone from his ear.

"Does that mean yes?"

Her smiled was a yard wide. The cops were going after Condescending Colon.

Then she paused. "He killed my brother?"

"Kitty, this has to be a one-way street right now. I can't tell you anything. Will you be talking to him soon?"

"Detective C. R. Payne, this is your lucky day. I'm walking out the door to see him right now. The paper is doing a big story on him and yours truly is the one anointed to interview him."

Now it was Payne's turn to be elated. He closed his eyes in quick gratitude. When he spoke his voice was low and calm and gave away nothing. "What are you asking him about?"

"I'm about to canonize him. I'm gonna give him the best blow job he's ever had." She paused. "Probably the only one."

"Can't you talk one minute without that kind of language?"

"Fucking right. What do you want, big boy?"

"You know better than to call me boy."

"Big fella."

"That's better. Here's what I need. You can't ask me any questions and you can't do anything with this until I say so. Agreed?"

"I told you when I found those keys someone threw them out on the way home. Was I right? Is he the son of a bitch who killed my brother?"

Payne did not speak.

"Okay," she said. "No questions. I got it under control. Agreed. I won't do anything until you say so."

"DMV says his wife has a black Mercedes registered in her name. I don't have enough PC to get a search warrant to look at it. And if I have a uniform stop her on a bogus traffic charge, Colin will have some silk-stocking lawyer throw out whatever I find. I need to know if his wife still has the Mercedes and if she is in town."

"Easy. What else?"

"Talk to him about his gun collection. See if he owns a twenty-two-caliber pistol."

"I told you in the Clermont Lounge he owned a

twenty-two. Did you call Key West?" She paused. "Whoops. No questions. Okay. Yes, I can do that. What about the party he was at that night? Want me to find out what time he left? We can get the time frame and see if he could have stopped at the station."

"Kitty, don't spook him. Don't give him anything."

"I'll ask him about his next book. That will activate his preen glands."

"He thinks he's got me running in eight different directions. And he's right. I want him to keep thinking that way. You've got to be careful. I have absolutely nothing that is strong enough to arrest him. I can't tell you how fragile the case is. In fact, I have no case. All I have is the knowledge that he did it."

Kitty did not speak for a moment. Payne thought he heard a sob.

Then he heard her voice, soft, but gathering strength as she talked. "I'll do this just as you say. I want your word that if it happens, the story is mine. And I want you to arrest him either at seven p.m., after the local TV news is off the air, or early in the morning so I can get it in all editions of the *Journal*. I want it on my time."

"If I can control that, you got it."

She nodded. "Hey, you're from southwest Georgia. Your word is good enough for me."

"You do this and I'll buy you the best dinner in town. You pick the place."

"My place. We'll do takeout, then make out."

Payne laughed. "You're always joking. Be careful with Colin. And call me the minute you get out of the interview."

"What do you mean, be careful? Just because I got blond hair and big tits you think I'm a bimbo? I'm as smart as he is."

"Kitty, I wasn't talking about smart. If I'm right, he killed two people in Atlanta, and one in Key West. When I said be careful, I meant be careful."

32

"Let's start with the book. How's *Street Smarts* doing?"

Colin smiled. Soft ball question. Kitty had begun by saying there would be no buddy-buddy stuff, that she was conducting the interview as if he were not a colleague, was not her nominal superior, and as if they did not know each other. It was to be a professional straightforward interview; everything was on the record. *Everything*, she emphasized. No asides, no putting-down-the-pen for him to clarify or explain. She thought she was being tough.

Silly girl. He agreed to everything because he could always dip into her queue, read the story, and if he didn't like it he could go to Don and have it changed. Simple.

"First, let me say I am surprised the paper is doing this story. It is a bit embarrassing."

Kitty's eyebrows climbed a notch. "Sometimes it is difficult to understand the news policy."

"Now, to answer your question, the book is exceeding everyone's expectations. It has taken off.

It has legs. It is jumping off the shelves. It is in its third printing and they are talking about a fourth. My agent at William Morris has persuaded the publisher to make the next book a hardback rather than a paperback. And they are predicting it will be a best-seller. I'm told the manuscript will be sent to Hollywood at the same time it goes to the publisher."

"Do you have a title for the next book? What's it about?"

He smiled. "You get two scoops here, things I've told no other publication. The working title is *Splatter*. It's an Atlanta cop book and it revolves around DNA testing in a homicide. I just decided on that yesterday. I became intrigued with DNA during the first O. J. Simpson trial. I found that very few people, even police officers, truly understand the significance of DNA and the incredible impact it is having and will continue to have on the fundamental nature of forensics. So while my book on the surface will be about a homicide, the back story will be about DNA work."

She scribbled rapidly. Without looking up she asked her next question. "Has the sudden success of this book surprised you?" She shrugged. "I'm jumping around a bit."

He smiled. "That's okay." He could see where she was going with that one. Wanted to make him look like success blindsided him. She was so trashy. That short skirt riding high on her legs. Big breasts unhindered by a bra. That trailer-park blond hair spiking in all directions. As for jumping around in the interview, she did not have the discipline of thought to pick an idea, develop it, then move on to another. She was scatterbrained.

"It is not uncommon for the better books to be sleepers. It takes a while for word of mouth to cause them to catch fire. Of course, I had hopes from the beginning. That's why I wrote the book, to make money."

She looked at him in surprise. "That's why you write? Not for fame or literary recognition?"

Colin laughed. He appeared to be in deep thought. "If ever I reach the stage where people in academia, those people in English departments who are the arbiters of such things, recognize me even as a minor writer, then I shall have failed. Because, you see, even to be recognized as an obscure writer or minor writer means they know who you are. And if that small incestuous lot knows who you are, then the great mass of book-buying people do not. I want the great mass of people to know who I am. I write to make money. I am a commercial writer. That's all."

Kitty nodded. Colin was such an unpleasant, self-indulgent, out-of-it, supercilious asshole who, deep down, was real shallow. She suspected his last little soliloquy was a play for the bleachers; designed to show he had no pretensions, that he was simply knocking out books for the money. Money was the last thing he needed.

"So you don't write on different levels? There

are no hidden psychological messages in your book?"

Again he laughed. "Kitty, my book works on one level only—the basement. What you see is what you get. I try to tell a good story, have strong believable characters, and to paint them against a big and bold background—the city of Atlanta. That is all. Nothing more. Nothing less."

She wondered if she was being too judgmental about his playing to the bleachers. She tried again.

"Who is your idol? What writer is your role model?"

He smiled. "If I could write like Jessye Norman sings—high, free, and clear with unimpeded power and authority—then I would die happy."

Nope, she wasn't being judgmental. One of the biggest racists she knew and he picks a black singer as his model. Yep, he is playing to the bleachers.

"I hear newspaper reporters, even TV people, talk about writing books. Many of them seem to think that cop books such as you wrote, police procedurals, are relatively easy. Several of them are working on Atlanta cop books. Worried about the competition?"

Colin laughed. "For reporters and freelancers to sit around talking of the books they will write is an onanistic sort of thing. They think that writing a cop book is easier than writing any other kind of book. But let me tell you something. It's just as hard, perhaps harder, to write commercial fiction as it is any other kind of fiction."

"You don't think they'll finish their books?"

"I call them stealth writers. We hear the noise they make. We are told they are at work but we never see them. Whatever they are dropping must be bombs because it is not books."

"You're obviously not worried about any of these people."

Colin held up an imperious finger. "Not in the least. Here's why. Most reporters don't understand the difference between truth and fiction. They don't understand that the story is more important than the facts. They don't understand that there is no connection between writing for a newspaper and writing a novel. They sit around talking. I sit around doing."

"That will upset some of them."

Colin laughed. "But not enough to galvanize them into writing a book. Only into criticizing me."

For almost an hour they talked in a desultory fashion about Colin's background, about his book, and about his work as a newspaper reporter. Then she began moving in.

"On national television and in national newspapers and magazines, the thrust of the coverage seems to be that you are a crime reporter, very wealthy, old Atlanta and all that, working for *The Atlanta Constitution* and covering a double homicide. Life imitating art. Every story and every clipping I've seen refers to you as the King of Buckhead and that gives the impression you are a bit of a playboy. Are you a playboy?"

"Of course not. Though, I must say, I rather like that appellation. It came from a police officer, you know. Actually I'm something of a homebody. If I'm not at the office I'm at home working on *Splatter*."

"Hobbies?"

"Not really. Only work."

"What about guns? You carry a gun and I've heard that you collect guns."

"You carry a gun, too. Are you a collector?"

"Colin, let's not be argumentative. I ask the questions and you answer them. Do you have a gun collection?"

"I like guns. I have a few. I wouldn't call it a collection. I try to collect guns used by law enforcement officers. I enjoy shooting."

She bent over her notebook. "What kind do you have?"

"As you know, I have a SIG Sauer nine-millimeter, which is used by the Secret Service to protect the President of the United States. I usually wear it. A forty-five, the 1911A model, one of the originals. I have it for historical reasons. A ten-millimeter like the FBI uses. A Smith & Wesson such as Atlanta issues. It's still in the box. A Glock, the weapon of choice for many agencies and, because of the large magazine, a weapon used for special protection details. I also have a few rifles like those used by different federal agencies. I have some weapons that require a BATF license. But I don't want to talk about those."

She looked at the list. Her pencil tapped the notebook. "You didn't mention a twenty-two. Do you have a twenty-two?"

He smiled and stood up. "How could I have forgotten my pride and joy. Maybe because I never shoot it." He walked across the room to the shelf under the bookcase and picked up a presentation box of thick wood covered with pickled blue leather. He pushed the silver latch to the right and opened the box. A .22-caliber pistol gleamed against a background of maroon velvet.

"This is my little beauty. It's a Walther TPH. Made in Germany. There are so few of these I rarely shoot it."

She nodded. That was twice he said he rarely shot the pistol. She looked at it. "What are those three notches on the grip?"

"I don't know. I bought it on the gray market. Guy who sold it to me said those were on it when he got it. Does look ominous, doesn't it. Almost like a toy."

"Why don't you shoot it? I know you go to the range."

"Too valuable. See the condition. Pristine. No abrasion. No marks. If you were to pull back the slide, the blueing is still there. It's not been abraded down to the steel by frequent firing. It's mint condition and I want it to stay that way."

He was too anxious to show the .22-caliber weapon to her; too anxious to talk about it. Whatever it was Payne wanted, he would not find it here.

Either he had not used the .22 at the service station or he had changed it in some fashion. Perhaps he had bought a new barrel.

"You said you enjoy shooting. Are you a good shot?"

"Damn good."

Why did she ask him if he was a good shot immediately after asking him about the .22?

He shrugged. "That sounds as if I am boasting and I don't mean to do that. Let me rephrase my answer. I shoot the SIG from time to time on the police range and they tell me I am a good shot."

If she used his first quote rather than the second, he would change it.

Kitty sensed his change of mood.

"You're married. Where is your wife?"

Colin smiled. "You've heard of wives being golf widows? Well, I'm a tennis widower. My wife is at the club playing tennis as she does every day. And she's very good at it. Competition level."

"Again, the national press has painted you two as something of Atlanta's glamour couple, the original power couple. One article mentioned that you may be the only newspaper reporter in America who drives a Range Rover. Does your wife have a Range Rover also?"

Colin smiled. "No, and I'm afraid you have broached a very sensitive topic. I'm glad my wife is not here."

"Why?" Her eyebrows raised.

Colin smiled and shrugged. "I was backing her

car out the other day and ran into the brick wall out back. Stupid thing to do. Virtually demolished the trunk and a fender. The car is in the shop, I'm afraid. And my wife is more than a little displeased with me. So if you see her, please don't mention my accident."

"Was it a Range Rover also?"

"No. She drives a Mercedes."

"What color?"

"The Range Rover? Green. British green."

"Her Mercedes?"

"Black."

His smile broadened. He sat back to enjoy the interview. This was going to be a bit of fun.

She smiled back. This was going as well as she had anticipated. She had noticed several things about Colin.

He was a *Cosmo* cover airhead.

And he had such a small package.

33

Richard Diaz held the telephone against his shoulder while he stared at the faxed copy of Colin's photograph.

"C.R.? This is Richard Diaz in Key West. I think you have a live one."

"He was in the restaurant that night?"

"Yeah. Big spender. Had lobster. Expensive champagne. Complained about finding hair in his food."

"Picky, picky."

Diaz laughed. "Your boy didn't like it. They said he was pissed when he left." Diaz paused. "There's more."

"Yes?"

"The homicide victim was the waiter for your suspect."

"That's pretty strong."

"Want to hear the kicker?"

"Lay it on me."

"While your suspect was paying his bill, the waiter went outside to meet him. He told another waiter to cover for him for five minutes, that he had to apologize on behalf of the restaurant. He thought your suspect was a rich guy, a guy who knew food, and he didn't want him to leave upset. Waiter didn't come back."

Payne shook his head. "He got killed for being conscientious." He paused. "Did the other employees of the restaurant say anything about the waiter that would indicate he was an aggressive sort of gay person?"

"I asked about that. They said no. Very low-key. Bright guy. Everyone said he was the most professional waiter in the restaurant."

"Richard, you did a great job in a short time. I appreciate it."

"The crime lab get the stuff we sent?"

"Yes. I'm waiting to hear from them."

"Let me know if we can help."

"Thanks, partner. I'll be in touch."

Payne hung up. He stared at the phone. Colin had killed the waiter. But all the evidence was circumstantial.

He still had nothing.

Big City and The Rev were laughing and reading aloud parts of Kitty's story on Colin when Payne walked into the squad room.

"Hey, young detective," Big City said. "Remember what we were telling you the other day about newspaper reporters. Well what we have here is one reporter performing a certain sexual act on another reporter and doing it in the pages of the newspaper where they both work." He shook his head. "God bless America."

The Rev looked up from where he had the paper spread across a desk. "You know, I thought Kitty had more sense than this. She's lost her mind. She needs to talk to Mister Jesus and get straight."

"Can I talk to you guys?"

Big City and The Rev looked at Payne, looked at each other, and—simultaneously and without speaking—stood up, extended their arms, and ushered Payne into their small office. Both of the older detectives, again without speaking, reached to close the door as Payne walked in.

He sat on the desk that took up one wall while Big City and The Rev turned their chairs to face him and sat down.

The Rev smiled. "Young detective, we got you an extension on holding on to your crime scene but you're going to have to give it up soon. Bible says it came to pass. Doesn't say it came to stay. You don't have a perp. So I'd say you got your ass in a crack again and you want us to get it out."

He looked at Big City. Big City nodded. "What do you want us to do?"

Payne took a deep breath. "You guys wonder when I'm going to forget about doing everything by the book. But I don't know any other way. Problem is, the book is not working. I got a perp but he is two steps ahead of me. As a matter of fact, he's used me. Unless I pull a rabbit out of the hat, he's going to walk."

Big City leaned forward, eyes burning, face intense. "You got a perp?"

The Rev leaned forward. "And he used you? He used a police officer? Who is this lowlife?"

Payne looked at the two detectives. "Colin Biddle."

Big City and The Rev looked at each other in disbelief. "The jerk-off newspaper guy?" The Rev asked. "The one who wrote a cop book?"

"He diddled you?" Big City asked.

Payne nodded. He looked at the floor.

Big City shook his head. "I've known him for years. Never thought he had the balls to shoot anybody."

"Surprises me, too," The Rev said.

Payne cleared his throat. "I've been talking to him from the beginning. Told him everything." He shook his head. "It was stupid, I know that. But I thought . . . well, I knew you guys did it and I thought it would help." He shrugged. "Then I found out he was the perp."

"You got enough to nail him?" Big City asked.

Payne shook his head. "I'm waiting to hear from Kelly Fite out at the GBI, but . . ." Payne paused. "I might as well tell you all of it. That newspaper story you were just reading?"

Big City and The Rev waited.

"I got Kitty to ask a few questions for me. He has a twenty-two but he may have altered the ballistics. His wife has a car like that photographed at the crime scene but he had an accident that destroyed the identifying characteristics."

Big City interrupted. "So if you get a search warrant, all it will do is tell him he's a suspect."

Payne nodded. "You got it. I also believe—but I can't prove it—that he had something to do with a judge turning down my request to get some videotape from WSB, some tape that was—still is—crucial to the investigation. He's also written stories that sidetracked my investigation."

The two older detectives stared at Payne. Big City put his hand on Payne's shoulder. "Young detective, I say this as your hero. You are the all-time winner of the dumb ass award."

Payne laughed. "I admired the guy while he was doing this to me. Now I don't have enough to arrest him. He's going to walk."

Big City and The Rev jumped up at the same time, both spinning toward Payne.

Big City laughed. "Only place he's walking is to jail."

"No slimy-assed newspaper reporter is going to get away with shooting two people," The Rev said. "Mister Jesus does not go along with that kind of behavior."

"I need your help."

Big City clapped Payne on the shoulder. "Don't feel badly. We did worse in our younger days. I don't remember when, but we must have."

"You've learned a lesson," The Rev said. "Deal-

ing with newspaper reporters is like walking blind-
folded through a barnyard. No way you're not
going to get shit all over your shoes."

The Rev shook his head. "What do you want to
do with Biddle? You want to spook him? You want
to fuck him over? You want to lull him a bit while
you take a final shot at getting enough to arrest
him? You want to force him into revealing he is
the perp? Or you want to do all of the above?"

Big City stepped in. "He wants to do all of the
above. It's an unnatural act when a bottom-dwell-
ing newspaper reporter takes advantage of a police
officer. I don't care if he's written five Nobel Prize-
winning books, been on *Larry King Live,* knows
the mayor, and is on a first-name basis with Mister
Jesus. He's got to be taught a lesson."

The Rev grinned. A slow beatific grin. "Then the
young detective is sitting in the right pew."

He looked at Big City. "Doesn't Biddle call you
sometime? Just sniffing around?"

Big City nodded. "He calls you, too. I've heard
you playing with him."

The Rev was still smiling. He held up his hands
as if pushing aside the heavens. "Gather around
the pulpit, my brothers. And hear the word."

Payne shook his head. "Nothing improper. I'm
in enough trouble."

The Rev looked at Big City in mock horror. He
turned to Payne.

"Who's your favorite preacher?"

Payne stared at him, confused. "What?"

"Other than me, who is your favorite preacher?"

"What has this got to do with . . . ?"

"Can you answer a simple question?"

"Okay. My favorite preacher . . ." He paused. "Other than you, of course, is . . . Ebenezer Cross."

The Rev nodded in approval. "Want to see him and his church make a million bucks?"

Payne stared.

"I ain't gonna lie," The Rev said. "He will be embarrassed. But he will wind up with what I conservatively estimate to be a million dollars." He smiled. "How'd you like to do that? How'd you like to know you helped your favorite preacher get a million dollars? Wouldn't you sleep good? Think of all the community projects he could fund with that money."

"Do I want to know how this is going to be done?"

The Rev shook his head. "No. All you have to do is play it straight. I'm gonna do my magic. When Biddle calls you, tell him the truth. In fact, I want you to try to talk him out of what he will want to do."

Payne stared.

"Go on about your business," The Rev said. "The apostles are taking care of it."

Payne paused. "You're sure?"

"Was Moses sure he could part the Red Sea? I'm going to part this sea of troubles, let you walk across on dry land, and then I'm going to reveal to you the promised land."

"You're full of it," Payne said. He walked from the room.

"True. But irrelevant." The Rev straightened his tie, then jabbed a finger at Big City. "Can I get an amen on that?"

Big City waved his hands overhead. "Amen."

34

"You the editor?"

"Yes. What can I do for you?" Don was lolled back in his chair, feet on his desk, watching CNN and knowing he was keeping abreast of the news.

"I'm calling about the double homicide on Cheshire Bridge Road."

Don put his feet on the floor and swiveled around, trying to find paper and pen. "Could you hold on a moment, sir?"

"Hurry up. I ain't got all day."

Don moved his stack of back copies of *USA Today* out of the way—best paper in the country, he believed—shoved aside the stack of *Wired* magazines, moved the two books about pop culture in America, and—there they were—paper and a pen. He pulled them across the desk, poised the pen, and said, "Okay, I'm with you."

"The police have found an eyewitness to the shooting. Guy riding by in a car. He's giving an affidavit."

"Has this witness identified anyone?"

"An officer transported him to the crime scene so he could put it all in context. They're putting together a composite that is photographic in its detail. Be easy for anyone to identify the perpetrator."

"Can you tell me who you are, sir?"

"No."

"May I ask how you know this?"

"What I'm telling you is either right or wrong. And it's easy to prove."

"You're right, sir." Don thought quickly. The gravelly voice used the words "eyewitness" and "officer" and "transported" and "perpetrator"—all words used by the police.

"Could I assume you are a policeman?"

"Assume anything you want."

The caller had to be a cop. Nobody else would speak to the editor of *The Atlanta Constitution* that way.

"I will pass this along to the reporter investigating the story. If he calls the policeman on the case, will the policeman talk to him about this?"

"He'll deny it." The voice paused. "The perpetrator is someone well known in this town. When the police arrest him it will be a big story."

"You're sure of that?"

"I said it, didn't I?"

It was a cop on the other end. No doubt about it.

"Could I ask why you are calling, sir?"

"Yeah, you could ask."

Click.

The receiver buzzed in Don's ear.

On the other end of the line, The Rev cleared his throat, shook his head from side to side, and in a mimicry of Don's voice said, "I'll pass this along to the reporter investigating the story." He laughed. "Investigating my ass. Colin Biddle couldn't find Rush Limbaugh in a phone booth."

Don quickly dialed Colin's extension. It rang four times, six times, eight times. No answer. He hung up and dialed the city desk. "Is Colin at work today?"

"No," said the assistant city editor, recognizing his voice. "He's working at home."

"Thanks."

He dialed again. Colin answered on the first ring. "Colin Biddle here."

"Colin. Don. I just had a phone call. The police apparently have a witness to the homicide. Someone was driving by and saw the person coming out of the store. They have a composite that I'm told is photographic in its detail. And the person who called—I'm certain it was a policeman—said the person is someone well known in Atlanta and that when he is arrested it will be a national story. I think you . . ."

Colin barely heard Don. His heart was thumping away, not so much from fright at being discovered as bewilderment as to how it could happen. He had blocked every possible avenue of pursuit, arranged it so the police had virtually no physical evidence and what they did have was no good, and rendered null and void their venture into videotape.

An eyewitness. Colin thought he had spiked that theory when he wrote a story and said the police were looking for a bright-colored Altima. Payne had said from the beginning he believed someone always sees the crime, that someone might have been driving down Cheshire Bridge when it happened. And there had been two cars that had come by that night as he was walking out to his car. He had bent his head, but it was possible one or both drivers might have seen him. His picture had been on national TV, local TV, and in the paper. But the odds were too great. It wasn't possible.

Or was it?

". . . case is about to break wide open," Don was saying. "So we're going to get it first and play it big. We're going to open up the front for you. You have twenty inches on the front and you can jump it inside and let it run as long as you think it's worth. I've already told the managing editor to pass the word."

A double shock. First, Don says there is an eyewitness who's putting together a composite and then he says Colin can jump a twenty-inch story from the front to the inside. There hadn't been a jump on the front page of *The Atlanta Constitution* since . . . since . . . when? The Gulf war?

"You can do some real writing on this one, Colin. Show us how a reporter—novelist—who knows the police like no one else in this town can do the job. Don't leave anything for television. We want it all."

Colin could not speak. He was running a half-dozen scenarios through his brain. Had he been identified? If so, why hadn't the police come after him? Were they waiting for the composite to be finished? Was this a trick? What were they planning? Instinctively he lowered his head and looked out the window and up and down the street.

"Colin, are you there?"

"Yes, Don. Sorry. I was thinking of how to handle this."

"Quickly is how you handle it. You know every policeman in Homicide. Call on your sources. They'll talk to you. You know how cops are. They don't make any money. They like to be on the inside. They look up to you. Work your sources."

"Yes, of course. I'll begin now. I'll call Detective Payne at the crime scene."

Colin prided himself on his ability to read people. He believed he could tell from the tone of Payne's voice if anyone was looking at him. Payne couldn't hide that from him. He would know. And then he would plan his next move.

"And, Colin?"

"Yes."

"Look at your watch. You're on a tight deadline. I want this for the three star. I'm calling the desk and tell them to open up the front for you. Write it in the first person. Run out the history of the case, how you opened up the conspiracy thing in the gay community, the trouble the police have had in solving this one. Young detective in over his head. You know how to do it."

"I'm on it, Don. Consider it done."

"C. R. Payne."

"C.R., this is Colin. How are you?"

Payne turned and stared out toward Cheshire Bridge. "I'm pretty busy right now. What can I do for you?"

Payne was preoccupied. He had nothing and he was going to have to give up his crime scene in a couple of days. His first case was about to go down the tubes.

"C.R., I'm told you have a witness."

"A witness? Who told you that?"

Payne was staring at the wall.

Colin laughed. "You know how it is. So who's the witness? What can you tell me about him?"

"I don't know anything."

Payne narrowed his eyes. What was that spot on the wall?

"It happened just the way you said it would. A person driving by saw the shooter. You don't know anything about an artist doing a composite? I hear the person is pretty well known around Atlanta and that you are about to have a big arrest on your hands."

Colin held his breath, closed his eyes, and listened with every fiber of his being for the tone of Payne's voice.

Payne took a half step toward the wall, stretching the phone cord as he continued staring at the dark spot. Reddish-black. When he spoke he sounded bored, distant. "Colin, I have no idea what you're talking about. You're on a wild goose chase. This is not a fruitful line of inquiry you're pursuing."

Colin paused. "You don't have a witness?"

Payne leaned closer to the spot and stared at it from a different angle. "Not that I know of."

"Investigation not going well?"

Payne leaned still closer to the spot. He sniffed. "Is that question for the record?"

"Just curious."

"For the record, the investigation is proceeding." Payne looked over his shoulder. He had rubber gloves in his briefcase. And an evidence bag.

"C.R., I can tell you have a lot to do, so I won't keep you. I had heard you had a witness and I wanted to run it by you."

"There is no witness. If there were, I would know."

"Okay. Thanks. Talk to you later."

"Bye."

Payne hung up the phone and walked toward his briefcase.

It looked like blood.

How did blood get on the wall?

And whose was it?

*　　*　　*

Colin took a deep breath. Maybe someone else in Homicide was working the witness and supervising the artist. Maybe they had run in one of the older guys to work with Payne. But Payne was right, he would still know about a witness.

What was going on here? Could it have been a whacko who called Don? This was too important not to pursue.

He dialed 555-3400—the homicide task force number. Michelle answered.

"Hello, Michelle. Colin here. Anything going on?"

He held his breath as she answered, his antennae quivering, listening for any indication in her voice, no matter how slight, that she might have overheard a conversation about him.

The attractive young black woman at the front desk smiled. "Hello there, Mr. Celebrity. You tell me. You know more than we do about what's going on."

Nothing there but her usual badinage.

"Lot of people around today?"

"Almost shift change time. Place is packed. I'll be glad when some of them go home."

"Big City around?"

Michelle laughed. "Yeah, for a change he's here. He has more off time than anybody I know. Wish I could get all the off time he has."

"May I speak with him please?"

"Yes, you may. Hold on."

"Homicide. Officer Lee speaking. How may I help you, sir?"

Colin laughed. "Hey, Big City. I see you remember the drill."

Several months earlier Big City had been working when his phone rang. He was overwhelmed by paperwork and in a bad mood. He picked up the phone and said, "What the fuck do you want?"

After a brief pause, a voice said, "This is the chief and here's what I want."

For two weeks Big City carried his radio in his holster and anytime anyone said, "Ring, ring," he had to pluck the radio from the holster, place it against his ear, and say, "Homicide. Officer Lee speaking. How may I help you, sir?"

He could not cross the squad room or the parking lot or walk down the hall without one of his fellow officers running up behind him and saying, "Ring, ring."

After two weeks the punishment ended. But he remembered how to answer the telephone.

"Hey there, famous writer. If I'd known it was you I'd have said, 'What the fuck do you want?' "

Colin laughed. "Anything going on today?"

"Nah. Nothing shaking."

"I heard there was a witness to that double homicide and that you guys are working up a composite."

Big City paused. "Who told you that?"

"Does that mean yes?"

"It means, who told you that?"

Colin smiled. Big City had not denied it. Somewhere out there was someone who thought he had seen something at the gas station.

There was a witness and a composite.

But Big City was talking to him about it. And he wouldn't do that if the composite were of the **real** perpetrator. What was going on here?

Had an eyewitness described someone else?

"I have my sources. I hear the composite is good and that a big arrest might be coming along soon."

"This place leaks like an old bucket."

"Why doesn't Payne know?"

"He wouldn't talk to you about it?"

"Said he didn't know anything about it."

"Well, I like that. Maybe that young trooper is learning how to deal with you people."

"Hey, Big City, tell me what you got. I'm on a deadline."

"Hold on. Let me close my door."

Colin readied his pen.

A moment later Big City was back. "Let me tell you up front that I think the whole thing is a bunch of hooey. I think the witness is bogus and if I were you I wouldn't get involved."

"Why do you say that?"

"Experience. Gut feeling. Whatever. I'm telling you don't bother with this guy."

"Let me decide."

"Just remember what I told you."

"Tell me what you have."

"Okay, the alleged witness is named Wilbur

Duke. Young guy. Says he was in Buckhead drinking that night and going down Cheshire Bridge about the time of the shooting. Says he saw a black guy coming out of the store. Tall guy. Well dressed."

Colin stopped breathing. Was Big City toying with him? Did someone walk up to the store after he was there that night, try to get in, then turn and walk away? Who could it have been? Whoever it was, the man was innocent. But if the cops had a witness who could identify this mystery person, that was a story.

"Supposed to be that preacher out at . . . what's the name of that famous black church? The one out on the south side of town? Holy Bethel AME. That's it. Ebenezer Cross is the preacher."

Colin threw his head back in exultation. It was all he could do not to shout with excitement. The cops had a witness who said he saw a famous black preacher coming out of the store.

What the hell had the witness been drinking?

It didn't matter. This would drive the nail in Payne's investigation. It was the last thing he needed to put this case away for good. Payne would be pulled off the case and there would be nothing left for anyone else to pick up.

"How can I get in touch with this guy?"

"Hold on. Let me make a quick call and see if I can get it. If you ever tell anyone I gave you this, I'll say you're a damn liar and I'll tell every police officer I know you are not to be trusted. You'll be cut off."

"Have I ever burned you?"

"You'd better not. Hold on."

Colin shook his head. These older homicide cops weren't all that impressed with him, or any other reporter, for that matter. Sometimes he had the feeling that they were even contemptuous of him and what he did. And he had no doubt that if he ever crossed one of them—particularly people like Big City or The Rev—that they would damage him in some twisted perverse fashion.

It was two or three minutes before Big City came back.

"Okay, I got a number. But I'm telling you again, I think this guy is crazy as a shit house rat. I wouldn't talk to him."

"But the police are talking to him and he has given a statement and he is working with an artist on a composite? Is that right?"

"We talk to everybody. Even newspaper reporters."

"Give me a break. Okay, did you get his number?"

Big City read the number. "This guy works strange hours. I'd call him now."

"I'll do it. And thanks, my friend. I owe you."

"Write straight."

Colin laughed and hung up.

Big City laughed. He turned and looked across the small office.

"Hey, Rev."

"What the fuck you want?"

"I abhor duplicity."

"This here is Wilbur Duke."

"Mr. Duke, my name is Colin Biddle. How are you, sir?"

"I'm fine."

"Mr. Duke, I work for *The Atlanta Constitution*. I write books, also. I'm calling about your experience the other Sunday morning. My good friends over at the police department tell me you might have seen the person who committed the two homicides at the convenience store. That makes you an important person."

"You a reporter?"

"Yes, sir. I am."

"I never talked to a reporter before."

"Well, I'm glad you're talking to me."

"You ever been on the TV?"

Colin smiled. "Yes, quite frequently, actually. As I mentioned, I've written a book and I've been on television talking about my book."

"You write books?"

"Yes, I do."

"I never talked to a book writer before."

"Tell me what you saw at the convenience store."

"Is it okay if I talk to you?"

"It sure is. The police gave me your number and

asked me to call you. They want you to tell me the same thing you told them."

"Well . . . if they said it was okay."

So, for about ten minutes Wilbur Duke talked to Colin Biddle. And when he was through, Wilbur Duke—whose real name was John McGriff—hung up, turned around, and said, "Boss, this line is burned. We need to cut it off."

Atlanta Police Lieutenant Mack McAlister, supervisor of the Vice Squad, smiled and nodded in agreement. "You did pretty good for a new guy."

McGriff nodded. "Thank you, sir." He paused. "Sir, could I ask a question?"

"Go ahead."

"What if the reporter calls the telephone company?"

"We have an arrangement with their security people. Anyone who calls about one of our undercover numbers will be told that the number never existed."

"Why did Homicide want us to do this?"

The lieutenant shook his head. "I don't know, I don't want to know, and neither do you. Wilbur Duke doesn't exist. That phone number doesn't exist."

John McGiff, newly graduated from the police academy and on his first assignment, smiled.

Colin Biddle was happy.

Once again he would have a front-page story breaking significant developments in a double homicide that had been the main topic of conversation in Atlanta for almost two weeks. And this time, unlike his diversionary feint into the gay community, he would be spot on. He was quoting a witness by name—not an unknown source—a witness who told him exactly what he had told the police; a witness who had identified a prominent black preacher as the mysterious man coming out of the convenience store.

Rather than doing one long piece, he would do a main story and two or three sidebars. And the sidebars would have enough hard information that they would have to go on the front rather than on the jump.

If he played it right, he could have three front-page bylines out of this one story. Colin smiled. Trips. Old-timers at the paper, the few who were left, sometimes talked of a former reporter having three bylines on a front page. They said it had happened once. He was about to do it again.

He was not worried about getting the story in the paper. The editor himself was pushing this one. Besides, the *Constitution,* like most newspapers, did not have fact checkers. They depended entirely upon their reporters. What a reporter was able to get into the paper depended on who the reporter was. Young reporters had no leeway. If they worked on a sensitive story, a senior reporter or an editor looked over their shoulder. But older experienced reporters like Colin had enormous leeway. Colin was a star. He was favored by the editor. He had written a novel. Not only would the editors not question his story, the copy desk wouldn't change a comma.

Colin picked up the phone, asked for information, then called the black preacher named by the witness. The interview was brief. The preacher denied everything. Of course, he denied it. Colin knew better than anyone that the preacher was not involved. But he had a witness who had named the preacher. His story was solid. He was covered.

He dialed the editor's office.

"Don, Colin here."

"Yes. Did you get it?"

"I got it all. Talked to the witness. It's dynamite. And, Don?"

"Yes."

"Forget the box on the front page. You'll want to strip this one across the top."

35

It was blood.

And in the middle of the blood was the desiccated carcass of a mosquito.

Payne used a small knife to cut into the plaster around the spot. He gently pulled out a core of plaster with the carcass in the center and carefully placed it into an evidence bag.

He sealed the bag and smiled. The old-timers were right: the crime scene reveals all. The police officer just has to know where to look and what to look for. He shook his head. Another day and it would have been too late. It might already be too late. DNA evidence takes forever to prepare.

It was a long shot, a very long shot, but it was all he had.

He searched his wallet for the card the woman at the GBI had given him several days earlier. The woman in serology. What was her name? He looked at the card. Peggy Haefele. He picked up the phone and dialed.

"Peggy, this is C. R. Payne, Atlanta Homicide.

We met last week when I was out there talking with Kelly Fite."

"I remember. What can I do for you, Detective Payne?"

"I've just found what I believe to be blood at my crime scene and I want to hand-carry it out to you. I know everyone says this, but this truly is an emergency. My case is about to blow up and this is my only hope. What is the absolute quickest I can get DNA results?"

"This is your lucky day, Detective Payne."

"How is that?"

"Up until several weeks ago, it took us up to six weeks to do DNA work. But the technology in that area, like everywhere else, is changing. We have new lab equipment, state of the art."

"And that means?"

"That means if you get it to me this afternoon I'll have the results sometime tomorrow afternoon or tomorrow evening. Do you have blood for a comparison?"

Payne sighed. "Not yet. I'll have it tonight."

"I'm familiar with your case." She paused. "If you get your evidence here this afternoon, I'll be here all night working on it. You can bring the blood for comparison anytime. But the later you get it, the later I'll have the results tomorrow."

"I'm on the way. Be there in a half hour."

He stared at the phone. "Now all I have to do is to get blood from Colin."

He had an idea.

*   *   *

Big City nodded as he listened to Payne on the telephone.

"You're going to need a court order to do that," he said. "That's one area where you can't cut corners. They'll throw it out of court in a New York minute. You got to have a court order . . . or . . ."

"He has to give his permission," finished Payne.

"Never happen. He's too smart."

"Wait a minute. Listen to this."

A few moments later Big City began laughing. "I don't believe this." The more he thought about what Payne proposed, the more he laughed. "I'm going to enjoy this."

"Will it work?"

"Risky."

"Tell me about it."

"You got anything else?"

"This is it."

"Everything on one roll of the dice?"

Payne sighed. "Everything. And if it doesn't work, well, I thought for a while I might wind up in Assaults again. Then I thought it would be the airport. But I won't be that lucky. With the mayor and the chief involved, the truth is I'll be back in Albany, Georgia, picking cotton."

"We don't allow good homicide officers to moonlight as cotton pickers. You go for it. I'll play it just the way you said. The Rev could talk to Mister Jesus all day and couldn't improve on your plan."

Big City laughed again. "Damn if you don't learn

fast," he said. Respect was evident in his voice. "You're gonna make a damn good homicide detective if you're not careful."

When Big City hung up he was still laughing.

Colin smiled when he heard Payne's voice on the phone. Colin was euphoric. "Hello, my man. How fares the republic?"

"Not too good."

"Case in the toilet?"

"Hope springs eternal."

"I was about to pop out and have a drink. Join me."

"I'd like that. That was why I was calling. I was abrupt when you called earlier but it was because I'm under so much pressure on this thing."

"You need to get away for an hour or so," Colin said magnanimously. "It'll give you some perspective. We can talk about other things. Then you'll be fresh with new ideas tomorrow morning."

"Where you want to meet?"

"How about Otto's?"

"Okay. How about now? I've had it."

"I'll be there in twenty minutes."

"Mind if I bring Big City along? He could use a drink."

Colin paused. Obviously, Big City had not told Payne of their earlier conversation.

"Sure. I'm buying."

"Twenty minutes."

* * *

"There's the King of Buckhead," said the bartender with a laugh as the three men walked into Otto's.

Colin laughed and waved. "How you doing? Bring my friends and me a drink." He looked at Payne. "I know you like single malt. What about you, Big City?"

"Hell, yes. A double."

"Three doubles."

"Three double shots of The Macallan coming up for the King of Buckhead."

Colin smiled. "I wish you'd stop that." It was clear he enjoyed the sobriquet.

The three men sat at one of the front tables. Several people who walked down the aisle from the front door spoke to Colin. Others saw him, nudged their companions, and whispered.

Colin held up his hand. "I'm going to make a pronouncement. A royal edict, if you will."

"Edict away," Big City said.

"We're here to get C.R.'s mind off his work. No shoptalk tonight."

Payne nodded. "I'm for that. I want to talk about positive things."

Big City looked at Colin. "I hear your book is doing well."

Colin nodded. He looked around the restaurant, then leaned closer. "Can I tell you something in confidence?"

The two police officers nodded. "It will hit the best-seller list of *The New York Times* Sunday.

That's tomorrow. It's the paperback list but it's still the *Times*."

Big City raised his glass. "Congratulations. I've never known a best-selling author before."

"Congratulations," said Payne, raising his glass. The three men tipped their glasses together.

Colin nodded in satisfaction.

"And my next book should be even bigger. A movie deal is in the works. And the publisher wants me to sign a two-book contract. He has asked me for a synopsis of the books."

"I saw Kitty's story. She mentioned your new book."

Colin smiled.

"You're nothing but good news, are you, fella?" Big City said. Colin did not notice the fires flickering in Big City's eyes.

"Things are going well right now." He wanted to tell them about the headline on tomorrow's paper. But they would hear of it soon enough.

"You told Kitty your new book is about DNA?"

Colin nodded. "I think the forensics angle truly intrigues people. Makes them feel like they are on the inside. This will be the definitive cop novel regarding DNA. My job is to take what can be a terribly boring topic, as you know if you watched the O. J. Simpson coverage, and make it a page-turner."

"How do you do that?" Payne asked.

"I used to think it was mastery of the topic; knowing all there is to know about it. And that is important, especially if the book moves into areas that the reader knows very little about. But now I believe that you have to have three ingredients: a good story, bigger than life characters, and a powerful compelling background."

"You know a lot about DNA?"

"I've done some research. But this story I've been working on, the one we're not supposed to talk about tonight . . ." He smiled at Payne. "It has taken a lot of time. But now I'm moving ahead on the research."

"I've done a hundred DNA cases," Big City said.

Colin looked at him. "What do you mean?"

"Taken samples. That's the fascinating part, not all the laboratory stuff. If you could get across to your readers about the little-known details of DNA evidence, people would buy your book by the thousands. Nobody knows how that is done. And nobody has ever written about how samples are taken. All anyone knows is those stupid-looking DNA bars on a light screen. About as much fun as watching grass grow."

Colin stared at him. "Tell me about samples."

Big City shrugged. "You have to have something to match blood samples with. You get it from a person's hair, blood, or saliva."

"How do you do that?"

Big City turned up his scotch and drained it. "You don't want to know. You're academic and removed from all the nitty-gritty stuff. Too rich. Hell, you're the King of Buckhead."

Colin was irked but didn't want to show it.

"You gonna buy us another drink or we have to buy our own after the first one?" Big City smiled at Colin. He looked like a demonic shark. Muted flashes of light could be seen deep in his eyes.

"Everything is on me tonight. You are my guests." Colin waved at the bartender, circled his finger in the air, then held up three fingers. He leaned toward Big City.

"I want to know about samples. All the details."

Big City studied him. After a long moment he said, "Tell you what. I'll show you. You can take notes. That way you'll have it firsthand. You can't write about it based on what I say. But if you experience it from a first-person standpoint, then what you write will be more powerful. This is my gift to you in return for the scotch."

"What do you mean, you'll show me?"

The bartender placed the drinks on the table. Big City picked up his scotch and motioned for Payne and Colin to do the same. The three tinkled their glasses together. "Put this puppy down the hatch and we'll all jump in my official police car and go down to Homicide and I'll take you into the bubble and show you what cop work is all about."

"Bubble?"

"Goddammit, Colin, I'm about to give up on you. You're a hotshot police reporter, write books that they're going to make movies about, and you don't know what the bubble is. Drink your scotch and we'll go."

"My car is here."

"Let Payne drive it. You ride in the police car. Get the feel of what it is like for a perp to be arrested and taken to the bubble."

"And let me get the feel of what it will be like to drive a Range Rover," Payne said.

Big City tilted his head back and drained the double shot.

Colin and Payne looked at each other. Payne shrugged and drained his glass. So did Colin. He tossed his keys to Payne.

"Come on, guys. I might even turn on the blue lights." Big City led them out of Otto's.

"You want authentic. We'll do authentic. Just the way we would to a real suspect when we wanted to get samples from him." Big City looked at Colin. "You up for that, famous writer?"

Colin nodded. He owed Big City for the tip earlier today. Owed him big. He couldn't afford to say no.

He smiled. "You going to walk me through it as though I were a suspect?"

"Isn't that what you want?"

Colin nodded.

Big City opened the door of the bubble.

The bubble was a small bare empty room in the back corner of the Homicide Squad's quarters. The walls were dented and kicked in dirty and showed smears of blood—signs of a hundred interviews, during many of which the person being interviewed had decided he had enough and that he was going to put an ass whipping on a cop and walk out.

Such a person always realized the error of his ways.

Big City pointed to a small straight-backed wooden chair in the corner. "Sit there." He looked at Colin. "I'll tell you something most people don't know. They see all these interrogation scenes in movies and that's a crock. We treat every suspect differently. You have to. Some asshole who comes in here with an attitude winds up leaving with a new respect for police officers. Someone like you who comes in, educated, wealthy, lives in Buckhead, we talk to in altogether different fashion. Usually, if someone like you were a suspect, we would have him sign a release that what he was doing was done of his own volition; that it was not coerced."

Colin nodded. "So his lawyer later on couldn't get the results thrown out or declared inadmissible."

Big City looked at Payne in pretended wonderment. "Did you hear that? Take back everything I said about him earlier. This guy is sharp."

Colin smiled. "What happens next?"

"Wait a minute." Big City picked up a single sheet of paper from a table in the far corner, wrote Payne's name at the top under the label of "investigator," and handed it to Colin. "I said we were going to do this by the book. You have to know what a suspect would be signing." He handed the paper to Colin. "This is a consent form. We can't get samples for DNA unless the suspect signs this form or unless we have a court order."

Colin looked at it. "You want me to sign it?"

"I want you to read it, tell me you understand it and that you are signing it voluntarily, and then sign it."

Colin read the brief form. "Is this the correct form? This says the blood samples, saliva samples, or pubic hair and head hair samples are for use in a rape investigation."

Big City took the form from Colin's hand. "They're interchangeable." He scratched out "rape investigation," replaced it with "homicide," and initialed it.

Colin smiled and shook his head. "This is all there is to it?"

"Whoops. Forgot. We have to Mirandize you."

Colin's eyes widened. He would have thought a senior homicide officer would be more professional. It all seemed so haphazard. He laughed. "Are you sure you've done this before?"

"Hundred times. Like I told you." He quickly read the Miranda warning to Colin.

Colin nodded impatiently. "I understand my rights as you have read them to me. I waive those rights." He smiled and signed the form. "For my book I need a cooperative witness."

"Yeah, but it's a lot more fun for us if the witness is not cooperative."

"What do you mean?"

"Sit down."

Colin sat in the single chair in the corner as Big City pulled on a pair of late gloves. Payne watched dispassionately.

Big City picked up a syringe. "I'm going to get some of your blood and if it turns out to be single malt scotch I'll kick your ass."

"What? Are you qualified to take blood?"

"I'm a qualified EMT. Renaissance man is what I am. Next week I walk on water. Now take off your coat and roll up your sleeve."

"You've done this before."

"Hundred times. You wanted authentic. You got it. Now come on. I don't have all night to dick around with some writer doing research. Payne and I got to go out and fight some crime."

Payne looked at his watch. "I'm behind schedule now."

For a brief second Colin was tempted to ask Payne what he had to do now that his case had blown up in his face. Instead he shrugged and took off his coat. "The things I do in the name of research."

"If you tell me it hurts, you're going to have to put that in the book, too. Otherwise you're lying and Payne and I will know it."

Colin rolled up his sleeve. "I'll let you know what I think of your technique."

"Watch me."

Big City tied a piece of rubber tubing around

Colin's bicep, felt for a vein, and deftly inserted the needle.

Colin nodded in approval. "I didn't even feel it." He watched as the syringe filled with blood.

"Told you I was good. But, hey, we got a problem here."

"What is it?" Colin was concerned.

"This stuff is red. I thought it would be blue."

Colin laughed. "I'm a mere mortal after all."

Big City laughed, jerked the needle from Colin's arm, and applied an alcohol swab. "Hold that in place for a couple of minutes while I take care of this."

"What happens to the blood?"

"I'll show you." He picked up two test tubes from the table. "Notice these have purple stoppers. For blood that is to be used as a DNA sample, we always use purple-stoppered test tubes. Two of them. Remember that. It's an important detail. Shows you know what you're talking about."

He pushed the top of the syringe and filled each test tube with blood. He turned his back to Colin and put the two test tubes inside a metal container. A plastic bag of ice was in the bottom of the small container.

"Now we do hair."

"I started to ask you about that. I saw it on the consent form."

Big City picked up a pair of tweezers in one hand and a small evidence bag in the other.

"I need twenty-five hairs. Gotta have the roots."

"Twenty-five?"

"See, already you're learning things you didn't know. Great detail stuff for the book. We don't need three hairs or eight hairs or ten hairs. Got to have twenty-five." He turned to Payne. "Young detective, hold this evidence bag. Colin, you remembering all this? Every step? Because when I read this in your next book it better be right."

"Owwww!"

Big City held up a tweezer full of long blond hairs and looked at them. He laughed. "We don't usually get three at once. But you've got a lot of hair. So I short-circuited the process."

He placed the hairs into an evidence bag and turned back to Colin.

Colin held up his hands. "That's enough. I get the idea."

"No way, Jose. You have to understand what a suspect is feeling each time we come back for more hair Usually, we would get a court order for this. If the suspect objects, we just hold his ass down and pull them out one by one."

Colin shook his head. "No more hair."

Big City held his arms wide. "I don't have the pubic hair yet. I need twenty-five hairs—with roots—from your head and twenty-five hairs—with roots—from your pubic area."

"What?" Colin crossed his legs. He looked at Big City and then at Payne. "Look, I got what I came after. I know the procedures. I now how it feels to have my hair jerked out. That's enough. No more. Especially not from my pubic area."

Big City stared at him. "Woosing out. Just as I suspected."

"The consent form mentioned saliva. You can get DNA from saliva. I don't mind spitting into a test tube."

"Hell, anybody can spit into a test tube. This is the part people will be fascinated by. Can't you see that scene in the book where the cops tell the suspect to drop trou. And then the details of extracting pubic hairs."

Colin shook his head. "No more hair. I have learned all I need to know for my research." He was emphatic.

Big City laughed. "Okay, but here's some more great detail for you. This is more for sexual offenders but it might work in your book. If a suspect has a mustache and we really want to fuck with him, we tell him that in each sexual encounter there is an exchange of body hair. We tell him he might have performed cunnilingus on the victim and that we are going to extract twenty-five hairs from his mustache. You think it doesn't hurt to have your mustache hairs jerked out?"

He gestured with the tweezers.

Colin winced.

"Sure you don't want to do the pubic hairs? The hair on your balls is different from that on your head." He paused. "You rich reporters do have hair on your balls?"

Colin held his belt. Very slowly and softly he said, "I get the idea."

Big City shrugged. He pulled off the latex gloves and tossed them into a waste can.

Colin relaxed. "Well, I must thank you. This will jump-start the research on my book."

Big City nodded. "Nobody but suspects ever go through that. It'll be the best part of your book. Great detail." He stifled a yawn.

"You getting sleepy?" Colin laughed. "Not as young as you once were?"

Big City nodded. "You young fellows can run rings around me. Two double scotches got me to nodding. And I got a big day tomorrow."

Colin thought of the morning paper. He looked at his watch. The early edition should be on the streets in an hour. If he drove downtown to the paper, he could call ahead on his car phone and have one of the secretaries bring a copy to the curb. He stood up. "I do, too. Better be going."

He shook hands with both police officers. "This has been a most enlightening evening. Great research. Great detail, just as you said. You've both added significantly to the book."

"Glad to help," Payne said. He held out the keys to the Range Rover. "Handles like a dream. I'm going to have one of those one day."

Colin smiled. "If you gentlemen are leaving now, I'll walk out with you."

"We've got to clean up a few things. You go ahead," Payne said.

"Night, guys. Thanks again."

"Thank you," Payne said.

"Night, buddy," Big City said.

The two officers watched as the tall handsome reporter walked out, the bright fluorescent lights over the door turning his blond hair white.

The door eased shut.

Big City smiled. The lights in his eyes were surging and pulsating like the aurora borealis. "Are we slicker than owl shit, or what?"

"You got the blood. What was that with the hair?"

"I was fucking with the boy."

Payne loosed a long sigh. Then he clapped his hands together and turned to Big City. "I've got to run it out to the GBI. They're waiting."

Big City shook his head. "I hope you're right. I never heard of getting blood from a dead mosquito."

"They finished painting the store the day of the shooting. If a mosquito bit Colin that night and he smashed it on the wall and we can do a DNA match with the samples we took tonight, then we've put him in the building the day of the homicide. He's already said he hadn't been in there in several weeks. Told me that the first morning. The DNA alone will convict him. But I want to be absolutely certain. I'm going to use the DNA to go judge shopping. I'll find a judge who will sign an order to produce that video. I have no doubt that if the people up at Oak Ridge can enhance that tape, even in the slightest, we will have video of him entering and leaving the store at the time the M.E. said the homicides were committed. I'll get a search warrant and see if there aren't some X-ray or chemical tests the crime lab can perform to show there was a deep scratch across the trunk of the Mercedes before it ran into the brick wall. If this DNA works, it will open the door to a flood of evidence."

Big City nodded approvingly. "You're learning."

"Yeah, but . . ."

". . . it all hangs on the DNA," Big City finished. "If that doesn't work out . . ."

Payne nodded. "Back to the cotton field for me." He shrugged. "A double homicide hanging on a mosquito's butt." He paused, stared at the floor, then looked up at Big City. "What do you think?"

Big City looked up as the lights from Colin's Range Rover flashed across the door of the homicide office. He nodded toward the disappearing lights.

"I know why he wouldn't let us have any pubes."

Payne laughed. "I do, too. He knew it would hurt."

Big City shook his head. "Nope."

"Why then?"

"He's got a teeny-weeny tallywacker."

36

"Kitty, C. R. Payne."

"Well, well, C. R. Payne. How you been, big boy?"

"I told you not to call me boy."

"I said big boy. That makes it okay."

"Who said so?"

"Jessie Jackson."

"You're right. That makes it okay." He paused. "What are you doing?"

"Playing with my Stiffy."

"Your what?"

"Stiffy. My cat."

"Funny name for a cat."

"He's all I got."

"In the mood for an offer?"

"Always."

"You know where the GBI is?"

"No, goddammit, I just came in on a turnip truck. I'm working nights at the Majestic Grill as a waitress and I don't know shit about Atlanta except how to find First Baptist Church and the Clermont

Lounge. Hell yes, I know where the GBI is. I'm a police reporter."

"Your mama should have washed your mouth out with lye soap."

"You didn't call to tell me that."

"Meet me out at GBI and I'll do what you've been wanting."

"You mean take my clothes off?"

"Kitty, you should be careful about what you say. Somebody's going to take you up on one of those comments."

"I hope so."

"Get out here. And bring your notebook."

Kitty paused. "For what?"

"You said you wanted the story when Colin went down."

"You're about to pop him." Then she remembered. "Oh, God."

"What is it?"

"He's running out a banner headline story tomorrow morning about the police having a witness and a composite. His story says Ebenezer Cross is the suspect. We sent it out on the wire. Hell, it will be on every TV station in town in the morning. It will be national news. We've had a couple of phone calls from big national papers wanting pictures of Colin. He's a hero of the republic. And by the way, you're quoted as saying there is no eyewitness."

"Ebenezer Cross?" Payne was mumbling to himself. "So that's how he will get a million dollars." He laughed. "What did you say?"

"You're quoted in Colin's story as saying there is no eyewitness. Makes you look like you don't know what's going on in your own case."

"There isn't."

"There isn't what?"

"There isn't any witness."

"What do you mean? It's on the front page."

"The story is wrong."

"Hey, it's on the front page of *The Atlanta* Fucking *Constitution*."

"One more time. Watch my lips. It's . . . wrong . . . Every . . . word . . . is . . . wrong."

"As Clark Kent would say, Holy shit. I need to call the desk and let them know."

"You think they will listen?"

Kitty paused. She sighed. "Under the circumstances, not if I gave them two affidavits and swore on a stack of fu—"

"Don't say it," he interrupted.

"So what do I do, C. R. Payne?"

"Meet me at GBI."

"My newspaper is about to take one up the ass. Right?"

"I'm not sure I would phrase it quite in that fashion. But, yes."

"That hurts my heart, C.R."

"There is nothing you can do about it."

"There should be something. This will embarrass every newspaper in the country."

"Kitty, the GBI."

She sighed. "Half hour. In the lobby."

"I'll be there. We'll go get some coffee and I'll tell you the whole story. And if you think Colin's story tomorrow is getting a lot of attention, just wait."

"I'll bring a six-pack."

"No. You're working."

"What does that have to do with it?"

It was 2:00 A.M. when Kitty looked up from her notes. She waved her hand at the waitress in the all-night truck stop and pointed to her coffee cup. "You want another?" she asked Payne.

"Yes."

Kitty held up two fingers.

"It all depends on the DNA?"

He looked at her and smiled ruefully. "On a squashed mosquito."

"Truth is stranger than fiction." She tapped the pencil on her teeth. "I didn't know you could do DNA with such a small sample."

"You can do it with less than half a drop. A pinhead."

"What do you think happened that night?"

"I don't know. I don't know if we'll ever really know it all. But he went in there to get gas. We got a picture of him at the pumps. Came off the tower cam at WSB. Something happened at the pump. Maybe he sprayed gas all over himself."

Payne stopped and pulled a notebook from his pocket. "I need to contact the dry cleaners where he goes. They can verify if he brought in a suit with gas on it."

Kitty stared at Payne.

He scribbled, put the notebook in his pocket, and continued. "If I'm right, a mosquito bit him. He smashed it against the wall. I don't know how he broke the cash register. Maybe swinging at the mosquito. Maybe swinging at the attendant . . . at your brother. Why he started shooting, I don't know. But for whatever reason, he lost it. Killed them both. Then he got the videotape from the surveillance camera, wiped down—"

"Pictures? Tower cam? You never told me that."

"I know. What gets me is that I showed them to Colin." He looked at her. "I wonder if you had seen them would you have recognized him." He shrugged. "Anyway, he wiped down everything in the store with what I now believe was a gasoline-soaked handkerchief and left. He still had the handkerchief in his hand when he crossed the parking lot. I saw it in the pictures and thought it was a container of some sort."

"I could have identified him." She waited a moment. "Doesn't matter now. You got him. What about the guy in Key West?"

"You were right. Colin did it. I don't know why. I suspect that he simply doesn't like gays. Maybe he feels threatened by them. Whatever it is, it doesn't take much for a homosexual to cause him to lose his temper. I'm not a psychologist. I don't know."

"Well, if he goes to prison, the boys in there will soon find out."

"That's a big if right now."

They drank their coffee silently.

"Let's go," she said.

"It's still hours before we will know."

"That's okay. We can sit in the car and talk. Ride around. Go back out to GBI."

When Payne opened the car door on the passenger side, Kitty slid inside, then moved across the seat to unlock the door on his side. She stayed by the steering wheel, her skirt rucked high up her legs.

When Payne got in he looked at her in surprise. She smiled and slid her left arm around his neck. "Drive around back. It's dark back there."

"Kitty."

"You're not gay, too."

He laughed. "Not by any stretch of the imagination. But listen. This is important. Move over to your side of the car. And pull your skirt over your knees."

She slid across the seat. She did not pull down her skirt. Payne reached over and tried to pull it toward her knees. It did not reach that far.

She sighed.

"I grew up black in southwest Georgia."

"I know."

"You don't know what it means, Kitty. You grew up down there, too. But you don't know what it means to grow up black and get a scholarship and come to Emory and then go to work for the city. We never escape our childhood. Never."

"So?"

"I don't want to be a stereotypical black man."

"I don't understand."

"Yes you do. Just about any black man who got a chance to make out with a good-looking white woman like you would break his ass doing it."

"But you're not." It was not a question.

He shook his head. "I've learned a lot about myself in the past few days." He looked out the window and did not speak for a long moment. "I could never please my father. I don't know if I ever told you about him or not. But he ridiculed me and demeaned me and told me I wold grow up to be just another sorry nigger. That's not a very good reason for me to want to succeed, but it's all I've got." He shook his head. "I have to prove him wrong. I have to succeed. Being a police officer is just the first step. I want to run for public office in a few years."

She seized his hand. "You'll win. I know you will."

He removed his hand from her grip. "Listen. My marriage failed. I have a daughter that my ex-wife will not let me see. I've failed as a father."

"But it's not your fault if—"

He raised his hand. "And I've thought for the past few days I was going to fail as a homicide cop. I still might." He looked at her. "But, Kitty, I can't fail myself. I can't fail as a man."

She shook her head in bewilderment.

"I'm not a stereotypical black man and I'm not going to become one. I don't want you to be upset. It has nothing to do with you. You are very attractive."

"Attractive, my ass. I'm a damn good-looking woman."

He nodded in agreement. "Kitty, if you were to make this offer a week from now I might take you up on it."

She bit her lip and stared at him. "What's C.R. stand for?"

He looked out the window for a long moment. "Caesar Roosevelt." He shook his head. "My mother, God bless her, is a good woman, a poor woman but a good woman. She never had anything. But she knew when I was born that she wanted me to get out of Albany and to be somebody. She named me Caesar Roosevelt. She thought having the names of two great men would give me greatness. My father was around but about all he did was criticize me. I was glad when he died."

He turned and looked at her. "You think that's an awful thing to say?"

"I think I understand."

"I never felt great."

Kitty did not speak.

Payne looked out the window. "The last time I was home she saw one of my business cards. With the logo and name of the Atlanta Police Department. She was very proud of that. But she didn't like seeing C. R. Payne on there. She understood. She told me that when I finally grew up, I would use the name she gave me."

Kitty sighed. She slid across the seat again, put her arm around his neck, and leaned her head on his shoulder.

"Life is shit."

He shook his head and laughed.

After a moment she straightened up, tapped him on the shoulder with a fist, and said, "Okay, your name has changed. I'm calling you Caesar from now on."

"My name is C.R."

She looked at her watch. "Let's drive back over to GBI and wait there."

He nodded and turned on the ignition.

She hit him on the shoulder again. "The offer will still be good next week."

He stared at her. Slowly he began to smile. She was leaning toward him when his pager sounded.

"Kelly Fite."

Payne moved from under the telephone kiosk so he could see the face of his watch. "Kelly, C. R. Payne returning your call. What are you doing working this time of the morning?"

"Hey, I'm really sorry. I've been out of town at an emergency meeting. I just got back and I'm in the lab catching up with rush jobs. Yours was at the top of the list."

"You've got the results from Key West?"

"Yes. And I have good news for you."

"Lay it on me."

"Two things. First, we have a definite match on the comparisons. The live round you found at the crime scene here in Atlanta came from the same weapon that ejected the casings found in Key West."

"No doubt?"

"None. Remember when I saw the live round and I talked to you about the marks on the rim? I said since I didn't have a second bullet for comparison and since I didn't have a weapon that those marks may or may not be significant?"

"I remember."

"The marks I found on the live round here were on both casings found in Key West. I wish I could tell you what caused them but without the weapon I can only guess. I think there may be an imperfection from the milling, maybe a burr on the breech face, that is causing the marks."

Payne paused. "Kelly, it would embarrass me to go into the details of what happened. But I have reason to believe my suspect might have altered his weapon to avoid a ballistics comparison."

"You mean he knows about rat-tail files?"

"Afraid so."

"Doesn't matter. If this is a burr on the breech face, it's not anything he would know about. You find me the weapon and I will get you a comparison."

"That's great news."

"There's more."

"Go ahead."

"The firing pin marks on the Key West casings indicate his firing pin is not perfectly aligned. It's tilted to one side. That means the firing pin marks on the shells are beveled."

Payne nodded. "And that means even if he did file the tip of his firing pin that . . ."

"I can still get a valid match from the beveled edge. Easy."

"These two points of comparison—the burr on the breech face, if that's what it is, and the misaligned firing pin—these are enough for a jury to put the shooter in jail?"

Kelly laughed. "You find me the twenty-two semiautomatic that ejected the live round in Atlanta and the casings in Key West and I'll put somebody in jail."

"Kelly, I'm going to send you a bottle of scotch."

"I'll take it."

Payne hung up. As soon as it was daylight, he would call about getting a search warrant for Colin's house.

Then he would wait for the DNA results.

37

On Sunday morning, two weeks after the double homicide, Atlanta awakened to the news that a witness had been found who had directed the drawing of a composite that identified the Reverend Ebenezer Cross, the charismatic leader of the eight-thousand member Holy Bethel AME Church, as the suspect being questioned by police.

Radio and television stations attributed the story to *The Atlanta Constitution*. Usually, when one medium breaks a story, others do not give proper attribution. Buried deep in the story will be something like "A local newspaper said" or "An Atlanta television station reported." It is only when the story is very big, when there is not time to do independent reporting to confirm the story, or when another medium is afraid of the story, that attribution is early and prominent.

Thus it was with the story about the witness. There was no doubt to anyone who saw the story on television or heard it on radio that the story had first been reported in the morning paper by the best-selling crime writer Colin Biddle.

Several radio stations did say that efforts to contact Wilbur Duke, the man quoted at length in Colin's story, were unsuccessful.

It was the headline story in the Sunday paper. A picture of Colin was part of the package. As was a little box of biographical information that talked mostly about his book.

And Colin had three bylines on the front page. He had accomplished the journalistic hat trick—trips, as reporters called it—which had caused considerable envy in the newsroom as well as enabling him to set a new record for his Tower of Power.

By 9:00 A.M. the editor's phone was ringing at home. It was Reverend Cross. He had talked to the mayor who had talked to the chief who had talked to Major Mickey Lloyd who had talked to Lieutenant Carter who had talked to Detective C. R. Payne who said he knew nothing of an eyewitness and that the reverend was not a suspect.

Then the news rolled uphill.

Reverend Cross informed the editor that he was going before his congregation to tell them that what they had read in the paper and seen on television and heard on the radio was a deliberate attempt by the newspapers to discredit black preachers and the black community.

"I'm going to light a truth fire, which you don't desire," the reverend said. "When the fire gets hot, we'll see what you got."

"I'm not sure I under—"

"What I'm saying to you is this: I'm about to light a fire under your white ass."

"But we can talk about this and—"

"Talk? I talked to your reporter and told him this infamous blast was from the devil himself. I told him he was roaming in the vale of speculation and consorting with unbelievers even to suggest such a thing. I told him I was at Grady Hospital that Saturday night in question; that I sat up all night with a parishioner who was dying of cancer. A dozen doctors and nurses and family members will confirm that. He kept saying the police had a witness. Well, Mr. Editor, I'm telling you that whoever this witness is, he is unknown to the chief of police or to anyone in the police department. It is all a tissue of lies. And, Mr. Editor, you have sown the tares of gossip and humiliation and now you shall reap the whirlwind of retribution. Good day to you. And may God have mercy on you for what you have done."

Don called Colin. Colin picked up the phone on the first ring and whispered, "Hello." He did not want to awaken his wife. He asked Don to hold while he took the call in his study.

"You better call your witness now and make sure he's staying in harness," Don said. "And check with the police. Get right back to me."

Colin was not concerned. He had his eyewitness.

But when he dialed Wilbur Duke's number, he

heard a recording saying the number was not a working number.

He then called a friend of his mother's, a woman who was a vice president at the telephone company. She put him on hold for several minutes, then came back and said, "Colin, you must be mistaken. Our computers show that is not a valid number. It has never been used."

There was no Wilbur Duke listed in the telephone directory. Colin called a friend on the larceny squad, a lieutenant, who, in turn, called the telephone company and was told no one by the name of Wilbur Duke had a number—listed or unlisted. Then the lieutenant called Georgia Power and was told no one named Wilbur Duke was listed anywhere in the metropolitan area as a customer. Same response from Atlanta Gas Light.

Colin called the newspaper and asked one of the editors to check the City Directory. No Wilbur Duke there. A state trooper was persuaded to tap into the DMV computer: no Wilbur Duke had a Georgia driver's license.

Colin could not reach Payne. He did find Big City. Big City laughed. "Colin, what did I tell you when you called me about that?"

"You told me . . . you told me . . ." Colin stammered.

For a moment Big City almost felt sorry for Colin. "I told you I thought the witness was bogus and that I wouldn't bother talking with him. Didn't I tell you that?"

"Yes, but I thought . . ."

"What did Payne tell you?"

"He said he didn't know anything about it. But I thought . . . I thought . . ."

"You thought you had a story and you were determined to run it. Right?"

Colin did not answer.

"Who the hell did you get your original information from?"

Colin cleared his throat. "Someone called the editor."

"Who?"

"I don't know."

"You wrote that story based on an anonymous phone call?"

Colin did not answer. He had lost his position in the universe and sensed that he was about to be spinning wildly out of control.

"Colin, you have fucked the monkey. But there's one thing you should be happy about."

"What are you talking about?"

"You have just raised a million dollars for Ebenezer Cross."

Colin slammed the phone down. Who the hell was Wilbur Duke? Even if he was a bogus witness, who was he? Why did he say he had seen the preacher coming out of the convenience store that night? Was he some crazy who had surfaced, told his story, then disappeared? But why?

There was no Wilbur Duke.

It was midafternoon when he called Don. The

editor's wife said he had gone to the office and that Colin was to meet him there as soon as possible.

Colin showered and dressed.

He was so upset he forgot to hide the videotape from the convenience store. It was left in the VCR.

It was almost two-thirty in the afternoon when Peggy Haefele came out of the lab and motioned for Payne and Kitty to follow her. Only her eyes revealed her fatigue. She was as crisp and neat in her dress as she had been the previous afternoon.

Payne was the same. Not a discernible wrinkle in his dark suit. His tie was snuggled up tightly. His coat was buttoned.

Kitty was another story. She looked as if she had been pieced together from an explosion in a Barbie doll factory.

"The blood you found at the crime scene was good," Peggy said. "We have unarguable results."

Payne nodded. He looked at Kitty. They walked faster to keep up with Peggy.

Kitty looked at Payne, raised her eyebrows, and mouthed, "Is he guilty or not?"

He put his fingers over his lips.

"The blood sample you got from the suspect was outstanding."

Payne looked at Kitty. He shook his head in exasperation. When would Peggy tell him what he needed to hear?

Peggy stopped and turned to Payne. "Detective, you have a matchup. Clear. Unmistakable. The person from whom you took the samples is the same person who left the blood at the crime scene. There is no doubt. To put it in layman's terms, every avenue of comparison checks out."

Payne choked with emotion. For a moment he could not speak. His hands were sawing up and down in the air. Then very slowly he said to Peggy: "You are absolutely certain? This will stand up in court?"

She nodded. "I've had far worse samples stand up in court. The perp can take this all the way to the Supremes and he'll still lose."

Payne turned to Kitty. He struggled to contain his emotion.

Kitty seized his arms. "Colin is fucked."

That broke the spell. He nodded. Payne and Peggy began laughing.

Payne clasped Peggy's hand. "Thank you for coming out here and working on a Saturday night. The GBI is first-rate. I'll find a way somehow to repay you."

"You want to repay me?"

"Name it."

"Arrest that man."

Payne bit his lips. He was afraid to speak. He waved and was gone. Kitty had to run to keep up.

"Wait. I want to ride with you."

They argued all the way into town.

"You have to wait until after six p.m.," she insisted. "It has to be on my time. This is not a television story."

"I don't work for the newspaper. I don't care about your deadlines. I want to put him in jail."

"You told me this would be my story if I helped you. You said that."

"Yes. I said that."

She held up her watch. "It's only four-thirty. If you arrest him now, television will break it on the six o'clock news. It's only an hour and a half. You can wait that long."

He did not speak for a moment. Then he turned and looked at her. "You don't want to go to your moment of glory looking like that. I'll wait long enough for you to shower and change clothes."

She smiled. "I knew he did it. From the very beginning, I knew it."

"How could you?"

"He's got a small package. Guy with a package that small would do anything to compensate."

Payne laughed.

"Can you think of anything else about his house I should know about? Something you might have forgotten from when you were there?"

"For your search warrant?"

"Yes."

She paused. "I don't think so. The thing I remember most vividly is his jumping up to show me his little twenty-two. He keeps it on the bookshelf near the TV set." She turned to look at Payne. "The VCR."

"The VCR? What about it?"

"It was turned on. I remember seeing the light. But there were no cassettes, no movies in sight."

Payne shook his head. "He wouldn't watch movies in his study."

"You're right. It would be in a bigger room. In case his wife wanted to watch."

"So why was the VCR on?"

"Who knows?"

He turned to look at her. "Kitty."

She looked at him, emotions flitting across her face. First, bewilderment, then understanding, and then horror. When she spoke her voice was very soft. "The videotape from the convenience store."

He nodded. "I don't know. The search warrant is specific. But if the tape is in plain sight, I can grab it."

She looked out the window. "I want to know only if you find it. That's all. I don't want any details of what's on the tape."

"Of course." He paused. "You saw his twenty-two?"

"Yes. He is very proud of it. A Walther. It's in a box on the bookshelf. You can't miss it."

Payne smiled.

Kitty sighed. She looked at Payne. Then she pulled down the vanity mirror on the rear of the sun visor and stared at herself. She pulled at her hair. She flipped the mirror up and sighed again.

"I do need to repair the damage." She paused. "You aren't very diplomatic."

"I'm not a diplomat."

She waited a moment. "My newspaper was embarrassed today. If we break the story about Colin, that will help us regain our reputation. Thanks for holding off on the arrest."

He smiled. "Thank you."

"For what?"

"For putting together more than two sentences without cursing."

She shrugged. "I thought a lot about what you said last night. And I decided I'm going to clean up my act. I'll get Colin's job as police reporter. So I'm going to slow down on the drinking and I'm going to keep my mouth closed where profanity is concerned."

He smiled.

"I know," she said. "I slipped at the GBI when we were talking to Peggy."

"I hope it lasts."

She turned to look at him. "I'm going to try to keep my legs closed, too." She settled back in the seat. "I've always had some sort of psychological yeast infection. I'd hump the corner of a table if nothing else was available."

"Do you have to say everything that flits across your mind? I don't want to hear stuff like that."

"I used past tense. That's history. I'm going to devote myself to being a good reporter."

He raised his eyebrows.

She shrugged. "There is one outstanding offer up in the air. I can't go back on my word."

*   *   *

Reverend Ebenezer Cross, two dozen parishioners, and Powell Armstrong, the most militant black lawyer in Atlanta, were in the editor's office when Colin arrived Sunday afternoon.

Reverend Cross was a tall muscular man with eyes like searchlights. The air around him seemed to crackle with his moral strength and the force of his personality.

Don beckoned Colin into his office. "You all know Colin Biddle, the reporter who wrote the story."

The reverend and his parishioners stared. Powell Armstrong, a smallish man with a neatly trimmed beard, smiled, stood up, and held out his hand. Armstrong was dressed as well as Colin. He was smooth and confident. "Mr. Biddle, we are going to get to know each other very well in the coming weeks." He nodded toward Don. "I was just saying to your editor that we clearly have a cause of action. Your story not only was inaccurate, you printed it after the police and the reverend himself told you there was no substance to your inquiries. You printed a story based on a fictitious source; a story you knew was wrong."

He poked Colin on the chest with a long black finger. "I believe a jury in this county will consider that malice. Prima facie." His smile broadened. "You do understand about malice in defamation suits?"

"Mr. Armstrong, I must speak to our corporate

lawyers," the editor said. "I can't speak for the paper until then. But, all things considered, I don't believe we will have to go to court over this. I think, and I shall so recommend, that we settle. That will be the best way for all of us to handle this."

Armstrong nodded. It was rare that a lawyer had such an obvious cause of action against a newspaper. For the editor even to attempt a bluff would, later on, do nothing but inflame a jury. It would add to the award for punitive damages. The editor knew that.

"Can I get an amen on that?" the preacher asked his parishioners.

"Amen," they said as one.

Armstrong looked at Colin. "There are some things that must be done, some things to show good faith that such an egregious act will not occur again, that one of the most prominent members of Atlanta's black community will not again suffer such humiliation because of the willful and reckless nature of a newspaper reporter."

"Just a minute," Colin said.

Don held up his hand and motioned for Colin to be silent. He nodded toward Armstrong. "We will do whatever is right and proper. We are good citizens. You can count on that."

"Don, we have to talk," Colin said imploringly. "I had a witness."

Don waved him away.

Everyone in the office looked toward the door

when they heard Don's secretary saying, "You can't go in there. They're having a meeting."

Then there was a moment of silence. The secretary said, "I'll open the door for you."

She opened the door and announced to the room, "A policeman is here looking for Mr. Biddle."

Payne entered. Don's eyebrows rose when he saw Kitty, hair neatly combed and wearing a conservative black dress with black high heels, follow the cop. She even appeared to be wearing a bra. A notebook was in one hand, a pencil in the other. A photographer followed, camera at the ready.

Payne looked at Don and badged him. "Official police business."

The parishioners were all ears. "The brother is here on police business," one said.

"Amen to that," said another.

Powell Armstrong, who seemed to have taken over even though he was in the editor's office, smiled and motioned for Payne to proceed. He and Reverend Cross watched with interest.

Payne stood in front of Colin and stared into his eyes for a long moment. "Colin Biddle, you are under arrest for the murder of Charles O'Hara, also known as Kirk Kitteridge, and for the murder of Alan Steadman. You have the right to remain silent. Anything you say can and will be used against you. You have the right to an attorney. If you cannot afford one, one will be provided for you. Do you understand these rights as I have stated them to you?"

He spun Colin around, deftly removed the SIG from the holster under his coat, and cuffed him.

Colin nodded.

Don was thunderstruck. "This is a mistake. He wrote a bad story. I know his mother. You can't—"

One look from Payne silenced him.

"You are way out on a limb, Detective Payne," Colin said. He was perfectly at ease. "You are letting your desire to make an arrest overshadow your good judgment. You have nothing. I'll be free in an hour."

"No bond on homicide cases." Payne spun Colin around again. "And I do have something. I have enough to put you away for a long time."

Kitty stepped forward. "Enough for you to meet Big Sparky."

Colin stared at Payne. "We'll see," he said weakly.

Reverend Cross looked at Payne and said, "Our God is a good God." He turned to his parishioners. "Let me have a big amen."

He got it.

Payne was staring at Colin. "Mr. Biddle, you never responded when I read you your Miranda rights. You know the rules."

"I understand the rights you stated to me," Colin said. "I want my telephone call."

"When we get to the office you can call your wife."

"She's playing tennis. I want to call my lawyer."

The photographer had been shooting from the moment he walked into the editor's office.

"Look at that," one of the parishioners said. "The brother has put the cuffs on the white man."

"For writing that story this morning?" another asked.

"No. It shoulda been. But it's something else."

"Let us rejoice," the reverend said. "Let us raise our voices in praise to God that His justice has been done. The word of God is swift and sharper than a two-edged sword. His will be done."

Kitty leaned over Don's desk. "I'm writing the story, Don. I've got the background, the details. I know what he did. You wanted a story about Colin that contained details no one else had. Well, I can give it to you. It's a story we have to do."

"You knew about this?"

"I'm a police reporter."

He nodded. "Do it. Play up the reverend's innocence in this matter. We'll give it the same play Colin's story had this morning. You got the front page."

"Excuse me, Officer," said the photographer. "I need your name for the cutline on this picture." He pulled out his pen.

Payne looked at Kitty. She smiled.

"I am a homicide detective for the Atlanta Police Department. My name . . . my name is Caesar Roosevelt Payne."

Kitty followed Payne out the office toward the

elevator. Payne had one hand on Colin's handcuffs and one on his arm.

Kitty looked at Colin. "Guess this means you're not the King of Buckhead anymore."

Everyone in the newsroom was standing up, watching, transfixed as the three waited for the elevator.

As the elevator doors opened, behind them in the editor's office came the rousing voice of Reverend Ebenezer Cross. His voice could be heard a city block away. "Let us praise God in song. Let us sing the hymn sister Jessye Norman has made famous. Raise your voices with me."

Kitty followed Payne and Colin onto the elevator. As the doors closed they heard the chorus rising from the editor's office . . .

"Greaaaaat Day. Great day in the morning. Greaaaaat day."

They could still hear the singing after the doors closed and the elevator began descending.

Payne looked at Colin and shook his head. "Gucci shoes. Perrier water. Now you. If this keeps up, I won't have any heroes."